CLOVER CASTLE

By Matt Burgin

EDITION 1 – May 2020

EDITION 2 – OCTOBER 2020

PHASE 1 - AWAKENING

CHAPTER 1
AUGUST 1963

THE BASE OF MOUNT SENTINEL,
THE UNIVERSITY OF MONTANA, USA.

On the side of Mount Sentinel, behind the University of Montana, lay a giant granite letter M. For 50 years it had been maintained by incumbent first-year students who whitewashed the granite and removed overgrown weeds and grass. But the enthusiasm of the 1960s student had waned to such a level that the football coach, John Carter, had been tasked with encouraging the current cohort of freshmen up the hill.

To reach the letter M, students would navigate a steep zigzag trail, consisting of 13 switchbacks from the base to the summit whilst carrying the tools required. The summer of '63 was unusually hot, making the trek up the steep hillside even more unappealing than usual. But 18-year-old freshman Jack enjoyed a challenge, so whilst other students gravitated towards the lighter objects, he volunteered to carry two large pots of whitewash up the hill; besides, he had an ulterior motive. Coach Carter was stoic, unanimated and difficult to impress, but, as he selected the football team, it was worth the extra effort to create a lasting first impression.

'Come on,' shouted the coach. 'This big letter won't paint itself.' And with those words of wisdom, he marched towards Mount Sentinel.

Halfway up the trail, as Jack strode enthusiastically alongside the coach, he was overtaken by another student also carrying two large pots of whitewash. Note to be outdone by his challenger, he widened his stride and soon they were out in front, with the coach and his entourage trailing in their wake. Jack waited until the final switchback before he made his move, but his fellow student was ready and accelerated away to victory. When he reached the summit, Jack dropped the pots onto the ground and bent over to catch his breath as the lactic acid built up in his muscles. Gasping, he looked up at his victor, who wasn't out of breath and hadn't even broken a sweat. He had blue eyes with short cropped blond hair, his naturally tanned face breaking into a smile. Looking as if he was trying not to laugh, he introduced himself.

'Hi buddy, that was fun! What's your name?'

'Jack,' he grunted,' Jack Marwood'

'My name's Carson. Carson Scott.'

CHAPTER 2

Jack's plan to ingratiate himself to the coach and win a place on the football team had been a partial success; he had made the team, but not as quarterback. The trials were an echo of the whitewash incident, with Jack and Carson going head to head for the coveted spot. Carson's strong right arm fired the ball through the air like a marksman's bullet, resulting in a victory equally as emphatic as the race up Mount Sentinel. Jack, an accomplished quarterback, had given it his best shot, but Carson's superior physical strength had rendered the contest a mismatch.

Although smaller in height than Jack, Carson had a broader more muscular build with his lower centre of gravity ideal for a quarterback. He was strong, with quick feet and excellent balance, and there were rumours of scouts looking at him for the major leagues. He was equally as solid mentally; nothing fazed him. Jack admitted defeat gracefully and, slotting into the position of wide receiver, he formed a formidable partnership with Carson on and off the field.

Shortly after the trials Jack experienced an unprecedented growth spurt which, in the space of just over a month, transformed his body. It began one night after training when he awoke with crippling pain all over his body. As the agony resonated through every muscle and into his bones, he was paralysed; unable to move or make a sound. He lay silent, motionless and terrified with sweat pouring from every pore, the pangs tormenting his soul until, after what seemed like an eternity, he passed out.

When he awoke the pain was gone and, having overslept, he jumped in the shower to cleanse himself of the night's cold sweats. But what had happened to him? Had he overdone it in training? Only a few hours ago he was in such agony it was impossible to imagine he would feel so invigorated just a few hours later. As the soapy sponge run over his body, he noticed his biceps were fuller and more defined than before and his chest had expanded in similar proportion to his arms; gradually he realised that his entire body had achieved an impressive increase in muscle mass.

The episodes continued over the next few weeks. It was difficult to say how many weeks, and how often they occurred; maybe 3 times a week for 4 or 5 weeks. But they were always excruciating and always resulted in a noticeably increased muscle mass. Despite the pain Jack was over the moon as his teenage body metamorphosised into that of a man. Jack lacked confidence with the opposite sex, but his improved physique, and performances on the football field, began to pay dividends.

Although Jack had wanted to be Quarterback, he was excelling as a wide receiver with his long legs and arms more suited to running and catching than dodging and throwing. Jack and Carson had developed an almost telepathic understanding on the field and were easily the best two players in the team.

But his muscle growth drew a lot of attention. Eventually, he was confronted by several of the team about how such a rapid increase could be down simply to hard work in the gym. Unexpectedly the coach came to his aid explaining that Jack had been building up for his new role of wide receiver with a special diet and exercise program called 'the Popeye routine', devised by the coach himself. He offered similar bespoke assistance to the rest of the team, catered to suit their individual build and position. Of the few who accepted the challenge, none stuck to their program due to the intensity of the physical exercise and a diet unpalatable for teenage consumption.

Jack couldn't understand why he had leapt to his rescue. It was uncharacteristic of the coach, who was so stereotypical of a former marine turned physical education teacher, with his detached and predictable style, that he was almost a parody of himself. Why had somebody seemingly so insular in nature, who he barely knew, shown compassion and lied for him? Maybe he had done it to keep harmony within a winning team? Or perhaps he was worried of suggestions that the muscle growth was illegally induced and wanted to avoid a scandal? Of course, he could have just asked, but that wasn't Jack's way; he would rather wonder in ignorance than instigate a confrontation. Maybe he was more like the coach than he realised.

As the muscle growth settled down, Jacks life was again disrupted as he experienced bouts of déjà vu. The episodes began immediately after the growth spurts stopped, occurring with similar frequency and were triggered by certain places or people. He would find himself vividly daydreaming about a memory he couldn't remember having; some were happy memories, but others were so dark he would run back to his room to hide the tears.

But with each episode his intelligence seemed to be increasing. Just as the nauseating bodily pain had resulted in increased muscles, the crippling psychological terror increased his most useful muscle, and his academic and sporting achievements at University began to mirror each other. But, how could déjà vu make him more intelligent? He couldn't even recall the memories. Were they even his?

He was worried by the frequency of the déjà vu and frightened by the nature of some of the episodes. Were these thoughts normal for someone of his age? It was his first year of University having relocated to Montana from DC on his own; maybe this disruption had been the source. He considered asking Carson if he had experienced anything like this. Like Jack he was well built physically. Maybe he had similar growth spurts before University, followed by déjà vu? But what if he hadn't? What if he had always been well built and had not had déjà vu? Jack would be the laughingstock of the Campus.

In the end he couldn't open up and discuss it with anybody, instead opting to research the phenomenon in the Campus library. He read many theories, such as crytomnesia; where a memory, although forgotten by the brain, is stored and randomly released; often associated with bouts of subconscious plagiarism. He also discovered links between déjà vu and schizophrenia, memory disorders, medication and the re awakening of experiences from previous lives. He was reassured to read that, whatever the reason, it was more common than he had thought, particularly in his age group.

Although there were similarities between the muscle growth and the déjà vu, he found the déjà vu more difficult to process. The pros and cons of the physical episodes were tangible; definitive pain, followed by obvious muscle increase. The déjà vu was different. Alarming mental episodes followed by a possible increase in mental capabilities. Possible, but difficult to gauge. Hopefully they would have one thing in common. They would be short-lived. But now he understood his problem better, maybe he would be able to handle the consequences. He certainly hoped so; it was the only blight on what was turning into an excellent Freshman year.

CHAPTER 3

As the team bus headed into town to celebrate their latest victory, Jack sat at the front next to Carson. With the cold February evening drawing in, Jack's reflection in the window was clear against the fading light outside. Aside from the muscles he was still the same all-American boy who arrived from DC in the summer: six-foot-tall, hazel eyes, brown hair; dressed in standard teenage attire - black Chuck Taylors; blue jeans, red zipped hooded jacket. But Jack wasn't looking at his physique; he was checking out his new hair style. He had decided to grow it and, for the first time in his life, he had a fringe. He nodded his head to one side, then the other, just to see what it looked like, remembering too late who he was sat next to.

'Are you looking at your hair again, you big poseur?' scoffed Carson, who sported a number 2 buzzcut, an unofficial part of the Grizzlies' uniform. 'Don't think me and the lads haven't noticed you're trying to grow it like the Beatles.'

'He's right, you know, they're all talking about your hair,' confirmed Coach Carter, sitting across the aisle.

Despite the coach's tough guy approach, his "work hard, play hard" philosophy meant his team did have extra-curricular fun. This evening they were heading to Sal's Place, a local bar and diner, to toast the victory. This was one of the benefits of the team's success - when accompanied by the coach, they were served beer. Even the local off duty police officers turned a blind eye.

But Jack was anxious. Although he had not experienced any déjà vu since he visited the library over a week ago, he knew that Sal's place had been a trigger point in the past.

They arrived at Sal's Place to find it unusually busy. That's not to say it didn't usually get busy, it was the mix of people forming the crowd which was unusual. But then, it was an unusual occasion: the Ed Sullivan Show was the most watched TV show in America, and tonight's guests included the Beatles. The scale of media publicity was unprecedented for a TV show, and the imagination of the American public had gone into overdrive.

As Jack sat at the team's table, he noticed the hype had worked: a cross-section of people had flocked in, from families eating in the diner area to young hippies and aging bikers at the bar. At the next table sat a group of beatniks, whom he disliked due to the superiority complex he felt was exuded by people of this subculture. To his mind, the only beatnik qualifications needed were to have read the latest Jack Kerouac novel and to dress like a Frenchman. He overheard a conversation about how the Beatles were a government project designed to undermine the spiritual quest of the beat generation. Their purpose was to destroy its soul and credibility by commercialisation; thus, confirming that his long-held opinion of all beatniks being idiots was true.

The furore surrounding the group's arrival in America fascinated him. It was as if they had arrived from a different planet, not country, and for such media attention to be lavished upon these four young men seemed unfair to other groups. Every newspaper and radio station were quick to champion them; every girl in America wanted to date them and every man wanted to be them. The bar fell silent as the TV show began and the Host started his introduction, but by the time the first note was played, mass hysteria had enveloped Sal's Place.

After the show, Sal's place was buzzing; girls were beaming with pride over which band member they would marry, with the men playing it cooler whilst secretly plotting to start their own band.

Turning to Jack, Carson asked, 'What did you think, then?'
There was no reply as Jack glared abstractly into space.
'Jack. What do you think? Are you OK?'
Jack sat bolt upright before heading through the crowded bar and out of the door, unaware of the disruption and spilled drinks created en route. Carson went after him, apologising along the way for the

manner of his friend's exit. Outside, a young girl remarked, 'If you're looking for your friend, he's around the back. He's drunk.'

Carson went around the corner to see Jack bent double, vomiting.

'Are you OK? What's up, buddy? Is it something you ate? It can't be the drink; you've hardly had anything. Did you feel OK after the game? Did you get a knock or something?'

'No,' replied Jack, 'I was fine up until then.'

'Until when?'

'Until I was watching the Beatles.'

'Well, how can that make you feel ill? You do realise that Beatlemania is something the papers made up? It's not real, you know,' quipped Carson.

Jack laughed. 'I know, but for the last few months I've been having some strange experiences, things that have been freaking me out. And I've had another tonight.'

'Like what, buddy?'

Jack was in danger of admitting the embarrassing déjà vu secret he'd planned to keep to himself, but Carson's joke had caught him off guard, causing him to lower his defences.

'Look, buddy, if you don't feel sick anymore, can we go somewhere else to talk? People will be wondering what we're up to round here.'

'Sure,' replied Jack, 'let's find somewhere round the front.'

Across the street from Sal's Place was a small park, close enough to be lit up by the streetlights - and to hear the aftermath of the British invasion - but distant enough for privacy. At the edge of the children's play area was a set of swings.

'So, what's the problem, buddy?' Carson asked, as they sat down on the cold wooden swing seats.

Jack stared across the park as he swung, causing the seat to creak under his weight.

'Look, it's nothing. I over reacted, that's all,' claimed Jack.

'I don't think so, buddy. I've never seen you look so pale; something's spooked you. I've noticed you've been preoccupied the last few weeks but nothing like tonight.'

Jack pushed his feet firmly against the ground, making him swing higher and the creaking even louder. How high would he have to swing to drown out Carson's questions?

'Look, whatever it is, I won't tell anyone. And we can sort it out. There's no need to be embarrassed; we all have our little quirks.'

Jack pushed against the ground harder still, swinging higher into the cold February air.

'OK. How about I tell you something embarrassing about me? Then you won't feel so awkward.'

'Like what?" enquired Jack, 'I thought you were perfect.'

Carson laughed. 'Nobody's perfect', he retorted, 'not even me. I have this odd thing I do. I know I'm doing it and it drives me nuts, but I can't stop it.' He paused, fishing for a response. Jack was aware of the bait but too curious not to bite.

'Well, what is it?'

'Step counting.'

'Step counting? What's that?'

'Well', answered Carson, 'I count steps whenever I climb stairs. I can't help it. Even if I know how many steps there are, I count them anyway. I'd hate to think how many times I've counted the stairs back home! I've thought about getting help for it, even thought about hypnotherapy once. Eventually I decided it was part of me and one day it might go away. Like I said, it drives me nuts. Anyway, your turn.'

Jack sat, rocking on the swing, thinking about what Carson had said. Was it true, or just a way of breaking the ice to coax him into talking? He was good at making light of situations and putting people at ease. Even if it was a deliberate tactic, would it be such a big deal to tell him? He put his feet on the ground, stopping the swing, and turned to Carson.

'Do you know what déjà vu is?'

'Yes, of course.'

'Well, over the past few months it's been happening to me a lot.'

'Is that it?" said Carson reassuringly. 'I don't think that's much to worry about.'

'It's not little episodes but prolonged feelings of it. I've been having funny experiences ever since I came here. At first, I hardly noticed them but recently, particularly since I had the flu a few weeks ago, they've been getting worse. It's random but certain triggers set off these feelings and I never know when it'll happen. There's something about Missoula, it feels so familiar. I don't even know why I chose this place, with all the options I had. It feels more like Missoula chose me. I thought I was getting over it but then it happened again in Sal's Place, tonight, much worse than I've had before.'

'So, what was the trigger this time?" Carson enquired.

'It was when the Beatles talked tonight on The Ed Sullivan Show.'

'Yeah', replied Carson, 'that was a bit weird. But I wouldn't worry about that. It freaked a few people out. I thought everyone in England talked like the Queen.'

'That's it, though. I didn't find it strange; it sounded familiar. Reassuringly familiar at first but then it left me feeling hollow in the pit of my stomach. Like that accent reminded me of something bad that had happened. It's ridiculous – I've never heard it before.'

'You probably have heard it before', reasoned Carson, 'but you didn't realise – perhaps when you were a kid?'

'Maybe you're right, but I don't remember.'

'Stuff like this happens to people all the time but they ignore it. You're just one of life's sensitive souls, buddy! Besides, you're becoming a little obsessed with the Beatles,' teased Carson.

'Shut up! That's ridiculous!' snapped Jack. 'Why would you even say that?'

'Whoa, calm down! I didn't mean to upset you, but you've been paying an awful lot of attention to all the media coverage lately - and that's without even mentioning the hair! Maybe you have caught Beatlemania after all.'

Jack shot to his feet, fists clenched, ready to fly. He glanced at Carson sitting calmly on the swing, trying to hide his smirk, and realised Carson was making fun of him to lighten the situation: a familiar tactic. Jack had taken it the wrong way; Carson had proved to be a true friend over the past few months; what's more, he was wise beyond his years, and although they were the same age, he acted like a big brother. Jack was an only child but could see his reaction was akin to how a little brother would react when teased by an older sibling. This realisation of immaturity embarrassed him. He also realised that had he started a brawl there would be only one likely outcome.

'OK', replied Jack, clapping sarcastically, 'you've wound me up like a cheap wristwatch. But you're barking up the wrong tree: I'm intrigued by the Beatles. Not particularly their music but with all the hype surrounding them. You could say I'm suspicious of them.'

'Suspicious?' exclaimed Carson, 'Of what? They are not real beetles if that's what you mean!'

Although not amused, Jack laughed dutifully at his friend's contrived attempt at a joke - it was the least he owed him after his overreaction. But his comment was part statement and part subterfuge to divert attention away from his own embarrassment; and Jack was inwardly ecstatic his comment had surprised Carson enough to distract his usually unflappable friend.

'Well, they're good musicians, look cool and write greats melodies backed up by top lyrics but ...' Jack paused. It was his turn to fish for a response.

'But what?' obliged Carson.

'But are they really that good?'

'You've just said yourself how good they are!'

'Good is one thing but look at the media coverage and support this group gets. It feels as if someone has pointed at them and said "Yes, these are the ones! Let's make these boys famous." Are they that much better than any other group or band out there?'

'Seriously, buddy, you think way too much. You could say that about anyone famous. What about Elvis Presley?'

'Yeah, but he really is that good.'

'Well, some people already feel that way about the Beatles. Man, if you were anything like this as a kid, I bet you annoyed the hell out of your parents! Anyway, do you feel any better?'

'I do,' he replied, surprised. 'But I still think there's something not right about the Beatles.'

'Well let's get back to Sal's Place then. I don't want the rest of the team thinking we've gone for a windy walk together!'

Sal's Place was in full swing when they returned. Even the Beatniks had forgotten how cool and intelligent they were supposed to be and were in high spirits despite the impending doom facing the beat generation.

'You need a beer,' announced Carson. 'Sit down, I'll get a pitcher!'

Their exit appeared to have gone unnoticed by the team, which could be explained by the amount of empty beer pitchers on the table. Glancing around the diner, he noticed Carson standing by the toilet door, having a heated discussion with the coach. They were too far away to be heard, but he could see the anguished expression on Carson's face. Jack had read that most people have a subconscious ability to lip read; he was no exception and had quite a knack for it but from where he was sitting, it was difficult to see what Carson was saying. He thought he picked out the words 'liability' and 'do it soon' but it was difficult to be sure. As Carson gesticulated towards Jack, he noticed Jack looking straight back at him. He turned to speak to the coach, who glanced backwards in consternation. The two separated.

Jack slumped in his chair. They must have been discussing his earlier conversation with Carson. He was angry that Carson had betrayed his trust; he could be cut from the team for not playing well without his friend labelling him a liability, and he was sure he would be out of next week's game. Worse still, he was annoyed he had considered Carson a big brother figure. For all his suspicions, he couldn't be certain of his betrayal; but recently he had started to feel there was more to Carson than met the eye.

He cast his mind back to when they met. Jack had never been beaten in a test of endurance, yet Carson had annihilated him on Mount Sentinel that day. He could accept that one day he would meet a bigger fish in the pond, but not to break a sweat was inhuman. The temperature was 30 degrees on an exposed mountain side and not one bead of sweat. Come to think of it, he couldn't recall ever seeing him sweat - not even in training.

As Jack mused on his friend's superhuman powers, Carson reappeared at the table with a pitcher of beer, his usual jovial self.

'Are you thirsty, Buddy?'

It was difficult to tell which was the larger, the pitcher or Carson's smile. But, despite the reassuring smile, Jack was beginning to wonder if his best friend really was the person he thought he was.

CHAPTER 4
Sunday 16th February 1964

Midway through the final quarter it was second down and ten, with the Montana Grizzlies sitting on their own 30-yard line. Jack had received a signal from Carson and knew the play was coming his way: his fears of being dropped had not materialised, and there were no indications from the coach or Carson that he was viewed as a liability. More importantly, there had been no more episodes of déjà vu, but none of which seemed important as he crouched forward, over the damp grass, waiting for the game to restart. As the ball was handed to the quarterback, Jack raced forward, and by the time it was launched skyward, he had advanced deep into the opposition's half. He knew when he caught it a touchdown was assured, but the throw was in front of him and he fumbled it into the cold air. The oval leather ball spun as he tried to juggle it under control until, with both hands, he clutched it. Wrestling the ball into his right hand, he was unaware of how much speed the fumble had cost him, and he didn't see a tackle coming as he was dumped, unceremoniously, onto the ground.

In the group crowded over him were Carson, the coach, the team doctor and a young medical assistant. Doctor Sam Johnson and the coach knew each other well: they were born and raised in the same neighbourhood and had attended the same schools and church. Now in their mid-forties, both stood at around six feet tall, though the doctor was slimmer in build and more laid-back in temperament. He possessed a sharp, dry wit, and was popular with the students, who had given him the nickname "Bones", after the doctor in a television series. Despite their common ground, the two did not get on well. Unlike his colleague, the coach was not popular with his students. Doctor Johnson's popularity was one of the many things that irked the coach. At high school, Carter's physical build had made him a better sportsman - and a more popular student - than the doctor. But the former glory days counted for nothing as his physical and sporting prowess were less important to the current students than a few well-chosen wisecracks. However, all this was a preamble to the main reason for the frosty nature of the relationship: the coach resented how their paths had diverged with the advent of World War Two.

Coach Carter was drafted into the army, experiencing front line action in Europe. Doctor Johnson, on the other hand, served his entire military career as a medical assistant at Fort Missoula, which was used as a prisoner of war camp for Italian soldiers. The coach saw this as an easy option and questioned the level of hospitality given to the enemy; the prisoners had nicknamed the fort "Bella Vista" - beautiful place – which stood in stark contrast to the backdrop against which he and his comrades had fought their own personal wars.

Much to his chagrin, not only had fate brought them together at the university, they had offices next to each other. Now, once again, they stood together, this time on the football pitch.

'Is he conscious, Bones?' Carson asked as the medic knelt next to Jack's motionless body.

'This should tell us,' he replied, reaching into his bag to retrieve a bottle of smelling salts. As he wafted the bottle under Jack's nose, the ammonia raised his heart rate, blood pressure and brain activity, causing a reflex to open his eyes.

'He's OK but he'll need a couple of minutes.'

'You've got three, the cheerleaders are on!' replied the coach.

But the smelling salts did more than open his eyes: they awoke subconscious memories in his barely conscious mind. Having no recollection of what had happened, he felt vulnerable as Doctor Johnson leaned over, his face just a few inches from his own.

'Jack!' he shouted, 'Jack. Are you OK?'

Oblivious to the crowd of people around him, Jack swung his arm around the medic's neck and pulled him to the ground. Getting him in a neck lock, he began to tighten his grip.

'Who are you?' shouted Jack. 'Wer bist du? Wer sind Sie tätig?'

Carson was first to react, followed by the coach, both pinning him to the ground. Jack returned to a state of semi-consciousness as the effects of the ammonia wore off.

'He's crazy,' the medic whispered as he crawled away, gasping for breath.

The assistant, frozen to the spot, broke his silence.

'What language was he speaking? Sounded German to me. Why would he be speaking German?'

'Because he's crazy, that's why!' screamed the medic, now sat on the grass, recovering from his ordeal.

'He's disorientated,' explained the coach. 'I saw all sorts of crazy stuff during the war. It's not unusual for someone who's been knocked out or is suffering from shell shock to start talking crazy.'

'But why German?' repeated the assistant.

'Perhaps it wasn't German,' Carson offered.

'Sounded German to me,' he persisted.

'You can speak German?' asked the coach.

'Well no, but ....'

'But nothing,' replied the coach, now irritated by the questions. 'You either speak the damn language or you don't ... and you don't. Are we gonna help him or stand here accusing him of being a Nazi? Let's get him to your office.'

'C'mon, Michael, give us a hand,' said the doctor to his assistant, gesticulating towards Jack who, after his brief outburst, was once again motionless on the floor. The two lifted him onto a stretcher.

'I'm coming with you,' said the coach. 'Carson –you call the plays.'

The medical centre was in a newly built single-storey brick annex on the opposite side of campus consisting of a combination of changing rooms, treatment areas and offices. Entering a room, they laid the stretcher on a treatment table. As they did so, the door swung open and in walked Sal Esposito. Sal Esposito was a big supporter of the team and the proprietor of Sal's Place. Although of Italian origin, he had lived in Missoula his entire life and was a well-known figure within the community - it was said that Sal knew everybody, and everybody knew Sal. He had several businesses but was most often at the diner; a social hub, attended by many locals including businessmen, politicians and police officers.

'OK, Michael', said the doctor to his assistant, 'I'll take it from here. You go back and watch the rest of the game, in case there are any more injuries.'

'But ... but what am I gonna learn if I can't help you treat injured players?' he protested.

'Look!' shouted the doc, 'What's the point in me having an assistant if he doesn't assist me when I ask? Now go!'

The assistant looked around, hoping in vain for support, before trudging back towards the football field.

'Is he OK, Bones?' Sal asked.

'Yeah, yeah, he's fine. Just unconscious, nothing to worry about. He could come around at any time.'

'We need to put him somewhere private until we can get a *greeter* to deal with him,' replied Sal, taking control.

'Like you should have done last week,' snapped the doctor, looking at the coach.

'What's that supposed to mean?' the coach snapped back.

'Carson told me what happened last week at Sal's Place. He warned you about it at the time and you did nothing. It's because of your ineptitude that we're in this situation.'

'What situation?' replied the coach defensively. 'Nobody noticed anything out there; they were too busy watching the cheerleaders prance about.'

'You don't know that for sure,' attacked the doc. 'Michael realised he was speaking German straight away, and don't assume your bullshit explanation will have convinced him of anything.'

'Well, if he starts asking too many questions, we'll have to deal with him as well.'

'We can't get rid of people every time you make a cock-up. He was displaying classic signs of awakening last week and you ignored it because you wanted him to play in the game tonight! I've always said you had bad judgement!'

'Watch your mouth, Bones. I gave him the benefit of doubt because of who he is. This guy's a hero, for Christ's sake. Not that you'd know what one of those is having spent the entire war in your own backyard, cosying up to the enemy.'

'Well, well, well,' laughed the doc. 'I wondered how long it would take you to get back to that old chestnut.'

'Shut up the pair of you,' growled Sal. 'We need to sort this out now and we won't do that with you two bitching like a pair of old women. The doc's right, though, you should have done something last week. This is your fault. You've put us in a compromised position.'

Backed up by Sal, the doc wasn't going to miss the chance to turn the screw on the coach.

'He's in the transition stage now. The last thing you want to do is put somebody in that state on a football pitch where he could be on the receiving end of a tackle. An impact like that could nudge him to the somnambulating stage. Can you imagine the problems we'll have if he wakes up like that? Bearing in mind who he is, we'd be in big trouble with the Council too!'

Sal agreed, 'He's right. We need to get a greeter here as soon as possible. This could go wrong. The sooner we erase Jack Marwood the better for us all. In the meantime, we need to make sure he doesn't wake up. Doc, you need to give him some green relaxant, now.'

'Oh, no!' the doc exclaimed as he scanned the room. 'I've left my bag at the side of the pitch.'

The coach couldn't believe his luck as, in a flash, the doc was now on the back foot. It was a stroke of luck he hadn't earned, but one he wasn't going to waste.

He laughed, 'How about that for judgement? You'd better get a move on before he comes around.'

'I won't be long,' said the flustered medic as he hurried out of the room with more haste and purpose than his assistant had ten minutes earlier.

'The game'll be over soon,' warned Sal. 'We need to put him somewhere while we wait, for the greeter.'

'My office is down the passage. It's private and secure.'

'Perfect. Then we'll tell the rest of the team he's gone to the hospital. Let's get a move on before he comes around.'

Jack's motionless body belied the fact that he had been regaining consciousness since being woken by the doctor shouting at his assistant; the shock caused him to open his eyes, which amid the panic in the room had gone unnoticed. Concerned by the conversation of his so-called friends, he closed his eyes and pretended to remain unconscious. But this was not easy as the content of the conversation had created a heightened sense of panic within his brain, he was sure they could see the fear on his face or hear his shallow, crackling breaths. His instinct was to make a run for it, but for now he remained still and regulated his breathing.

Now on a trolley, it wasn't only fear which flooded his brain but questions too. Why was he so important to these people? Why did Coach Carter think he was a hero? Why were they saying he spoke German? What is a greeter? Why did they want to erase him? But before he had time to ponder, the trolley stopped.

'Put him over here,' said the coach.

Jack needed to make his move before the doctor came back. He knew the layout of the office and now was the perfect time. The annexes were a couple of years old, with large windows overlooking the playing fields through which he could escape. He began a countdown from five before using his only weapon: the element of surprise. He only had one chance. The countdown began in Jack's head, but, as he braced himself, the sound of a door closing and the turning of a key in a lock ended his plan. He could still hear voices, but they were muffled and unclear. When he opened his eyes, he was alone in the store cupboard.

The store had been set up as a mini office by the coach to hide himself away when he didn't want to be disturbed which, with his insular nature, meant he spent more time in the cupboard than the main office. It had a window, but it was small, high and difficult to escape through. The random assortment of items in the store was such that even the medical trolley did not appear out of place. Pulling the trolley over to the window, he locked the wheels and climbed on. With the light fading, the deserted field would indeed make an ideal escape route.

Opening the window, he put out his left leg and tried to slide through, but his clothing became snagged. Realising he was still in his football kit; he climbed off the trolley and began to strip. There was no shortage of clothing for him to change into: T-shirts, tracksuits and even a couple of the coach's own jackets hung on a coat stand. The jackets were easy to identify with the coach's motif embroidered onto them. Jack assumed he must be part Irish as the motif was a black cat over a four-leaf Clover but, whatever it meant, it was too distinctive to take. He was thinking clearly now; his earlier panic having given way to calm deliberation. He put on a blue sweat suit and began loading a kitbag with a coat and another sweat suit. Quietly, he opened the drawers of a desk and rummaged through the contents. Into the bag went a Zippo lighter, a box of matches, a pen knife, a first aid kit, some wire coat hangers, a tin cup, two empty water bottles, a small sheath knife, a blanket and a length of frayed gym rope. He found a compass, which he placed on the desk, to avoid damage. Unsure of where he was heading, he chose the items he thought he would most likely need.

With time against him, he must make his move; but struggled to get the kitbag through the window. It was snagged on a metal point forming part of the window latch, so with the knife he began to unscrew the latch. The screws came away easily and the latch, now attached only by the surrounding paint, was prised away from the frame. Again, he pushed the bag through the window and, this time, with a little persuasion it fell onto the grass outside.

Remembering the compass on the table, he climbed from the trolley before hearing voices in the other room. The locked door had three Georgian wired vision panels obscured with black card fixed to the frame with sticking tape. Picking away at the tape with his fingers, he revealed a small corner of glass at the bottom of a panel. Doctor Johnson had re-joined Sal and the coach, and in his hands, was a large hypodermic syringe. The needle had a beam of green light projecting from it. He had never seen anything like it before but knew it was the green relaxant. He was transfixed by the light beam until a rap on the main office door snapped him out of his trance.

Jumping onto the trolley he tried to force his way through the window, but it was too tight; he couldn't get out. He removed his clothes and threw them out of the window, and now dressed only in his underpants and shoes he attempted to escape. He felt the rough surface of the unpainted wood behind the removed ironmongery rub against his groin as he slid through the gap between the frame, and as a splinter stuck in his inner thigh, he was relieved he had done a dummy run on the kitbag. His attempt to exit with any level of control was futile, and with his trailing leg still inside and his centre of gravity outside, he cascaded out of the window. Landing on the bag winded him, but with no time for self-pity he picked up his bag and clothes and ran semi-naked into the cold Missoula night.

CHAPTER 5

Sprinting through campus grasping the bag and loose clothing, Jack more closely resembled an errant lover fleeing an angry husband than a man on the run. Despite this predicament his state of mind was relaxed and assured. He was a man running towards something not away from it. As a strange, unseen force filled him with calm, for once he chose to embrace the feelings of déjà vu.

Soon he had a decision to make. He was heading towards the woodland at the base of Mount Sentinel, which would afford him the security provided by immediate cover of the trees, but before he could reach it, he had to run across two training pitches. Approaching at speed, he realised how a semi naked man running out in the open would draw attention to himself. On the other hand, was it more dangerous to stop and risk being caught?

He headed out across the open fields, deciding maintaining momentum was the better option. The journey was brief and soon he stood protected under the cover of the surrounding tree canopies. As he began to dress his eyes scanned the playing fields for his assailants. He assumed that the knock on the door had come from the 'Greeter' and it would not be long before his disappearance was discovered. Although relieved, he was surprised to see the field and surrounding area empty. But surely, they must be on their way, they must be closing in?

The navy blue sweat suit gave him both warmth and cover under the blanket of darkness. He headed north to an old deserted Army Training area he knew of, which would be an ideal place to shelter and regroup. By now he had realised that, in his haste, he had forgotten to pick up the compass.

The lack of compass was more inconvenience than disaster as, although his journey time would increase, he could navigate North using the stars and trees. He wasn't sure how he could do these things: he just knew he could. Come to think of it, he had never been to the deserted army training area before but knew it would be there when he arrived. Having neither the time nor inclination for questions, he embraced the feelings he previously feared; he was in autopilot. He was sleepwalking to safety. As his journey progressed and he became confident he was not being pursued, his mind turned to food and shelter.

He was acting quickly and efficiently to accommodate his now basic hierarchy of needs. The need for shelter was urgent as his destination was too far to reach tonight. His best chance of shelter would be to either find a natural undulation in the ground suitable to cover over with branches, or to find refuge in a cave or nook in the rocks. He left the shelter of the trees and headed off toward rocky ground. Although late, the moon cast a faint light over the valley. Faint, but enough for Jack to survey the area. He identified a recess in a rock face which, although narrow, was wide enough for him to squeeze through. Inside was sheer darkness but sheltered. Perfect, but he knew that he may not be the only one to appreciate the caves potential. Having strayed from the trees he had ventured into bear territory. Jack knew a lot about bears, as did anybody living in the area. Not knowing a lot about bears was fatal. There were differing opinions as to whether bears hibernate or not. It was widely accepted that they slowdown in winter and take long naps with a decreased heart rate but, unlike hibernating animals, they will wake up quickly, hungry and at full strength if startled by loud noises. Jack preferred to consider them heavy sleepers rather than actual hibernators. Tentatively he took out the Zippo from his pocket, opened the lid carefully and gently spun the flint.

The cave was smaller than he thought, but big enough for his needs. Looking up there was a small gap through which he could see the night sky. Although not waterproof it was well ventilated and bear free. Shelter established; food was the new priority.

Jack's concern about bears within the area was justified as their population had remained stable despite the increase in the humans. This was due largely to the plentiful food supply on offer. As Missoula sat at the convergence of five mountain ranges alongside the Clark Fork River, it provided a cornucopia of potential food on land or water.

The mountain ranges were home to grazing elk and mule deer alongside many birds such as turkey, grouse, pheasants and partridge. From outside the cave he could see a small river a few hundred yards away. These rivers were well stocked with a variety of fish, many simple to catch without traditional fishing equipment. They could be eaten raw or easily cooked and were protein rich. Given the hour, he decided a fish supper was the obvious solution.

The reflection of the moonlight cast shadows on the riverbed providing the light he needed to spot his shadowy prey. Tickling is neither an unusual or difficult way to catch trout with overhanging shelves provide good shelter for fish to hide and become trapped. Spotting an ideal location on the opposite bank, he headed upstream. To ensure there were fish under the overhang they must be guided there. As fish naturally escape downstream Jack approached from upstream.

He entered the water in a deliberately clumsy manner as, to force the fish to take refuge, they must be aware of the danger. The river was narrow and knee deep, and as he waded across and he could see the shadows of the fish deciding which option to take. Upstream? Downstream? A speedy exit or low-key retreat? The shadows decreased by the second as they chose their strategy; but Jack only needed one under the ledge. By the time he reached it he was unsure if any fish had gone under. He thought he saw a fish, but the moonlights reflection on the river caused eye flashes. He was no longer sure if he was seeing the fish or the temporary spots in his vision. Although he could see an outline, it was too dark to identify what kind of fish it was. Trout would be idea, but the yellow perch which also frequented these rivers had the natural protection of spikes running down their backs and next to the gills. The spikes were not venomous but could easily pierce the skin. Despite having the good sense to procure a first aid kit from the store, this was an injury he could do without. That said, yellow perch were tastier than trout.

Now was the time for stealth as he crouched down slowly next to the overhang. He could see the large shadow in the water was too big to be a perch. By now he was kneeling in the water with hands wide apart and arms outstretched in a V shape. Carefully avoiding the head, he scraped his hands along the riverbed, using his body as a natural barrier. Moving his hands together he pointed the fingers on one hand upwards, like weeds gently floating on the riverbed. He had identified its position accurately and gently stroked the underside of the belly. As he did this, he steered it into his other hand as it floated contently in the river. Soon he had one hand under its head and the other close to its tail. Suddenly Jack grasped the wrist of the tail and head simultaneously and, in one seamless action, threw the unsuspecting victim onto the riverbank.

    Back on dry land he crouched over the fish to discover a large Rainbow trout, about 3 pound in weight. He looked up towards the heavens, to show appreciation for his bounty, and then struck the fatal blow with a nearby rock.

    Returning to the cave he changed into dry clothing before going in search of fuel. He knew that peat would burn long and intensely but produce little smoke. He searched around treed areas where vegetation had grown over rocks to find a suitable source and, using the knife he dug below the wet top layer, down to the dry fibrous substrate before removing several sections. He carefully replaced the top layer of wet green vegetation to mask his extraction.

    Soon he had a warm fire onto which he placed 2 coat hangers, cooking the fish on top. He poured water, into the metal cup to boil free from any contaminants upstream. A nearby dead animal, not seen in the darkness, would cause serious illness. The hot water would also be welcome as the evening temperature continued to fall. As he set about making a warm bed with the contents of the bag, he was proud of how he had adapted to his circumstances. He had acquired food, water and shelter as second nature. The old Jack would have spent the evening searching for answers, but the new Jack didn't need too. He was stronger, smarter and better than before. He didn't know why - and he didn't care. It was too late to contemplate. It was futile, serving only to deprive him of valuable sleep. But more than that, for the first time in his life, he felt himself.

CHAPTER 6

Awaking cold but dry, he packed his meagre possessions and continued north. By early afternoon he was on target to make his destination before dark; until he found himself at the top of a cliff. It was 100 feet high, split in the middle by a shelf a couple of metres deep. To the east the cliff continued as far as the eye could see; to the west it decreased until it met the ground. The westward journey would be safer than climbing down, but at the expense of daylight. It was difficult to gauge how far west the cliff merged with the ground, but it could take an hour in either direction, possibly even two.

He removed the rope from the bag. It was a typical 3-strand twisted gym rope made from hemp, with a steel bow shackle on one end and resin coated the other and was the heaviest item in the bag. The end near the bow shackle was frayed, explaining why it was in the coach's storeroom. Cutting through the frayed rope, he unwound the strands forming the twisted construction. Tied together they would reach the shelf below, but he would need the same length of rope again to reach the ground. If the rope were tied at the top it couldn't be retrieved, leaving him stranded on the shelf below. There was a solution, but it was risky.

Below the secured rope he would tie a "suicide" knot, like the sheepshank knot climbers use to shorten lengths of rope. With the sheepshank, if the tension was not maintained the knot dropped out. The deadly variation with the suicide knot was that once the rope was cut, should the tension be released so would the rope; thus, he would only remain safe on his abseil if the rope remained taut. He would have to do this twice.

But it was a risk worth taking, so without hesitation he threw the bag onto the shelf below. With the rope's strands tied together and the top of the rope attached to a rock, he began to form the sheepshank knot. Standing at the summit of the cliff, he leaned backwards to test the robustness of the knot, and with a quick flick of the knife, the sheepshank became the suicide knot.

Slowly, he shuffled down the first rock face, ensuring the tension of the rope remained taut, until he reached the ledge. As he stood, overlooking the beautiful valleys, he was gripped by an unseen force, ethereal in nature. He untied the rope from his waist and threw it over the edge, followed by the bag. The suicide knot had done its trick; he had retrieved the rope, yet he had purposely tossed away his lifeline. Crouching over the edge, he spun around, gripping the rock face with his fingertips, and free climbed to the base.

What surprised him was not his climbing ability but the cursory manner with which he greeted his latest accomplishment. Discovering the hidden knowledge and skills he mysteriously possessed was now second nature to him. But he knew these skills weren't new to him, they were just forgotten, lying dormant - waiting for him to summon them. They had become disconnected but, somehow, he had tripped a switch, sucking them into his psyche and creating a suit of armour to protect him.

Ditching the heavy rope beneath a cluster of rocks, he continued his journey.

As early evening beckoned, he arrived at an opening with lush grassland and a small river. Although it felt achingly familiar, he entered a state of confusion, sensing he was close, or possibly even at his destination, but could only see trees, grass and the river. There were no buildings or indication that any structure had even been there. Walking down a sharp slope and out into an opening next to the river, he conceded that the sixth sense which carried him north had deserted. The river reminded him of his need for food and water and, with daylight beginning to fade, would be a good place to set up camp. In the meantime, there was no benefit standing out in the open motionless and bewildered, so he retreated up the slope and into the shelter of the trees.

After a brief reconnaissance, he began to build a bivouac. He found a tree to form the main structure, which was deep enough into the surrounding woodland not to be seen and to give protection from the elements and had a fork at the perfect height to support the spine of the shelter. A nearby rock protruding from the ground would be ideal to build the fire next too and would screen it from vision, whilst reflecting heat into the shelter. To minimise his trail, he used naturally fallen branches, until soon the spine and supporting members were securely in place. Searching for larger branches with foliage to provide cover he, once again, found himself at the opening next to the river.

Beside the stream was a clump of trees, standing in isolation in the open grassland. The trees were uniform in shape and size and equidistant from each other. The more he looked, the more at odds they looked with their natural surroundings. Entering the trees appeared to distort the woodland and he couldn't decide whether there was something ahead that was moving or whether it was still. As he approached, he realised the object was still and it was his movement making it appear to shift. The object was a small building, and the visual anomaly was caused by a reflective cladding material, giving the appearance of a big mirror. This was it. This was what he had been looking for.

The reflective cladding angled backwards, so his reflection was only visible when standing directly in front of it. Walking around, the interaction between the cladding and surrounding trees formed an effective camouflage. He was awestruck by its beauty and ingenuity and contemplated how the trees must have been grown in this formation to camouflage the building before it was even built. Exploring the structure for a means of entry, he touched the cladding, and run his fingers down it until they stopped an inch from the ground. Underneath, he felt a length of rough sawn timber but although it gave a clue to the construction it didn't help to gain entry. Pacing the rectangular perimeter several times, he could see no door. His brain knew more, but he needed to release his subconscious. Could it be part of Montana's military past? Is this why he was drawn to the University? Where was his déjà vu when he needed it?

Montana was a military town established back in the late 19th century to protect settlers from Native American Indians. The focal point Fort Missoula was steeped in history, with its service ranging from housing the Buffalo Soldiers in the 19th century, to detaining

Italian and Japanese prisoners of war during World War Two. It was rumoured that the fort and surrounding woodlands were used by special services from all over the world for training exercises. It was suggested that the vast woodlands and European style climate had drawn in military teams from Great Britain, although these rumours were never proven. Either way, there had been no significant military presence in Montana, either official or rumoured, since the Second World War. But the structure before him, with its sophisticated construction, and secluded location, must have a military origin.

Maybe the entrance would be situated on the narrowest and least visible façade, most likely the corner, to utilise the joint? After examining the four corners, he noticed a shadow line three feet in from one of the corners. Instinctively, he pressed the bottom right-hand corner. Click! He did the same at the top left-hand corner. Click! It was only a couple of millimetres, but the panel had been sunk into the structure. Again, he pressed the middle right-hand side and with one final click the panel swung open to reveal a timber door with a keypad. Immediately, he tapped in a code: 2-2-2-5-5-5-6-6-6-8-8-8-3-3-7-7, took a breath and pressed enter. The random numbers were more recognisable to the keypad than to him and the door clicked open. At last, the déjà vu was back. A light activated as he entered what appeared to be the sleeping quarters, with three single bunk beds.

It was clear from the dust, stale smell and dankness of the room that it had not been used for some time. This suited Jack, but he was concerned his pursuers would also be aware of its existence. He knew he had been here before and, with his surroundings becoming familiar, he noticed two TV screens built into the wall, above which was a sign saying – REFUGE POD No. 552. Pressing a red button on the left-hand TV, the screen lit up, displaying a sequence of labelled red boxes. As he touched a box labelled "Air con" a barely audible whirring noise began, and the box turned green. Next, as he touched "Cameras", a screen on the right displayed images of the exterior of the building. The cameras must be on the trees to the outside of the clump as he could see the surrounding area. Next, he pressed "Themes" and was prompted to select one. The list was seemingly endless, but he settled on "Aqua".

At this, the left screen transformed into a giant fish tank, its life-like appearance and explosion of colour transfixing him. A message appeared on the screen:

"ACTIVATE 1 KM WARNING?"

Jack selected "YES"

"ALARM WILL ACTIVATE WHEN 1KM RADIUS BREACHED"

The unit provided shelter, warmth and security, with the unexpected bonus of electricity. He expected visitors at some point, but he had left little in way of a trail and was in an area accessible only on foot. Besides, the luxury of a 1KM warning would give him time to evacuate. Scanning the many small surveillance screens, he realised he was alone, for now at least.

The size of the room accounted for around half the floor area. There was a second door, opposite the entrance, probably for toilet and washing facilities, but he hoped there would also be a supply store. He knew that any items left behind would be of intrinsic value and may have perished in the years since it was last used. A military unit would have stored weapons but there was little chance any would have been forgotten. Despite his "glass half empty" approach, he hoped for a forgotten gun. With the opening of the door, more dankness seeped into the sleeping quarters. With no light automatically activated this time, he fumbled around in the dark, finding a pull cord dangling from the ceiling. The handle spun around as he failed to grasp it, until clutching above it, he wrapped it around his knuckles and pulled.

'Hello,' smirked the coach, sitting on a chair in front of him. 'What took you so long?'

Confidence is an imposter which empowers those in possession and destroys those who are not. Even those in possession should be wary of the speed at which it can take flight - usually at the precise moment it is most required. If it could be captured and bottled, in an elixir that did not result in a hangover, its inventor would indeed be wealthy. Standing there dumbfounded, Jack could have done with a couple of spoonful's himself.

'Great unit isn't it?' the coach continued, gesticulating around the room. 'Hard to believe it's been here now for over fifty years, except for the smell, of course. They were manufactured secretly in one of the timber mills around here, in two pods, and flown over by helicopter. Inside the timber walls are battery panels that store electricity generated from the reflective cladding, which is essentially one large solar panel. But then, you already knew that, didn't you, Stanley?'

'What …? How did you get here? … Stanley?' Jack stammered, unable to decide or articulate which aspect astounded him the most. Adding further to his confoundment, sitting next to the coach were the doc and Sal.

'He doesn't know who Stanley is,' remarked Bones, turning to Sal. 'But he's found his way here and remembered the code, so he must still be in the early somnambulating phase.'

'How did you remember the code? Was it the code word you remembered or the numbers that spell it out?' asked Bones.

'What?' replied Jack. 'Numbers. Why?'

Turning to the coach, Bones continued: 'Looks like you got lucky again. That luck of yours will run out one day!'

The coach laughed. 'Maybe, but not today. And speaking of luck, I've won the bet too. I had thirty-six hours, so I am the closest?'

'Yes,' replied Sal. 'But I reckon Bones would have won had he not forgotten to pick up the compass.'

'He didn't pick up the compass? You told me he'd taken it out of your drawer!' the doc exclaimed.

'He did,' laughed the coach, lighting up a cigar. 'But then he left it on my desk.'

'Well, that's not fair,' protested Bones. 'You deliberately misled me! That must have added a few hours to the journey.'

'Maybe, but I didn't lie!' he claimed, whilst unsuccessfully attempting to blow a smoke ring.

'And you can put that damned thing out, too. It smells bad enough in here already,' the doc complained.

'Don't get your knickers in a twist - it's not like any of us can get cancer from it or anything. You're annoyed cos you lost the bet … again,' teased the coach.

'Maybe. But it bloody stinks and it's getting in my eyes. Think of other people for once; there are five of us in here, not just you!' he snapped back.

Until that point, Jack had stood rooted to the spot, immobilised by the relative absurdity of the conversation. Considering the calamitous effect this could have on his life, he was alarmed by the trivial manner of these people he used to regard as his friends. Even more alarming was how long it had taken him to realise he had underestimated the number of people there were in the room. So long, in fact, that by the time the penny dropped, it was already too late, he had not checked behind him. He cursed his schoolboy error as he knew it was unlikely that the doc had accidentally revealed an extra presence in the room - more a conspicuous signal. In an instant, the mystery person behind him took two steps forward and, with one click, intravenously administered a foreign liquid into his neck. The medication took immediate effect, and he slumped to the floor.

Lying on the floor, although paralysed, he was still conscious. When he fell, he had seen a flash of green light from the corner of his eye; he had finally succumbed to the green relaxant. But with the doc in front of him, who had administered it? As he began to lose consciousness, he could see a fifth pair of feet in front of him. They were clad in white Adidas training shoes with three red stripes. These trainers were issued to all the football team and often got mixed up, causing squabbling between the players. To stop the bickering, the coach had ordered every player to write their name on the tongue of the shoe. As the trainers walked towards him and then stepped over his motionless body, he saw Carson S written on the tongue. With this revelation, as he slipped into unconsciousness, any remaining doubts he may have harboured about the depth of his betrayal were extinguished.

CHAPTER 7

Opening his eyes, the bright light beckoning him suggested death was his new state of being. But he wasn't dead: somehow, he knew what dead felt like and this wasn't it. He occupied a deep sense of relaxation but was having trouble adjusting his vision. As his focus began to return, he noticed the bright light was coming from the ceiling rather than a celestial origin. The entire ceiling was a giant light diffuser, giving an equally distributed illuminance throughout the room, and although he hadn't realised it at the time, a subconscious bounce in his brain told him this unusual style of lighting was the same as that in the sleeping quarters of the mirror-clad army base.

He was in a state of hyper-relaxation, and despite periodic attempts to sit upright, he remained motionless, his body happy to stay in a pleasant state of flux. An attempt to raise his hands was interrupted by the sound of people entering the room, and Jack once again closed his eyes and played dead. The door opening mechanism created a soft swooshing sound, which combined with the barely audible footsteps made it difficult to establish how many people had entered, though he quickly sensed they were standing over him.

'I haven't seen you since Christmas. What did you get up to?' asked the first voice, a man approaching middle age. He didn't have a discernible accent, although there was a faint whiff of New Yorker in there. Without giving a chance to reply, he continued: 'Yeah, I spent most of it in Italy. Tuscany, actually.'

Oh, that's nice,' replied a second voice, a woman, younger than the man, with a soft British accent.

'Yeah, I've got a little villa on a mountain side, with a magnificent view of the Med.'

'Oh, that's nice,' repeated the British woman, engaging out of politeness rather than genuine interest.

'Well I say little but it's actually quite big, four bedrooms and a small pool. Well, not that small. Have you ever been to Tuscany?'

'No, but I've heard it's quite nice and ...'

'Yes, yes,' he interrupted. 'I go for the culture. Drive to the mountains to search out a few hidden gems. The food is to die for. You ought to see my car – a Maserati 3500 GTi Coupe. Red. Fair rips round the mountainside.'

'Oh, that's nice,' repeated the woman, reverting to default.

'Yeah, if you ever fancy a visit, let me know; I'm over there a couple of times a year. We could whizz up to Pisa in the Maserati – do the Tower and have a spot of lunch.'

'Er, yes, thanks, sounds nice,' she replied uncomfortably. 'I'll have to get back to you. I have a couple of trips planned and don't have much time off left.'

'OK, I'll hold you to that,' he replied, seemingly unaware she was not interested.

'Anyway, have you read your notes on this patient?' she spluttered, changing the subject.

Throughout the conversation Jack had become increasingly agitated. This was the second time he had been ignored and trivialised whilst in a state of semi-consciousness. This time, he had been forced to witness an anaemic and thinly veiled chat-up attempt.

'No. I only got called back up a couple of days ago,' replied the man. 'Must be something serious though if they're sending for me.'

'You're right,' agreed the woman. 'Do you know who he is?'

'I don't recognise him,' came the reply.

'Well, here, have a look at my notes then. You really should have looked before.'

For once, the man was briefly lost for words.

'OK. I didn't realise. So how long has he been here?'

'He was brought in by the Greeters 72 hours ago.'

'OK,' replied the man, regaining his composure. 'So, what stage of the awakening is he in?'

'He's not. He's moved into the somnambulating stage. Quite advanced, I understand. He escaped before the Greeters got to him and had to be tracked down. Took two days to catch up with him.'

'WHAT! But what about his mentors? Where were they when this was happening?'

'Well it's all in the notes, as I said. But basically, there were a few factors leading up to it which created the perfect storm.'

'Like what?' came his anguished response.

'Well first he had a bad bout of influenza and he took a treatment for it that contained Amantadine ...'

'Amantadine? Amantadine? What were they doing letting him take that? We must get that taken of the recommended list.'

'Well they can't watch him 24/7 - he did it himself, bought it off the shelf in a chemist in the form of cough medicine. Obviously, with his age and the drug he started to get flashbacks, which he thought to be déjà vu.'

'So why didn't they bring him in then?'

'Because the mentors didn't spot it and as he didn't mention it to anybody this carried on for a few weeks.'

'A FEW WEEKS ...?'

'Then one night he had a vivid flashback, prompted by hearing a familiar accent. He freaked out and confided in one of his mentors. Then a week later ...'

'A WEEK LATER!' exclaimed the distraught man, who by now had taken to loudly repeating the last few words of the woman's sentences.

'...a week later he was caught by a hard tackle during a football match.'

'A FOOTBALL MATCH!? What the hell was he doing playing football? He should have been brought in three times by now. Why wasn't he brought in when he confided in the mentor? What's the point of placing mentors there if they are not going to relay information back? This is madness.'

'Well, like I say, there's more in the notes but that's the abridged version.'

Clearly not listening, he continued: 'Do you know how much the chances of success for retrieval are reduced in the somnambulating stage?' he ranted. 'It's impossible to quantify.'

'Well it says 78% in the report, as per recent studies done by the Council,' she replied.

'Yes, yes ... exactly, that's what I would have said. And they expect me to sort this mess out?' he continued.

'Well, it is quite a mess, which is why they sent especially for you.'

'That's right,' he claimed, no more adept at spotting sarcasm in a voice than he was lack of interest. 'But I'm not taking the rap for this if it goes wrong. Oh no. I'm going to tell them straight. Come on, I need you with me as you've read the notes. Let's sort this out!'

A few faint footsteps and the swoosh of a door later, Jack was alone again. During the conversation, he had experienced tingling sensations throughout his body and could feel that he was regaining consciousness. He hadn't attempted movement while he had company, but now alone, he opened his eyes and sat upright. Sitting on the edge of the bed, he noticed the soft and tactile nature of the mattress. Presiding beneath a smooth matt black fabric cover lay a soft fluid base. At first, he thought it was water but as he removed his hand, the viscosity of the fluid returned it to its original state too slowly to be water. His mind was still unable to fully function as he sat prodding the mattress, watching it slowly reform. He recalled the conversation between the man and woman. Again, reference was made to Greeters and a somnambulating stage, but he was still no wiser about his fate. His life at the university was a farce, with his best friend placed there to monitor him, and his déjà vu triggered by a cough medicine.

Sliding off the bed onto the soft grey rubber flooring, he realised he was barefoot. In front was a glass entrance door, his reflection revealing he was no longer in his sweat suit but a skin-tight white hooded suit. The suit was covered in a rubber webbing, making it comfortable and warm to the touch. Next to the door was a keypad like the one at the army base, but it couldn't be the same code, could it? He remembered the comment Bones had made: *'How did you remember the code? Was it the code word you remembered or the numbers that spell it out?'* At the time it made no sense but now, looking at the pad, he realised the number represented a letter depending on how many times it was pressed. He began to enter the number whilst memorising the letters.

2,2,2, - C - 5,5,5, - L - 6,6,6, - O - 8,8,8, - V - 3,3, - E - 7,7, - R.

C-L-O-V-E-R. CLOVER? He frowned as he realised the 'clue' was useless but took a deep breath and pressed enter. Click. Click. Click. Click. Click. Click. He knew on the first click it was the wrong code but continued pressing to be sure, his firmness increasing exponentially with each press.

The room was bright, clinical and sparse. The structure of the bed below the mattress was minimalistic, with a translucent thin sheet balanced on a centre pedestal. The sleekness of the base appeared to lack the strength or balance to support the mattress but somehow it did. A TV screen positioned in the centre of one wall displayed images of outer space, looking down on Earth. The screen's surface was harder and cooler than the one in the refuge pod. He caressed it with his fingertips, running both hands in a transverse circular motion to activate the surface.

Swooosh.

A startled Jack pirouetted sharply to see three people entering the room. He was more alarmed by the presence of the one familiar face than the two complete strangers. Standing next to Carson was a lady in her early twenties and a middle-aged man, whom he assumed to be his earlier visitors. They were also dressed in white body suits but different to his; they were thicker, with padding and a diamond cross stitch and a royal purple stripe running down the outside of each arm.

'How are you doing, Buddy?' Carson piped up. 'All this must seem weird for you?'

'Buddy. Buddy? You can stick your Buddy. Would a Buddy sneak up behind his friend and pump him full of drugs?' Jack shouted.

'Yes, he would if he had too. If it was to help him in the long term.'

Jack was expecting an apology and was angry with Carson's reply.

'You expect me to believe that? I saw the Doc in the changing room, with a fancy syringe full of a green liquid. I know that's what I was injected with and I know it was you who did it because I read the tongue on your trainers.'

'Well there you go, Buddy, I injected you with Green. It's when you get pumped with Red that you should be worried,' Carson laughed.

'What?! I'm supposed to be thankful for being injected against my will, from behind, with God knows what because it's green and not red? What does that even mean? I want answers and I want them now!'

The young woman chose this point to strategically interject.

'Hello, my name is Poppi. Pleased to make your acquaintance,' she stated, holding out a hand.

The softly spoken British accent confirmed her presence in the room earlier. Her pale, flawless complexion complimented the ebony black hair resting on her shoulders, and a reflection of light revealed a soft touch of coral. The suit complimented a slim, lithe figure whilst accentuating her gently curvaceous hips. Like many Americans, Jack loved the British accent.

'Were you here earlier?' Jack enquired.

'Yes, yes, I was,' she replied, her firm handshake belying its petite, delicate form.

Reassured by Jacks reception, her male accomplice edged forward, also offering his hand. He was slim and middle aged, with a receding brown hairline, greying on each side. The tight suit revealed a fledgling paunch, perhaps the result of his recent pasta consumption.

'And I am Professor … er, Erik. My name is Erik,' he announced.

To Jack's surprise, Erik displayed a distinct Northern European accent, probably Dutch, thus eliminating him as the earlier dime-store lothario.

'Oh, OK, so you weren't the other person here earlier then?' he replied shaking his hand.

'No, that was Payne. He's feeling unwell, so I've replaced him.'

'Replaced him to do what? Unwell? Sounded like he was on the verge of a nervous breakdown to me. What do you want from me? What kind of professor are you anyway?' By now he was rattling out questions like bullets from a machine gun. 'Where am I? What are Greeters? How do I know how to do all this stuff and where to find the Army base? And how did you know I would be there?'

'Whooa, Buddy,' Carson interrupted. 'That's a lot of questions right there in one go.'

Jack turned away and again began caressing the TV screen.

'You were doing that when we came in,' Carson remarked. 'Why?'

'I was trying to change the theme on the TV screen. The other one was much easier, it had red buttons on the bottom. I was trying to change it to the fish tank again, I find it relaxing.'

'TV screen? That's not a TV screen,' replied Carson in bewilderment.

'Well what is it then?' asked Jack.

'Well we call it a window!' laughed Carson sarcastically.

'A window!' laughed Jack, louder and even more sarcastically. 'So, I suppose we are in outer space and that is planet Earth over there, then? Are we floating through space on a giant spaceship, like on Star Trek?'

'Well', said Carson sympathetically, 'pretty much so except it's a space station not a spaceship. I thought you knew where we were.'

'Did Spock beam us up?' roared Jack.

'Well no. Those things don't exist. The very idea that you can transport matter through space is ridiculous, that's just TV. And it's Scotty that beams them up, anyway. We flew up on the shuttle.'

'The shuttle – so what's that then? An aeroplane that flies in space?'

'Yes, exactly, except it's covered in heat resistant tiles and insulation to form a thermal protection system so that when it re-enters the earth's atmosphere ...'. Carson stopped talking. Looking at Jack he realised he was already suffering from information overload. Any more would be unnecessary waffle.

'But I've seen these before,' claimed Jack. 'In the mirrored place. They *are* TV screens. We *can't* be in space. How is that possible?'

Once again, Poppi had chosen her moment to re-join the conversation. 'He's right, Jack. And deep down you know he is. It may seem strange, but we'll explain everything in the fullness of time.' Her voice was calm, her accent reassuring. 'You may not realise it now, but Carson is a good friend to you, possibly the best friend you will ever have. But before we have time to explain, we need something from you.'

'What?' he questioned.

'Information,' she replied sternly.

'But I don't have any information.'

'Not in your conscious brain. But locked away in your subconscious mind is information that is vital to us, vital to everyone on that planet over there,' she proclaimed, dramatically pointing at Earth.

'She's right, Jack,' confirmed Erik before pausing for so long that Jack wondered if he had spoken purely to remind people of his presence. Finally, he continued: 'But we must do it now. This should have been done weeks ago. The longer we leave it the more likely it is the information will be lost forever.'

'You must trust us, Jack. You must,' pleaded Poppi. 'I promise, once we have the information, we will explain everything you want to know. But first you must take this leap of faith and help us. We're all on the same side.'

Jack looked through the window, the reality dawned he was indeed looking at Earth. Though this sounded highly improbable, was it unthinkable? He was aware of NASA's Apollo space program, developed to land men on the moon by the end of the decade. These people weren't NASA, though. From what he had seen they were at least 50 years ahead. The coach had commented at the army base that the unit had been there for more than 50 years, yet it possessed technology superior to anything he had ever seen. But was his situation so bad? What did he have to lose? It's not like he could escape this time. Not only was he prepared to take this leap of faith, he was becoming increasingly excited about it. Maybe the decision was made easier by the remaining green relaxant in his blood stream, but he decided he would play ball.

'Come on man, snap out of it. We need this information now. Stop messing around!' yelled Poppi, unaware of how badly timed and inappropriate her outburst was.

Jacks epiphany had convinced him to co-operate, and he was only moments away from divulging this; but instead they all stood silent, shocked by her unexpected rant. It was only then that Jack began to feel the whole scenario was more than a little staged; Poppi and Erik had been acting out a good cop bad cop role to persuade him to comply, but Erik had fluffed his lines, and she had taken it upon herself to take on both roles. Maybe his acting ability was rusty due to his last-minute substitution for the Tuscany guy. Whatever had just happened, rather than feeling annoyed, Jack was both amused and reassured. Even with the seriousness of the situation he found it comical and, besides, there was something about Poppi he trusted despite her overacting. For all the fancy technology, they weren't the putative geniuses he had assumed, and they lacked the most basic of interpersonal skills. Perhaps their over-reliance on technology had made them forget how to deal with people face to face?

'OK', announced Jack, suppressing his laughter, 'what do I have to do?'

'That's my boy,' cried Carson.

'Thank you, thank you, Jack,' Poppi gushed. 'You're doing the right thing.'

CHAPTER 8

Jack was taken to the 'Awakening Room', which had a similar layout but with a table, TV monitors and technical equipment in one corner.

'Lie down here please, Mr Marwood, and try to relax,' Requested Erik, pointing at a bed in the middle of the room.

The base of the bed was sturdier than his previous berth, but the mattress was the same. Jack lay down and began to relax.

'So, Poppi, you promised to tell me everything I need to know. You can start by telling me why I have information inside my head that you need to save humankind!' Jack demanded.

'That's not what I said,' came Poppi's riposte. 'I promised I would answer your questions *after* we have the information. The less you know about it now, the less the information will be further compromised.'

'She's right, Mr Marwood,' Erik stated.' Are you comfortable?'

'Yes, I'm fine, but it all seems a bit one sided to…'

'OK then, listen carefully' he continued.

Erik had his game face on. His persona had changed since Jack's compliance - he was in his comfort zone. It was difficult to say whether the perfunctory way in which he verbally expressed himself was down to personality or his accent, but, either way, he delivered his instructions direct, sparingly and at speed. Jack knew Poppi was right in her comments and trying to get information from Erik was an exercise in futility; so, he would have to trust them to keep their end of the bargain. Erik continued his monologue: 'The information you have is locked away in your subconscious, and Poppi and I have the task of finding this information in a relaxed and uncompromising manner. We will extract it as cleanly as we can. To do this we will send you into a state of deep hypnosis. There is no danger to you in any way. But I must emphasise that we will only have one opportunity to do this; once you awake from your state of hypnosis this information will be gone. Although it's the responsibility of Poppi and I to guide you to your starting point, once you begin you will be on your own. For this reason, it's vital you enter this process of your own free will. If you are not in favour, or feel in any way coerced, the process will not work, and the information will be lost forever. Do you understand what I have said, so far?'

'Yes,' he answered.

'Are you compliant in nature?'

'Yes.'

'Then we will begin. The next voice you hear will be Poppi. I will monitor your journey for our records,' concluded Erik before walking off in the direction of the table.

'Hello Jack. How are you feeling?' Poppi asked, with her now familiarly soothing voice.

'Good. Relaxed,' he replied.

'I'm going to pop a hood on for you.'

She attached a hood to his suit, which was slid onto his head, sweeping away a lock of protruding hair from his fringe with the seamless grace of an artist. Jack lay with eyes half open as Poppi produced a small electronic device roughly the size of a cigarette packet; but much thinner. She stared intently at it before touching the surface with her fingers. It was difficult to see the display from his position, but it looked like a miniature TV screen.

'What's that?' he enquired.

'Well', she replied, 'without getting too technical, we call it a heartbeat.'

'A heartbeat?'

'Yes, that's not the technical term but it's what we like to call it, because, like a heartbeat, we all have one and it's become such an integral part of our lives that it's hard to imagine how we would exist without one!'

'But what is it? I've never seen one.'

'You have but you don't realise it yet. It's a fantastic piece of technology. It comes as standard, with default settings, which, over time, become synchronised with you. This information is transferred wirelessly via satellites and kept on a central computer, so if you lose it or it breaks, you can regain the data accrued. On full charge the battery lasts up to 4 months but is recharged either by sunlight or artificial light. So, unless you're floating around in deep space, you'll be fine,' she explained, passing the unit over to Jack. 'This is a new unit set to factory default settings. Put your thumb in the middle, please.'

It was light in his hand with a smooth, gleaming glass screen and non-slip rubber back. As he placed his thumb in the middle of the screen, a message appeared 'Downloading……..'

'What's happening?' he asked.

'It has thumbprint recognition so whoever assigns their thumbprint to a unit becomes its owner. Now it can now only be activated by you and is currently downloading all your relevant information from the central database. Once it's complete we can continue.'

'What do you mean? How can it have information on me? I don't understand,' he quizzed.

'It has information on you because, although you haven't realised it, you're on our database. It has all sorts of information, like your preferences for music, food, books, and contact details. Stuff like that.'

'Contacts. Why?'

'So, you can call them from the device or send electronic letters. It also has a global tracking system, so we always know where you are.'

'Seriously', laughed Jack,' you can phone people up on this thing?'

'Phoning people is one of its most basic functions. But look, Jack, you don't need to understand too much now; all will become clear soon. You must trust me. All you need to know is that this is an amazing piece of kit which can save your life.'

'Wow!' exclaimed Jack, 'I thought you people were about 50 years ahead of us, down there. But a tiny wireless telephone, that's way more than 50 years ahead! Do you have any more stuff like this?'

Poppi's eyes lit up, 'Well, there are three cool pieces of kit we use in the field. They are the heartbeat, the skin and the Bivou-Mac. The heartbeat you have already seen and the skin you are wearing.'

'This? What's so special about this? Although I must admit it is comfortable,' he commented, stroking the soft rubber ribs.

'Well it's the ribs which make it such an effective tool. I can't remember the exact name of the composite material but it's basically a super-rubber. The back of the heartbeat is made of the same material as the ribs and when in contact will send currents to each other. For example, the suit will communicate to the heartbeat information such as heart rate, body temperature and increased breathing patterns. In return, the heartbeat reacts by raising or lowering the temperature of the suit in line with the user's requirements. So, when carrying out a physical activity, the skin lowers the temperature of the suit, thus reducing sweat and increasing performance. The suit will also work out the ideal heart rate for the wearer, based on body mass index. If exceeded, a gentle warning vibration is emitted. When fine-tuned, over time, to a person's idiosyncrasies, it's proven to increase strenuous physical performance by 81%. More in some cases.' She explained.

'It's also a great bit of kit for running up mountains on a hot summer's day!' hollered Carson from the other side of the room.

'YES!' exclaimed Jack. 'That would explain a lot. It was the first time in my life that I'd been beaten so easily at anything physical and you never even broke sweat.'

'That's right, buddy – I could have done it all again. No problem.'

'So, if I'd had one of these suits on with a heartbeat, then I would have won!' Jack mused.

'Ha, ha, steady on, buddy, it's not all down to the suit, you know?' retorted Carson.

'Maybe not but all the cards were stacked in your favour. Who knows, if I'd had one of these suits, maybe I'd be quarterback?'

'You keep telling yourself that, buddy. You sound like the young athlete from Greek mythology. He was jealous of another athlete who was so successful and popular there was a statue of him in the village square. He was so fed up with second place that every time he was beaten, he went into the square at night and chipped away a little at the statue until one night it collapsed and killed him. What was his name now …?'

Was Carson's belligerence deliberate, or an attempt at humorous banter? Maybe Carson's attitude was born of insecurity? When they met, he was a far superior physical specimen to Jack and the only player in the team who, had the body of a fully developed man; physical attributes which gave him the advantage during the trials for quarterback. Had Jack's recent transformation unwittingly threatened his friends' position as the alpha male? Jack mused on how the football trials may have had a different outcome if held today.

'Gentlemen, gentlemen, let's put those handbags away,' interrupted Poppi, stepping in with the authority and timing of an experienced boxing referee. 'I'm sure you're both excellent quarterbacks and score plenty of goals - or whatever it is they do. Besides, Jack, I haven't yet told you the suit's best little trick.'

'Go on …'. It would seem Jack could never resist bait.

'It's bulletproof!'

'Bulletproof? How can rubber be bulletproof?'

'Like I say, it's a super-rubber. But you'll have to take my word for it as I won't be firing a bullet at you just yet,' she laughed.

'Didn't you say there were three cool things?'

'Oh yes,' she remarked. 'I forgot about the Bivou-Mac. You've heard of a bivouac?'

'Yes.'

'And a Mac?' she continued.

'Well, obviously.'

'The Bivou-Mac is a coat which can transform into a one-person tent. Fully waterproofed, with a highly insulated foil inner skin to reflect and maintain body heat. Along with the other two items, you could survive anywhere providing you can find water and food. I hear you are partial to a bit of trout?'

Before he had time to answer, the heartbeat gave two shrill beeps.

'It's time to continue,' announced Erik, who had a knack for blending into the background.

'Here we go, Jack,' said Poppi. 'The heartbeat has downloaded your personal information and data. I just need to pop it into its little pocket.'

She reached over and placed it in a pocket on the shoulder of the suit, which had gone hitherto unnoticed by him.

As it slid snuggly in, she informed him, 'I've put the heartbeat in relax mode for you. That will help you get to where you need to be. Like we said, there's no danger to you, but the heartbeat will track your vital signs anyway.'

As he lay back, the vibrating suit did indeed help him relax.

'Before I go under', croaked Jack, 'there's one thing I would like to clear up with Carson. Are you there?'

'Yes, buddy, I'm here.'

'That story you told me about step counting …'

'Yes, buddy.'

'I didn't believe it for one second!'

Carson laughed. 'It's a true story, buddy. I never lie!'

His head was raised by the mechanical bed, and his eyes blinked rapidly as his lids become heavy. Poppi was staring searchingly into them, her gaze fixed intently, seemingly without the need to blink. He was transfixed by her deep blue eyes, which hinted at both beauty and coldness. She took his hand again, gentler than before, putting the underside of her fingers beneath his and gently caressing the top of his knuckles with her thumb. The cumulative effect of Poppi, the vibrating suit and the surroundings made his eyelids hopelessly heavy. He managed one final gaze into her eyes before surrendering.

'You are very tired… tired… tired… and will go to sleep… sleep… sleep…' she whispered before repeating 'You are very tired, tired, tired and will go to sleep, sleep, sleep.'

Letting go of his conscious self, Jack floated backwards as his mind disconnected from his body. He was aware of Poppi's presence; she had now become a guardian, guiding him along his esoteric journey.

'What is your name?' she orated.

'Jack.'

'Full name?'

'Jack Marwood.'

'What is your designation?'

'Designation?' he queried.

'Nomination, calling, job.'

'Er … student.'

'What is your current domicile?'

'Domicile?'

'Where do you live?'

'Montana.'

'Town, state and country?'

'Missoula, Montana, USA.'

'What is the year?'
'1964.'

After a brief pause her oration continued but quicker and with an increasing level of authority.
'NAME?'
'Jack Marwood.'
'DESIGNATION?'
'Student.'
'DOMICILE?'
'Missoula, Montana, USA.'
'YEAR?'
'1964'

Again, she continued:
'NAME?'
'Jack Marwood.'
'DESIGNATION?'
'Student.'
'DOMICILE?'
'Missoula, Montana, USA.'
'YEAR?'
'1964.'

By now, the force of her questioning had raised her status to the level of haranguer.
'NAME?'
'Jack Marwood.'
'DESIGNATION?'
'Student.'
'DOMICILE?'
'Missoula, Montana, USA.'
'YEAR?'
'1964.'

The sermon continued:

'You are NOT Jack Marwood. You are NOT a student. You do NOT live in Missoula, Montana, USA. It is NOT 1964.'

Again, a short pause before further confirmation: 'You are NOT Jack Marwood. You are NOT a student. You do NOT live in Missoula, Montana, USA. It is NOT 1964.'

Then again:

'You are NOT Jack Marwood. You are NOT a student. You do NOT live in Missoula, Montana, USA. It is NOT 1964.'

Again, she continued:

'You need to find the beginning. You need to start your journey. Your journey is important, but you are safe. You need to join your friends and begin your journey. You are on the south-east coast of Uruguay. The year is 1945. Do you see your friends?'

'I can't see anybody,' he whispered weakly.

Once again, he was cross examined: 'You are on the south-east coast of Uruguay. The year is 1945. Do you see your friends?'

'No.'

'You are on the south-east coast of Uruguay. The year is 1945. Do you see your friends?'

'Wait, wait. I think I see two people in front of me. Yes, Yes I do.'
'Do you recognise them?'
'Yes, I do. Of course, I do. I've known them for years.'

She returned to her original line of questioning:
'WHAT IS YOUR NAME?'
'Stanley Webster.'
'WHAT IS YOUR DESIGNATION?'
'Special Operations.'
'WHAT IS YOUR CURRENT DOMICILE?'
'Sheffield, Yorkshire, England.'
'WHAT IS THE YEAR?'
'1945.'

And again:
'NAME?'

'Stanley Webster.'
'DESIGNATION?'
'Special Operations.
'DOMICILE?'
'Sheffield, Yorkshire, England.'
'YEAR?'
'1945.'

By now she was relentless:
'NAME?'
'Stanley Webster.'
'DESIGNATION?'
'Special Operations.'
'DOMICILE?'
'Sheffield, Yorkshire, England.'
'YEAR?'
'1945.'

'Welcome back, Stan, it's great to hear from you again! You are at the starting point and ready to begin your journey. We will be with you throughout your journey but only in an observational capacity. We will not be able to interact with you directly, but you can interact with us. For the journey to be successful you must provide us with a regular, articulate narrative of events as they happen. Everything you see, everything you think, you must share with us. Without this your journey will not be successful. Do you understand?'
'Yes.'
Again, she repeated her previous comments:
'For the journey to be successful you must provide us with a regular, articulate narrative of events as they happen. Everything you see, everything you think, you must share with us. Without this your journey will not be successful. Do you understand?'
'Yes.'
For the final time she confirmed:
 'For the journey to be successful you must provide us with a regular, articulate narrative of events as they happen. Everything you

see, everything you think, you must share with us. Without this your journey will not be successful. Do you understand?'

'YES, YES. I understand!'

'After I have countdown to zero you will not hear my voice again. You will begin your journey. You will begin your narrative. Good Luck! 5 – 4 – 3 – 2 – 1 – ZERO……….'

He was on a beach. He could see two people running towards him carrying a dinghy. The vision was hazy and disconnected, with the booming countdown still ringing in his ears, causing more confusion. But as the voice in his head disappeared, his two friends became clear, as if emerging from a cloud. As they were almost upon him, he could see them very clearly. He knew what to he had do. He had a story to tell.

CHAPTER 9

Stanley's Narrative
June 1945

I can see John and Mouse on the beach, carrying a dinghy. They run past me, towards the trees and put the camouflage cover over the dinghy and slide it beneath the undergrowth. The beach is secluded but long and exposed; but we are far enough south of the target to have landed without being noticed, so hopefully the intel is robust. We have a long trek ahead of us, through rough terrain, accessible only on foot. But this is what we've trained for, and I can't think of two people I'd rather have by my side. We head north-westward into the dense woodland, led by John, with Mouse and me behind.

I've never been to Uruguay, but it's as I'd expected from the mission briefings back in Liverpool. Most of our physical training took place in the relative obscurity of the countryside of Missoula, but we were also stationed in Florida to acclimatise to the humid subtropical climate. June is one of the cooler times in Uruguay and it reminds me more of Missoula, or a spring day back in England, than it does Florida.

The geography and climate make this an ideal place for our mark to set up home. It's flat with many sources of water and is similar in area to Great Britain, but as most people live in a few built up areas, there are vast areas of unpopulated space - ideal for a high-profile European troublemaker to disappear. The country borders Argentina and Brazil, both of which could be crossed, and would suit anybody fleeing crimes committed in Europe.

'Oy, oy, oy,' exclaims John. 'Are you managing to keep up with me?'

We're now far enough into the cover of the trees and far enough away from our target to afford ourselves a bit of banter. John Carter is born and bred in Missoula, which comes in handy when we're stationed there. Between him and his friend Sal Esposito there isn't a person they don't know or place they can't get into; we've had some great downtime in Missoula. I know it's only a matter of time before

Mouse responds. Not to disappoint, he answers in his droning scouse accent,

'Alright, soft lad calm down. I'm having to slow my walking down so I'm not treading on your heels. Plus, I'm down wind of you so I don't want to get too close and caught in the crossfire. We all know what Carter rhymes with, don't we?'

'How old are you?' John replies. 'Grow up.'

'Just saying,' Mouse sniggers. 'I noticed you had beans for tea last night and I bet your bergen is packed full of them too. I'd hate to be in your Bivou-Mac tonight.'

'Look, that joke's wearing a bit thin now and it wasn't funny the first time. Carter rhymes with farter, so what? Big deal. And the next time you crack that one in front of a young lady, I'll crack you. I was in there, the other night, and she couldn't take me seriously after that.'

'Like hell you were in there. You were throwing yourself at her, but it was me she was looking at. You don't think she was falling for that stupid fake posh accent you use when chatting the birds up, do you? What's it supposed to be, anyway? English? Sounds more like Australian to me.'

'Bull crap. After you? Ha! Why have a burger when there's prime beef available? And there's nothing wrong with articulating your words when speaking to a young lady. Just because nobody understands your ridiculous accent. And you could try calling them ladies not birds. At least I sound like a gentleman, not a redneck from some freezing cold dump in the North of England! No offence, Flash!'

'None taken,' I reply, laughing.

I've had the nickname Flash for a year. It's better than Carter the farter, which Mouse is desperately trying to get to stick, much to John's annoyance. I'm called 'Flash' ironically as I'm laid-back in nature, which is something you couldn't accuse either of these two of. Mouse's real name is Gerry Shaw, but I came up with his nickname, even though John claims he made it up because of Gerry's stocky but small build. I was the first to call him scouse, then scouse mouse and finally Mouse. He seems to like it, particularly as he's proud of being from Liverpool, and it stuck. I know the comment about some dump up north will have riled him, so I can expect this banter to carry on for a while.

'No offence. No offence? How can you say that, Flash? He's talking about Sheffield as well as Liverpool, you know.'

'No, he's not, Mouse. He's always enjoyed Liverpool when we've been and I'm pretty sure he's never clapped eyes on Sheffield.' I say, attempting to conciliate the situation. 'He's winding you up because he doesn't like the nickname. He knows he can get at you with comments about Liverpool just as you know the farter thing winds him up. You're both as bad as each other and just as easy to wind up. Anyway, it was me the girl fancied the other night, not you two squabbling old women!'

As they laugh, I know I've stopped the bickering before it got out of hand, and despite the petty arguing, we're a tight bunch. When you work under high stress conditions you become close and together form a different entity with its own dynamic. As I'm the one who keeps the group together, I've been described as the glue, but I prefer to think that together we're as strong as concrete. John is the aggregate – big, solid and providing strength. Mouse is the sand – small and abrasive but gets everywhere and fills in the gaps. Me, well I'm the cement that holds everything together, of course: generally inert but just add water and wait for the chemical reaction. Despite the banter, we'd die for each other - which is just as well considering where we're heading.

We're well trained and compact, so it's hard to imagine any mission being unsuccessful. All three of us are Clover Caste, which makes each of us equal to at least 50 normal people. I think that's a conservative estimate, and when you factor in the training, superior equipment and technology, you could say we're as hard as coffin nails. This mission is different to the others, more challenging. We know for certain that the high-profile target is also Clover Caste, which is unusual. Not only that, but he is Leaf Level 4 Caste. Me, John and Mouse are only Leaf Level 1, so he is three Leaf Levels higher. This can be offset to a degree as being on Leaf 4 he has more to lose, and there are three of us. But either way, many of the benefits of being Clover Caste are gone. This is the biggest challenge we've faced but we're at our most prepared.

Being up against another Clover is already evident. On a typical mission we'd use our heartbeats for basic functions like navigation and communication. The *Normals* are unable to intercept our superior technology; this is not the case when up against a Clover Caste operative. To avoid interception, we must use the heartbeat in low power mode with the GPS turned off. Low power function reduces heat emission, which can be detected by heat sensors miles away. This function still enables interaction between the heartbeat and skin, so our body temperature and bodily functions are still monitored. Even on safe mode the heat emitted can be picked up from a 5-mile radius so, we'll be approaching the final 10 miles with the heartbeats turned off. So, it makes sense to set up camp outside that radius and to enjoy a good rest, utilising the heartbeats temperature and relaxation modes. John navigates from the front with a magnetic compass and a paper chart.

'You could do with a nickname, though, John,' I say. 'It's always handy for a Clover to have a nickname - but one you're comfortable with.'

'How about Lucky?' John replies. 'I think Lucky suits me.'

'Seriously?' howls Mouse. 'Seriously, you're trying to give yourself a nickname? Only an American would do that!'

'Well I'll have to if neither of you two can come up with one,' he adds defensively.

'Anyway, looking at the chart, we're just over 10 miles away from the target, so we'll set up camp here. There's a small river over there for water and plenty of cover beneath the trees.'

We're deep in primary forest with no sign of humans ever having set foot here. Johns right, it's the perfect spot. We put down our bergens and start to form the makeshift camp. Without looking I know they're doing the same as me; we've done this so many times before in training it's instinctive. Sure enough, I look up to see that John and Mouse have removed each of their Bivou - Macs, erected the small robust tents and fixed them to the ground. We've formed a triangle, a small triptych fort, within which the fire will be built, to share the warmth and reduce its visibility.

While John prepares the fire, Mouse wanders away from camp with a couple of containers to collect water. 'I'm going to see a man about a dog,' he says before disappearing. He always says that when he goes to collect water. Or pass water, come to think of it. I wonder what he'd say if he ever actually went to see a man about a dog?

'So, do you think there'll be any more Clover Caste there, other than the target?' I ask John, as he pulls a peat briquette from his burgen and places it on the bed of rocks forming the base of the fire.

'Can't see it myself. There's no doubt he's got rogues working with him. He couldn't have got this far without them. But he's such a high-profile target now they will be avoiding direct contact with him. What do you think?' he replies.

'I agree. He'll be there with a small band of Normals. The fewer people who know about this place the better for him. Reports are that all the contractors used to build this place were killed and dumped in the forest after the work was completed; once they've seen it, nobody leaves the site alive. He's completely ruthless.'

'Ruthless. Is that another word for crazy?'

'He's crazy alright. Textbook megalomaniac,' I conclude. 'Are you looking forward to trekking through the forest tomorrow without the skin to cool you down?'

'Yeah, should be a challenge doing it old-school. I'm looking forward to it, but in this humidity, be prepared to sweat like a five-dollar whore!'

'Well, you'd know more about that than me,' I counter, laughing.

'Did someone mention whores?' chirps Mouse, whose light-footed approach in his camouflage skin I'd failed to notice. He's returned with the water, the concertina containers bouncing up and down in his hands. I notice the water in his left hand is green, so he's already added the purifier. John grabs the clear container, for cooking and hydrating the peat. He measures it out and pours it over the briquette. We stand and watch as it gradually increases to twenty times its original size. We've done this many times, but there's something therapeutic about the process. While there are many sources of fuel out here, the subtropical climate results in a high-water content, producing unwanted smoke; if the correct ratio of water is added to the peat, it's smokeless and gives out high-intensity heat.

'So, do you fancy a little treat for tea tonight?' enquires Mouse.

'What do you mean?' I say. 'We have our protein packs. I thought that was the plan. And some beans.'

'Yes, but wouldn't you prefer to eat this?' he boasts, producing a large fish from a bag concealed behind him.

'Wow look at that!' John exclaims. 'How did you manage to get that? You were only gone two minutes.'

'The rivers full of them. They were practically jumping into my arms. I don't think they've many natural predators, and I reckon we're the first people to set foot here.'

'But we can't eat that!' I protest. 'We don't even know what kind of fish it is – we could get food poisoning! And cooking it will make a smell. We need to stick with the original plan of protein packs and odourless beans. What's the point of going to the trouble of bringing our own food, peat and purifying the water if we take risks like that?'

'We could always run a quick scan on the heartbeat,' suggests John.

'No, we can't,' I reply. 'We would have to turn the signal on to access the database, which could be intercepted. '

'Everyone knows it has to be on for at least a minute before it can be intercepted. It would only take a few seconds to scan the fish,' he proffered.

This is the thing about John that winds me up: he's the most knowledgeable and hardworking guy I've ever met but prone to major lapses in judgement. He says that I worry too much and that I am one of life's thinkers. As if to reinforce this point, as I'm thinking about how to further articulate my contempt for his idea, he turns on his heartbeat and scans the fish anyway.

'Yes, its fine to eat,' he announces.

'I can't believe you did that!' I scream. 'You've put us in danger. And what for? A fish.'

'Look, buddy, it's you raising your voice that's putting us in danger. It's off now and wasn't on for more than a few seconds. Nobody could have picked that up. I'll bet you 50 bucks that when we wake up tomorrow morning we're still alone.'

'Maybe. But that was an unnecessary risk. Sometimes I wonder about your judgement.'

'Well sometimes I wonder about the size of your testicles,' is his repose.

I turn to Mouse for support, but he has his back to me whilst preparing the food. Sensing my gaze, he reassures: 'Don't worry, Flash, I'll fillet the fish so that it doesn't smell when we cook it.'

I know Mouse agrees with me, but he doesn't like confrontation. Banter he could do all day long, but he's uncomfortable standing his ground on more serious issues. As much as I like John, I've more in common with Mouse. A lot is to do with being English but some of it's down to personality, and though I'm seething inside, I must concede that John is usually right about these things.

The silence is deafening as we sit around to watch the cause of our squabble cook on the fire. I won't admit it, but I'm reassured that the fire is smoke free and there's no smell. Mouse breaks the silence:

'How come this guy has managed to cause so much trouble then? He's as mad as a hatter, so how's he got so many people to follow him?'

John, who's an expert on the subject, responds:

'It's historical. Dates back hundreds of years before we had the Clover Council. Do you remember the myriad armies from history class, Mouse?'

'Well, sort of,' is the unconvincingly reply.

'Well do you know what a myriad is?'

'A lot?' Mouse quizzes, equally as unassured.

'Well, kind of. That's what it's come to mean over time, but its literal meaning is 10,000. So, a myriad army is an army of 10,000. Back in the old days, before the Council, each Clover was assigned their own myriad army of 10,000 Ants - or Normals as you call them. This worked well if individual Clovers either worked alone or grouped together for the common good; to bring forward society, often benefitting the Ants

- as much as the Clover Caste. The problem is when you have individuals wanting to benefit their own cause at any expense.'

'Yes, I understand that, but how does he get so many Normals to follow him into doing bad deeds?'

'Well, Mouse, it's simple. Most Ants are easy to predict and will follow direct and strong suggestive persuasion. There are many techniques and this guy uses them all - but he's particularly fond of mass hypnosis, which is a technique we've been using for hundreds of years to control the masses. It's because it can be so easily exploited for the gain of the few that the Council was formed in the first place. We Clover are far more advanced than the Ants, but we need each other and must live together. We mustn't adopt a superiority complex; they're not our subordinates or slaves for us to boss around and manipulate. This is why I'm a great believer in the Council and the fairness and balance they provide.'

'I understand all that,' Mouse confirms. 'But how they can go along with such atrocities with little or no resistance.'

'That's because you are looking at it through your eyes; Clover Caste are advanced and better educated. You must remember that the speeches he makes are set against a backdrop of poverty and starvation. These people are so desperate to survive and look after their families that they will do anything to achieve this. So, what he does is isolate one sector of society and subliminally make them the scapegoats for all the misery that he himself is piling upon the masses. It's this transference of blame that's his biggest weapon. He puts thoughts into people's heads by carefully scripted speeches, repeating key words three times for maximum impact. The strange thing with the Ants is that a lot of people will collectively believe a big lie much easier than an individual will believe a small lie. They find the suggestion of the masses irresistible, with few strong enough to resist. Those who do realise that if they voice their opinions too loudly, they will end up in the same situation as the people they are trying to help. These are basic tactics used for hundreds of years by us to manipulate them for our gain. As I said, the fundamental reason the Council came into existence was to put a stop to such abuse of our responsibilities. Who knows where we would be now if it wasn't for the Council, and we went back to the dark days of the myriad armies? And with the powerful weapons and technologies we now possess, who knows where that will lead?'

'Anyway', Mouse Responds, 'if you feel so much empathy with the Normals, why do you call them Ants? They aren't little worker ants to do your donkey work for you.'

John sighs before continuing. 'Didn't you learn anything at the School of Enlightenment? They're not called Ants because of the insects. That's political correctness gone mad. The term Ant has been used for thousands of years but has recently been turned into a derogatory term by the liberal elite to show how caring and benevolent they are - or rather want to be perceived. That's not where the term Ants originates from; Ant derives from an abbreviation of the word Anthropos, which is the ancient Greek work for human. Despite what you've been indoctrinated to think by the do-gooders, there's nothing condescending about using the term Ant. Of course, I realise that when I use it, people feel uncomfortable, which is the main reason I continue to do so!'

As I stare at the fire, I'm beginning to feel guilty at my anger toward John. Perhaps the reason I have more in common with Mouse has nothing to do with personality or even nationality; maybe it's because I will struggle to ever match the gentle humility John has toward all humankind, let alone have such an understanding that I could articulate to others so eloquently. He's a true scholar of the Clover Caste and life in general. So, what if he scans the odd fish when he shouldn't?

CHAPTER 10

Gulping down the delicious fish I feel guilty about my overreaction. As Mouse passes John his plate, he can't help having another dig.

'I've put fewer beans on yours than ours; there isn't much fresh air in those Bivou-Macs as it is.'

John doesn't react, instead choosing to stare into space before sighing,

'Mmmm, this fish is nice.'

After giving us our food, Mouse settles down with his own.

'Well, Leaf 4 is a long way off, but I know what I want to do,' he announces, shovelling food into his mouth. 'I'm going to be a musician,' he adds, before looking up to gauge reaction.

He looks up to gauge reaction. As Clover Caste spend much of Leaf Levels 1 to 3 planning for Leaf Level 4, it's not surprising that Mouse has brought it up. Sitting around the campfire, ahead of a deadly mission, is an ideal time to focus our minds on the future and remember why we are putting ourselves in harm's reach. We've discussed this topic before, but Mouse has changed his mind since last talking about it, when he wanted to be a surfer living in Australia.

'Don't you think it's a waste?' John replies.

'No, I don't', Mouse defends, 'I intend to enjoy Leaf 4. Work hard, play hard - that's what I think. I'm gonna work hard for the Council and this'll be my reward. Earlier, when you were talking about the Normals' behaviour, you accused me of seeing it through my own eyes not theirs. I thought it was hypocritical as you're the worst person I know for being pig-headed.'

Touché. Although I show no emotion, I'm egging him on. OK: Mouse changes his mind a lot and it's difficult to keep up with him, but John always belittles his ideas. This time John looks shocked and shapes his mouth to reply, but Mouse has already moved on.

'I want to start a group back in Liverpool with three of my mates. I'm gonna play lead guitar and sing. We're gonna spend ten years touring the world, meeting women and drinking beer. We'll be so successful that everyone will know who we are, and all the girls will fancy us. With the backing of the Council there's no reason it won't work.'

'Are you gonna be like an English version of the Ink Spots?' I ask.

'No, much better than that. More like Woodie Guthrie, but in a group. At the end of it all I'll have so much money that I can do what I want with the rest of Leaf 4.'

'I can't see it working; it's a silly idea,' dismisses John. 'The only way to make real money is to be a solo artist like Frank Sinatra or Jimmy Dorsey. Plus, I can't see the Council going for it.'

'What do you mean silly? Don't you think most of the singers and big bands making money now are Leaf 4s? Of course, the whereabouts and identity of Leaf 4s is treated by the Council with discretion. But a large chunk of the rich and famous must be bankrolled by the Council. These are people who have served the Council well and are now being rewarded, and I bet they haven't done anything as big as I'm doing now. Frank Sinatra must be, for sure? Not just singers either, but actors, sportsmen, TV personalities. What better way to be rewarded for years of hard graft than getting paid lots of money to do something you love!' Mouse argues, standing his ground.

'Sportsmen!' scoffs John, 'You can't make someone a good sportsman. Even the Council can't do that you, have to have talent.'

'Yes,' replies Mouse impatiently, 'I know that. I'm not saying all Leaf Level 4 Clover can be sportsmen, but those that are capable of it can be helped. Besides by the Final leaf we will have built up four lifetimes of muscle memory. Physically speaking we will be superior specimens to the Normals. What an individual Clover may lack in natural talent, they will make up for in speed and strength.'

'He's got you there, John,' I laugh, 'So, what about the rest of Leaf 4?'

'Dunno yet. But it will involve kids. Lots of kids. What about you, John? You dismiss my ideas, but I bet yours has something to do with the Council, doesn't it?' responds Mouse.

'Well I know what I'm going to do', John pipes up, 'and no, as it happens, it doesn't have anything to do with the Council. I want to be President of the USA!'

'Ha, ha, ha,' laughs Mouse with derision. 'That would have been my second guess. You're so predictable! You do, of course, realise you'll be at the back of a very long queue for that one. And you must also realise that every single president and presidential candidate in the history of the USA has been Clover Caste. It was the Council who invented the president of the USA - and the government - to maintain democratic control when we moved away from the myriad armies.'

'Wow, that's amazing,' John replies, impressed.

'I thought you, of all people, would have known that.'

'I do, Mouse, but I'm amazed that you managed to stop staring out the classroom window for long enough to learn anything. For once you've impressed me!'

As these two lock horns, a metaphorical lightbulb appears above my head.

'I've got it!' I screech.

'Got what? If it's catching then don't come near me,' Mouse says, drawing upon another favourite from his often predictable but seemingly endless Liverpudlian joke book.

'A nickname for John. How about the Cat?'

'Why?' John enquires.

'Because you two are always arguing like the cartoon cat and mouse. So, it's either that or we nickname the pair of you Tom and Jerry!'

'I prefer Lucky,' he moans, before returning to his favourite subject. 'Anyway, Mouse, did you know that the Clover have lent a helping hand in much of the history of the USA? For example, during the War of Independence, against the British, some of our best generals trained the patriots in advanced armed combat techniques and military strategy. They were at a disadvantage to the British as they had no government, army or infrastructure and would never have won the War without our help.'

'But why should we help?' Mouse questions. 'Maybe they wouldn't have won the war because they weren't meant too. It's OK you talking up the Council and how they help the Normals but what gives us the right to decide who should win each war?'

Mouse is giving as good as he gets tonight. It's usual for them to have heated discussions but of a trivial nature. Mouse avoids serious confrontations with John, particularly about anything to do with the Council. John is a big believer in the Council, and anybody prepared to stick their head above the parapet and say differently should expect to be shot at.

John counters: 'Well what about the American Civil War, which followed 100 years later? You can't argue that the Council helping to abolish slavery was a bad thing. When the war seemed to be reaching a stalemate, they released a little technology to help it along.'

'What technology?' I ask.

'They passed the reloadable rifle onto the Yankees, so they didn't have to reload after every shot. The Ants technology is primitive compared to ours, so every now and then we help them along with some technological innovations. We helped the war finish quicker, saving lives and improving the quality of life immediately.'

'Throw them a few crumbs, you mean?' baited Mouse. 'But if they are as equal to us as you say they are, why don't we give them all the technology we have? We should even come clean about who we are. I agree with the abolition of slavery, but again we have chosen sides and won that particular fight.'

I don't agree with what Mouse has said – and I don't think Mouse does either– but I know I won't have long to procrastinate before John comes to the defence of the Council.

'You don't get it, do you, Mouse? You don't understand the control and balance the Council brings. How old were you when you found out you were Clover Caste?'

' Sixteen.'

' Sixteen – the same as me!'

'You already knew that,' Mouse protests. 'We were in the same class in the School of Enlightenment. All three of us were. It was only 10 years ago'

'Exactly, exactly. So, if we were in the same class then, how come you understand so little?'

Again, Mouse protests: 'I wasn't as interested as you. Besides, you were the class know-it-all; you knew more than the teachers by the time we left. In fact, you seemed to know more than a lot of them when we started. It's you that's odd not me. You're obsessed!'

Again, I keep my own council, but I agree with Mouse. John knew more about the Clover Caste when he started than I did when I left, a year later. He has a way of making you feel stupid when it comes to the subject. He's no smarter than me; I got better grades in most of the other subjects but as Clover Culture was the main one, he emerged with the better academic reputation.

'I knew about the Clover Caste when I arrived because in the brief time between being *greeted* and going to the school, I read up on the subject. I didn't sit around questioning my existence and crying into my surrogate mother's apron. When I was there, I grasped the chance to learn as much as I could from the mentors and teachers. I realised what a privilege it was to be Clover Caste and wanted to learn as much as I could from experienced peers. You chose not to grasp the opportunity as I did. I think that was a mistake but then that was up to you. If you'd have paid closer attention, you'd realise that you're missing the whole point.'

'Go on then,' Mouse coaxes, producing a fake yawn. 'Tell me the *whole* point then. I'm *dying* to know!'

'You keep asking why the Council interferes with the status quo, as if it were the Ants who have made things this way. That's not the case. The current state of things is a result of thousands of years of the Clover Caste using our greater knowledge and technology to make things better for us, *not* the Normals. The Council is levelling things out. We talked about the American Civil War and the War of Independence earlier. They are both great examples of why the Council need to get involved. Before the War of Independence, the largest concentration of Clover Caste was in Northern Europe. Groups of Clover Caste joined together with their myriad armies, their goal being to form a hegemony.'

'What's a hegemony?' I ask.

'A dominant group with influence over all issues in society. The holy grail for these Clover was to create one global hegemony to control the world. To do this they had to pool resources and join their respective myriad armies to achieve this common goal. During this period, they used their skill sets to sail around the world claiming land for themselves. The big problem they had was ambitious individuals working together with other like-minded individuals. It's a tricky paradox to master. Becoming selfless in the short term for longer-term individual gain can be impossible where greed is concerned. They say there is no I in team but there is an M and an E. Sure enough the hegemony became fractious and splinter groups began to appear over different areas of Europe. The groups in France, Spain and Portugal continued to acquire land relatively close by. The British faction was more ambitious, claiming land further afield, including America, building up what became known as the British Empire. Inevitably, there were squabbles between the armies for land and dominance.'

'So, our forefathers were a bunch of greedy, land grabbing megalomaniacs?' I ask.

John replies, 'Not all of them. You see we're different to the Ants in our DNA but not in personality. For each one of us wanting to rule the world there's many more who just want to live peacefully. History will always remember the fighters and troublemakers before they do the peacemakers. While the disruptive Clover were forging ill-fitting partnerships with others in pursuit of the coveted hegemony, many more were getting together peacefully to lay down the foundations for what was to become the Clover Council.'

'Yes, I remember this from class,' I find myself saying. 'Wasn't the original declaration made in remote headquarters on the west coast of Ireland? The Gammadion Agreement?'

'That's right, Flash. Well done. Do you know why it was called the Gammadion Agreement?'

Although John is the same age as me, I feel like I have just been sent to the top of the class by my teacher. Unfortunately, as I can't remember why it was called the Gammadion Agreement my moment of glory is short-lived. I know I've been taught this during Enlightenment, so I rack my brain before finally admitting defeat.

'No, John, I can't remember. Why was it called the Gammadion Agreement?'

'Because it was during these meetings that the gammadion cross was formed. We all know why the number 4 is of special interest to the Clover Caste, so they created this cross as a sign of unity. It's made up of four Greek gamma letters fixed to each other. Over time, this became known as the swastika, which means "lucky object".'

'But what's all this got to do with the Civil War and War of Independence — and the Clover getting involved?' snaps Mouse, now visibly frustrated with John's meandering narrative.

'Because North America was discovered and colonised by the British Clover. High level Clover were rewarded with large areas of land, worked by their myriad armies. They became rich on the back of this slave labour. Now this was nothing unusual because it's how we'd been working for thousands of years. But the tide was turning.'

'How?' I ask.

'By this point levels of communication across the world had increased, and the voice of the masses began to drown out the noisy minority. Most didn't agree with the practice of the myriad army, instead preferring a democratically elected Council. So, a plebiscite was held, and the first Clover Council elected. To celebrate this new direction, the four-leaf Clover replaced the swastika and we became known as Clover Caste, rather than the Gammadions. As part of this process, the USA was designated as the first true democracy in the world, but for this to happen the British colonisation and the practice of slavery had to be removed, which is why, to this day, America is the land of freedom and opportunity.'

'Sounds like propaganda to me,' Mouse replies. 'You're like a party-political broadcast on behalf of the Clover Caste. This story is one sided. The fledgling democracy was spearheaded by George Washington, who we all know was a wealthy Clover landowner. So how is this true democracy when we are still putting our own people in the positions of responsibility *and* withholding technology from them?'

I can see by the look on his face that John is exasperated with Mouse, but he continues anyway.

'Look, Mouse, there's always going to be a ruling class within any society and - whether *you* like it or not - this *will* come from within the Clover Caste. Things are more democratic and better all-round since the Council. There are still some who prefer the old Gammadion days and won't accept change, which is why we're in this position now. Do you think this guy we're after has the interests of the Ants at heart?'

'So', I respond, 'you're saying that this guy, and the people helping him, are a subculture of our Caste that yearns for the good old days of the Gammadions?'

'That's exactly what I'm saying, Flash,' he purrs. 'You can see the big picture, not like some people! Most people see history as a set of outdated, uninteresting facts, but it's one of the most powerful tools in the world. History has a habit of repeating itself because we seem incapable of learning from previous mistakes. To a degree, you can forgive the Ants such mistakes because of their short lifespan, but we should be wiser. Flash is spot on, there *is* a subculture of our Caste out there refusing to learn from past mistakes. They hide among us in plain view but secretly yearn for days long past. They still secretly call themselves the Gammadion Caste and use the swastika as their symbol.'

'So, in effect that's the whole reason we're sitting here now!' I conclude as the metaphorical light bulb once again appears above my head. 'This guy still sees himself as Gammadion Caste! Its history repeating itself!'

'As you say in England, Bango!' exclaims John.

'Bingo, you idiot,' frowns Mouse.

'Bingo, bango, whatever,' smiles John. 'Flash understands. Anyway, we have a big day ahead of us tomorrow. Time to go to sleep.'

As I lie in my Bivou-Mac, I wonder what will happen tomorrow. John's visitation of history has clarified why we are here and what we are up against, though part of me wishes he hadn't bothered. The task ahead now seems bigger and I can't help wondering why we've been chosen to carry out such an important mission. Am I ready? Am I good enough? This guy is Leaf 4 for Christ's sake! If they picked up John's signal when he scanned that damn fish, we may not even wake up to find out. I'm thankful for the soothing, relaxing vibrations of the Heartbeat. Without it I'm not sure I'll get to sleep.

CHAPTER 11

'Wake up, Flash,' John whispers, shaking me awake. 'It's time to get ready.'

As I emerge from the Bivou-Mac, John and Mouse have already packed away their temporary abodes.

'I thought you could have a lie in, Flash, so you'd be in a better mood when I remind you about the 50 bucks you owe me.'

'What for? I don't owe you 50 bucks.'

'Yes, you do. I bet you we'd still be alone this morning after turning on my heartbeat yesterday!'

'OK', I admit, 'you were right, and if we get through this in one piece, I'll give you the money!'

One of John's annoying traits is his gloating. He didn't have to bring the fish up but chose to do so to prove a point. But that's why he makes his little wagers; he doesn't need the money; he just wants everyone to know he was right. Still, he shouldn't have scanned that fish, whichever way you look at it. As if reading my mind, he passes me a protein pack and remarks, 'Here's the protein pack you missed out on yesterday – you can eat it on the way. Yum, yum!'

In stark contrast to yesterday, the climate is subtropical and, without the heartbeats to cool us, we make slow progress through the forest. John again leads the way but this time there's no jovial banter to break the monotony. As the close, humid conditions sap sweat from my body – and, with it, the strength from my legs - my mind focuses on the task ahead. I consider our plan in painstaking detail: the intel, the execution, the exit strategy. Of course, much will depend on the accuracy of the intelligence, but we've worked on many scenarios. I've a mental image of the compound we're looking for from the mission briefings; it's a hamlet of three buildings isolated deep in the forest. Building one is a large stone residential structure. Building two is something of a mystery but possibly a workshop or storage facility. Building three is located near the top of the hillside and is a multipurpose building serving as a lookout and water collection tower.

With John raising his hand, I realise we must be close. I've been so focused on the task I hadn't noticed the toll taken on my body, but as we stop, I notice the beads of sweat pouring down my forehead. I take a swig of water, emptying the bottle, and wipe the sweat from my brow; but he rubber web on the sleeve of the skin is waterproof and rather than soaking up the salty water from my brow, smears it around my face instead. The other two are faring no better, with Mouse looking as though he's taken a shower. A wry smile passes between us as we open our bergens to search for a change of clothes.

The training in Florida has paid dividends in acclimatised us for this moment, but although the temperature during training had seemed hotter, I feel more drained now. I don't know if this is due to the terrain or the humidity but a jelly-like feeling in my legs suggests it may be down to nerves. Once changed, I wipe down my forehead with a cloth. Our bags contain bottles of an effervescent fluid designed for quick rehydration, which we drink. I scan around, looking for a place to hide the bergens.

We're at the top of a rock face above the valley which is home to the hamlet. I'm panicking; I'm not ready for this. I need to know more about what lies in the valley. John picks up my bergen to hide it and sensing my fear he reassuringly puts his hand on my shoulder and smiles. With our property hidden, he beckons us to the edge of the rock face.

Peering over, the beauty of the landscape rolling out before me is breath taking. Below are hilly meadows covered in lush vegetation, gloriously punctuated with splashes of multi-coloured flowers. Red flowers grow in abundance on a nearby tree. The meadows stretch gradually downhill towards an estuary; within its reflection are all the imaginable shades of green. Beyond the estuary a sprawling mountain range defines the horizon, separating the land from the pale blue sky. Our steep ascent up the hillside gave no indication it was harbouring such a hidden gem. It's a beautiful location for a hideaway. I see the three buildings ahead: the dwelling is not what I was expecting to see in the midst of meadowland in Uruguay, and although the location is unusual, it's the European style of the architecture which has caught me off guard. The stone is irregular in size, with pieces so big I'm at a loss to figure out how they were transported here; but it's an accurate reflection of the flamboyant opulence often associated with our target.

Closer to the rock face is a stone water tower, even more impressive than the house. It's circular, with eight rectangular legs around its perimeter, supporting a reservoir at the top. The legs are joined by a simple arch construction, transferring the loads down the structure. I marvel at the large keystones and wonder how they ended up here. Fixed to one of the legs is a ladder leading to a platform around the reservoir, which must be an observation point. The wooden planks sit on metal gallows brackets attached to the stonework, forming an octagonal walkway. At the bottom of the valley sits the third mystery building, which I'm guessing is an electricity generation facility. Between the tower and the third building runs a narrow timber trough, perhaps for water to run down at high pressure and spin a turbine to generate electricity. Solar panels are simpler but would be spotted by our satellites. What strikes me the most is not the genius or beauty of the buildings but the lack of movement within the site; I haven't seen a single person in or around any of the three buildings.

Turning to John I mouth the words 'What do you think? Where is everyone?'

John shrugs his shoulders and mouths back: 'Not sure. Do you think it's a trap? Do they know we're here?'

Mouse wags his finger in front of his face to draw attention, but I can't read his lips. He has a habit of talking too fast which, along with his accent, makes it difficult for even an accomplished lip reader like me to understand.

'Speak slower,' I reply, pointing to my mouth.

'There's only one way to find out,' he mimics. 'Let's go.'

John nods: I nod back. This is it! We pull over the hood from our camouflage skins for maximum protection. We must descend a 30-foot rock face to access the meadows. The face is flat and easy for climbers of our competence, but we'll be exposed and must choose our moment carefully. As always, John goes first and is hidden safely in a bush in an impressively fast time. Mouse follows in a similar manner

– but not as quick. It's clear as I make my descent that the face has been quarried; it's artificially flat and covered with chisel marks, which make good footholds. Landing at the bottom, I see a large semi-cut block of stone, surplus to requirements and partially covered in vegetation.

The vast cliff face is where the stone for the buildings was extracted. So, the mystery surrounding the origin of the stonework is solved, but where are the missing people? The others nod as I point to the rock face and mouth the word 'quarry'. We give each other the thumbs up and set off in different directions; having been allocated one building each, John heads for the water tower as I head downhill towards the mystery building with Mouse until he peels off toward the dwelling. As I continue, I can't help looking back at the stunning dwelling, built in the Classical Order of Architecture and would not look out of place on a hillside in Tuscany.

I can't see anyone in the immediate vicinity, even Mouse has disappeared. But then, the camouflage skins have been designed for this environment: as well as cloaking visibility, the skins give us protection from attack. Our target will be wearing one, so I'll aim for his hands, feet or face. If I'm lucky, I'll catch him with his hood down, but being Leaf 4 he's unlikely to make such a mistake.

There's a small track next to the water trough, between my building and the water tower. They're overgrown rail tracks, used for transporting building materials down the hill. This building is more elementary than the other two, with solid walls and small window openings. Despite the intelligence reports of its high-level safeguarding, I still can't see another living soul. My heart beats faster and I start to panic, again. It must be a trap. Where is everyone?

The windows are small and high, so access will have to be through a door. Has the target been tipped off and the site abandoned? I doubt this is his only personal citadel in South America. But if he's fled, did he do it in a rush or did he have time to rig traps? Maybe when John turned on his heartbeat, they picked up his signal and fled. If he's gone, the mission's a failure. We're all failures. So why am I hoping this is the case?

At the far side of the building is an area covered in camouflage nets. Maybe he's growing drugs to finance his warmongering. It's the perfect environment to grow marijuana and with little chance of being disturbed. I hear a humming sound coming from beneath the covers; perhaps a machine used for cultivation? They must be here, harvesting the crops. But who's helping him? Maybe the workforce is farmers from the local villages? Gun in hand, I edge towards the netting and sweep it aside to reveal rows of green rectangular metal boxes. Each box is six feet high, with two large fans visible through perpendicular meshing. There are hundreds of them whirring away in the fields. But still no people. The cables lead to the main building via a channel in the ground covered over with timber boards. The boards are easy to lift, and I see black insulated electrical cables. So, I was right - this is an electrical generation farm – but instead of using water powered turbines they're using warm air. Ingenious! A sharp cracking noise from the house on the hill startles me. It sounded like a gunshot. I'm worried for the others but I must check my building first. The wooden door is ajar so, crouch on my knees and push it open.

CHAPTER 12

The door swings open, revealing a lobby with four doors. The cool air inside is a welcome relief from the energy-sapping, breath-gasping humidity outside. A chill spirals down my spine as the warm river of perspiration is replaced by a cold trickle juddering across my body. The quiet coldness of the building radiates an aura of bad omens; I sense a place within which bad things happen.

Three of the four doors are labelled. The two to the right are a store and a toilet, with the unlabelled door to the left. In front is a "Cryogenics Lab". What's cryogenics? A light automatically triggers as I enter, revealing a bigger lab than I'd expected. It's even cooler than the lobby with no windows or smell; but what I see ahead disturbs me.

There's ten large silver cylinders in two rows of five, one down each side of the room, with a door at the far end. The cylinders have a full-height glass panel to the front with cables rooting out at the base. With photographic evidence taken I should move on, but I can't take my eyes off them. A clear liquid fills the cylinders almost to the top with a silver bag floating inside. The size and shape of the bag suggests there's a body inside. At the top of the cylinder is an illuminated panel displaying -125 C, with "Dewar 1" handwritten on a sticker below. If this is the temperature of the liquid inside, it must be liquid nitrogen.

All ten of the cylinders, are occupied. As I reach the door at the far end of the room, I notice a store to the right with black metal gates discreetly set back from a full-height stone wall. Behind the padlocked gates are metal canisters stacked up to the ceiling which are blank except for the letters LN2 printed on the side; and must be the liquid nitrogen tanks used to fill up the Dewars.

Behind the door is a small landing with a door opposite labelled "Perfusion Room" and a set of stairs leading down to a basement. The door to the perfusion room is pressure sealed requiring force to release the handle. The hissing of expelled air gives way to a blast of icy cold as it swings open. The shiver that shoots down my spine is due only in part to the temperature: mostly it's due to the pale, lifeless body sprawled on a stainless-steel medical trolley. It's the naked body of a man in his mid-thirties, around six feet tall, with a muscular build and dirt under the nails on his hands and feet. His dark hair and features suggest he's local, but his skin's so pale it's almost translucent.

The four-wheeled trolley has two blue perforated plastic straps fastened around the body, with a large steel circular light above. Stored in a compartment below the mattress is electronic equipment. Beside the soil-stained feet is a metal shelf, clipped to the frame of the trolley, with a clear glass bottle with a bright orange plastic lid containing a white liquid labelled "Ultra Cool Cryoprotectant". Next to it is a blue metal gun-shaped object with a pointed end. Attached to the base of the gun is a blue rubber hose. On the man's face are two small puncture marks. Could these have been made by the gun? But the gun only has one point; and why is there no sign of blood? The pale complexion of the body suggests it's been drained of blood post-mortem. But why would anybody carry out such a macabre task? There's a panel in the floor, with a hoist fixed to the ceiling. The body must have been hoisted up from the basement. Or maybe it's going to be lowered there. Judging by the dirty nails and physical build of the body, it could be one of the workmen used to build this place. The trapdoor heaves slightly as I exit the room and head for the stairs.

The open plan basement covers the entire footprint of the building, with an area partitioned off for electrical cabling and manifolds harvesting the electricity. Next to this is a large refrigeration unit which, as I open it, sends another chill down my spine. Dressed in a skin designed for a warm climate, I've been extremely cold since entering the building and I'm now shivering profusely - having resisted the temptation to turn on the Heartbeat. The unit is filled mainly with blocks of ice, so I decide not to enter to avoid the door closing and sentencing me to an icy death. In the right side of the refrigeration unit is a shelf with a large brown box sealed with tape and with the word "Frogs" written in large black letters. Frogs? It can't be a box of frogs. Common sense beats curiosity as I close the door.

The basement is even colder than the room upstairs and doesn't feel any warmer than the refrigeration unit. At the far end are two areas covered with blue curtains hanging on a curved steel rail, the curtains and clinical disinfectant aroma reminds me of a hospital. My heart pounds with fear in anticipation of what horror lies behind the curtain. Not allowing my angst to breed, I yank open the curtain to my left to reveal a large tiled bath. The bath is half-filled with water and ice. But that's not all that's in there: partially submerged is another male body, similar in size and appearance to the one upstairs. His wrists and ankles are fixed to a steel mesh sheet by brown leather straps. Dead bodies don't need restraining, so this poor guy was put in here alive. His mouth and nose are above water, so he hasn't drowned, but it wouldn't take long to die of hypothermia in these conditions. He also has dirty nails. But if they are the workers, it makes no sense to torture and kill them by such elaborate means. By now I'm beginning to feel like a contestant in a perverse quiz show: *So, what lies behind curtain number two?* I yank the second curtain, preparing for the worst. Another body? Off course there is. Lying prostrate on a medical trolley is yet another young man, again with dirty nails. Attached to his arms are needles and tubes, sucking any slim remaining chance of life out of him. I'm shaking: is this because of the freezing cold or the horrific sights I've seen? I don't know why but I peer deep into his eyes.

'Who are you?' I ask. 'Shorry I couldn't 'elp you.'
My speech is slurred and I'm so tired; I don't want to move any more. If I curl up into a ball to warm up, this will all go away. My hands are pale; my breathing is fast and shallow, my vision blurred. The skin is no use against the cold without the Heartbeat - but I can't turn it on without it giving off a signal. I start to take off the skin, thinking this will warm me up. What am I doing? - I'm not thinking straight. From my training, I realise I'm showing classic signs of hypothermia - not from training for this mission though, from a little job we did in Russia. Who'd have thought I would suffer from hypothermia in the middle of South America? I need to get outside but I'm disorientated and stagger forward, colliding with a stone pillar. Knocked to the floor, I've no choice: I must turn on the Heartbeat, my hand is shaking so fast I can't hold it straight. I press my thumb against the screen, but it isn't

working. I keep pressing - but nothing. Of course: when on a mission we use a code number for security, to stop the enemy accessing it with the digit of a dead man. How could I forget something so basic? The hypothermia – that's how. I still don't have the strength in my arms or legs to stand and slump back to the floor.

 What's the code? What's the code? I knew I wasn't ready for this mission. They said I was, but I knew I wasn't. But why should they care? To them I'm collateral, they see my life as sacrificial. In a state of delirium, I start to laugh as the cold floor reminds me of an expression Mouse uses. He moans when he sits anywhere cold, claiming he will get piles - or the "Duke of Argyll's" as he calls them. Yes, of course, Mouse! Mouse gave me a tip for picking the six-digit Heartbeat code. He's soccer crazy and says the best way to remember a code is to think of a famous victory for your team. The first two digits are the score and the next four are the year. Mouse is a Liverpool fan, but I support Sheffield Wednesday, who I used to watch with my surrogate dad. They won the FA Cup in 1935, a famous win that the whole city turned out to celebrate. What was the score? Well, that's easy: it was 4-2. That's it – the code – it's 4-2-1-9-3-5. God bless you Mouse! It's strange the things you remember under pressure; I can barely recall my own name, yet I can remember a soccer match from over 10 years ago. Sliding the Heartbeat into the wrist pocket on the skin, I tap in the six-digit code. Despite my almost numb, quivering fingertips, I manage to prod it correctly. The display shows my body temperature at 31 degrees, triggering the suit to raise it to a normal level. The impact is instantaneous, with the Heartbeat targeting the key areas of heat loss first – primarily my head – before washing over my whole body: immediately, a warm rush envelops me from head to toe. I raise the inside of my wrists, pressing them against my forehead, warming my face. My feet start to itch with the new-found sensation of warmth but at least I can feel them now.

 I don't understand what's going on in this building. What kind of person kills someone in freezing cold water and then sucks the blood out of them? Is he a vampire? Regaining my body temperature and composure, I swallow a couple of protein capsules stored in the suit. The powder has a swift impact as I feel my strength return, still on the floor, but ready for action. The level of detail, even in the basement, is extra ordinary for a building this isolated. At the bottom of the walls are timber skirting boards, the wood must have been taken from the forest. Likewise, the doors, frames and surrounding architrave will have come from the same source. A monumental amount of skill and sweat would have been required over years to achieve this finish. It strikes a chord with John's comments about this guy commanding a myriad army.

John! Mouse! I must find them. Back on my feet, I head over to the nearest cadaver to check for fang marks. Of course, there are none. What an idiot! What was I thinking? As I exit the basement, I realise I haven't taken any photographs. I want to get out; I don't have the patience anymore, so I take a few in a rush. Who cares if they're blurred? Fleeing up the stairs, a sharp pain shoots up the back of my right leg, causing me to trip; I've pulled my hamstring.

The injury hinders my movement as I continue my exit through the corridor and then the room with the eerie Dewars. Back in the entrance corridor, I am about to leave before realising I only went through one of the four doors. I'm not interested in the toilet or store, but the other door isn't labelled, so I slowly open it. Please, God, no more corpses! The room is a small, well-lit laboratory, with Bunsen burners and petri dishes. In one of the dishes I notice a dissected frog. So, they must really have been boxes of frogs. Had I entered this room first I would have found it bizarre and alarming, but by now the benchmark of weirdness has been raised to such heights I find it disturbingly mundane - I'm just relieved there are no more dead bodies in here. I'm soon outside and heading towards the residential building in search of Mouse.

Running up the hill, the tightness of the hamstring burns into the back of my thigh, but at least I'm mobile - even with a limp. The warm, humid conditions are a welcome opposite to the previous climate. Despite my training, I'm underprepared, unravelling as the mission progresses. I don't care: I just want to get out. There's a chance the signal on my Heartbeat has alerted the enemy to my movements, so I've no option but to pray for the best as I head for the main door to the dwelling. It's unlocked and flies open as I enter the palatial and extravagant entrance hall, the centre piece being a lavishly carved wooden staircase with artisan crafted newel posts and banister rails. There is an open vaulted ceiling with two timber trusses exuberantly supporting the roof.

    I notice a body slumped under the stairs … it can't be. No! It can't be … it's Mouse.

CHAPTER 13

The mark is a couple of yards from Mouse. There's been a struggle. He sits slumped against the wall, wearing ill-fitting khaki shirt and trousers. From the short sleeves and baggy shirt, I see he's not wearing his skin, so maybe he wasn't expecting us after all? But if not, where's everyone else; and where's John?

Blood seeps between the fingers of his right hand as he clutches the left side of his body. His breathing is shallow but he's alive. His head is fixed, his gaze focussed upon me. He's in a bad way and with no weapon poses little danger, so I turn to Mouse, who's sprawled on the ground with no sign of movement. I sit down and drag him over my lap. I don't want to believe that I'm too late.

'Mouse,' I whisper, slapping his face. 'Mouse. C'mon man. Wake up. When we get out of here, I'll take you to watch Liverpool. My treat.'

I can't find a pulse; I must be missing it in my panic. I can't see what's wrong with him. There's no blood and he was wearing a skin.

I pump his chest to revive him: 1-2-3. 1-2-3, stopping only to give him mouth to mouth. I pray he'll wake up and joke about the mouth contact. But nothing.

I take a bottle of smelling salts from my suit, unscrew the lid and look up to the heavens for divine help before holding the bottle under his nose. Theres no involuntary body jolt caused by the chemical assault on the nervous system. I try again, but nothing happens. He's dead.

In tears I wrap my arms around his neck, and pulling his head towards mine, I whisper: 'See you in the next life, pal. I'll make sure you're looked after. You're a hero.'

This sombre mood mutates from despair to an anger fuelled by hatred. But I'm fortunate: the birthplace of my vitriol is only yards away and powerless to defend himself. To put the glazed cherry on top of the cake, I'll be a hero when I kill him.

He looks different to how I'd imagined: I knew he wasn't tall but he's smaller than I thought and with a slighter build than I'd expected. He's removed his distinctive moustache, but the hair is still the same, jet black and swept to the side. Inside I'm fighting the disgust, a volcano of fury ready to erupt, but my training kicks in. I must complete the mission; Mouse mustn't have died for nothing. This moment of lucidity reminds me of my vulnerability; I can't be sure I'm alone and don't have much time, but what I need to do won't take long.

The photographic evidence is important, and I meticulously capture him from an array of angles. As he opens his mouth to speak, I stick in a buccal swab, twisting it firmly around his cheeks. The head of the swab is a large cotton bud on a stick, surrounded by a narrow plastic cylinder with a lid. With the sample collected, I pull the stick into the cylinder until the lid clicks into place; I snap the stick, so it's easier to carry. The containers have tiny holes for ventilation to stop the sample from going mouldy. There's a strict protocol for collecting samples, which was repeated time and time again in training. I'd thought we'd spent too much time on such a simple procedure but now in the field I understand. As I remove it from his mouth, he tries again to speak but I put the second swab in his mouth; this time shoving it to the back of his throat, deliberately to cause pain and discomfort. As I remove it, he's coughing and dry vomiting, with saliva dripping from both sides of his mouth.

'You've no clue,' he taunts in a barely audible whisper as I pull hairs strands from his head and place them in a small plastic bag, which I seal.

'You've no clue who you're up against,' he continues. I'm surprised to hear his accent is English. This must be a ploy to throw me to gain advantage. Maybe he thinks I'll let him live if he's English.

'I know exactly who I'm up against!' I snap, feeling the dormant volcano beginning to re-ignite. 'I know all about you and your people.'

'You know nothing,' he replies, his gaze now shifting from mine towards the corner of the room. I turn to see what he's looking at but there's nothing there.

'Then tell me what I don't know,' I demand.

'You can't tell me what to do. You people make me sick. You turn a gift into a curse. You deserve everything coming your way. And it *is* coming your way.'

'What? What's that supposed to mean?' I reply.

'Ask your friend,' he hisses, his smirking eyes cast in Mouse's direction. 'He's dead but still less stupid than you.'

The inner volcano erupts, and I can't remove my hands from his neck. Despite being defenceless, choking the life from him is justified, right? He's a monster, an architect of tyranny responsible for taking and ruining millions of lives. Who am I kidding? This is revenge for Mouse – and it feels good.

'Flash, Flash! Let's go, let's go.'

I've never been so pleased to hear John's voice. Relinquishing my grip, I spin around to see him kneeling next to Mouse. As he looks at me in desperation, I shake my head apologetically.

'What happened?' he quizzes, his voice cracking.

'I don't know how but he's dead,' I gasp, still shaking. 'Where've you been? What's at the water tower? Was anybody there?'

'No, it was empty. It was exactly that: a water collection tower with a treatment area to turn it into drinking water and what looks like the beginning of a water turbine mechanism, which isn't complete. What about you? What was in your building?'

'It was a laboratory full of dead bodies. Sick and disturbing. This guy was insane. I've just done the world a big favour. I'll tell you more when we get back.'

'Have you got the samples to prove it's him?' John enquires.

'Yes: buccal, hair strands and photographic.'

'Let's go, then,' orders John, taking control.

'But what about Mouse? We can't leave him here!' I protest.

'We can't bring him with us: the meeting point is five kilometres away; there's no way we can carry him that distance. He's dead. He would understand. The mission isn't complete until we get those samples back. The mission is all that matters. We're collateral, pawns in their game. What we have done will save many more lives. For all his moaning and bullshit, Mouse understood the big picture. We'll see him again one day. Right?'

I know he's right, but I hate the ease with which he can let go. For him the Council comes first, second and third - way above trivial considerations like friendship.

'Let's go,' I screech, heading for the door.

Five kilometres should take 15 minutes, fully fit with my skin and Heartbeat working together. But with a pulled hamstring, who knows?

'What's wrong?' asks John, as I lag.

'Hamstring.'

'OK, I'll take the back, can't have you falling behind. He might not be on his own. I don't want to lose you as well.'

John's right, as always. Not only about me being vulnerable but also about others being here. None of this makes sense. Why would he be out here on his own? If they knew we were coming, he would have been the first to evacuate; if we'd got here before he'd had the chance, he would have been protected by a wall of Normals - and he would have had his skin on. Maybe he went mad and killed them all; I suppose he could have run out of people to experiment on; or maybe word got around in the villages about workers not returning. Maybe the workers saw what was happening and ran away. Who wouldn't run if they caught a glimpse of what was happening in the bottom building?

Despite the injury we're making good time. We're on the lookout for a sanctuary pod; but the lightweight units are clad in solar reflective mirrored panels and are difficult to spot. But what if they know it's there and are waiting for us?

'We're being followed,' John pants from behind.

'Seriously?' I reply. 'Why do you think that?'

'I can hear something, but I don't want to look around. Keep running. We can't be far away!'

I hear two sharp cracks from behind followed by a couple more. Although it sounds like the snapping of twigs, I know from the rhythmic cadence and dull echo they are gunshots. I haven't been hit and hearing John's footsteps, neither has he: the skins are bulletproof, but an impact is excruciating and at close range will knock a moving target off their feet. A shot to the head, I'm told, is as painful as being hit in the testicles with a baseball bat - fortunately, I've never experienced either and would like to keep it that way. The gunshots seemed close, but I didn't see any impact on the nearby trees or sense the bullets whizz past. Remembering the training I focus ahead, resisting the temptation to return fire; instead, I meander my run erratically between the trees to make the moving target a more difficult prize to attain. John will be doing the same.

'Keep going,' he shouts from behind. 'Keep going.'

My eyes focus on my feet as I tread through the dense forest undergrowth: one slip and we're doomed? The river of sweat returns to my forehead as we head for the opening in the forest. I know the pod is at the other side, within touching distance, but the opening will expose us. Should I go around the edge of the forest, beneath the trees, or head straight for the pod?

'What shall I do, John?'

'Straight on, straight on, I'll cover you. You open the pod. I'll return fire. Don't look back, focus on the pod! Get the evidence in the pod!'

Emerging from the shelter of the trees, we're open to attack and, as I catch sight of the pod, the battle begins. The unsheltered surroundings offer little sound attenuation, creating a symphony of gunshots, with the distant and random echoing of the gunpowder's sonic boom making it impossible to guess what's going on. I arrive at the pod with such speed I can't slow down and collide with the end panel; as I bounce off, the cover panel springs open to release the keypad. I notice my hood is down, I must have forgotten to put it back on. It's a schoolboy error, but I've got away with it. I hammer in the code.

CHAPTER 14

As Jack awoke from the hypnosis, he sprung forward. Startled, disorientated and gasping for air, he was unable to ease the palpitations and hyper-ventilation. He was suffocating in his own paranoiac imagination which conjured vivid images of a plastic bag wrapping around his head. Panic struck, he put his hands to his mouth. There was nothing there, but still he struggled for breath.

'Relax, everything's OK,' a familiar voice reassured, one hand gently taking his, another hand softly caressing his forehead. Poppi's voice triggered a cognitive response within his soul, reducing the crippling fear and nausea multiplying within his core. Would he have been so quick to relax had it been Carson or Erik to offer comfort? Stupidly, it seemed to him, the crux of his recovery came from his feelings toward Poppi. But how could that be? They'd only met a few hours ago. He didn't believe in love at first sight - that was for the weak-minded. He had read, with little consequence, how men can be induced by women to think and do things against their natural order. It was not fathomable that he could be one of those people - not under any circumstances. Or was it? Maybe she had hypnotised him in more ways than one?

As calm returned to his body, the fog beneath his cornea lifted. Behind Poppi were the same people who had been in the room when he was put under her spell, and they been joined by the coach, who stood next to Carson. Poppi's intervention had calmed him, but the coach's presence reignited his unease. The coach and Carson were subdued. He noticed the coach was unique in wearing normal clothes, not the standard-issue body suits donned by his associates. His faded blue jeans and brown leather jacket were his usual attire, but suddenly the trademark cat on a four-leaf Clover motif on his jacket screamed out to Jack. Were Coach Carter and John 'Lucky Cat' Carter from his hypnotic state the same person? The hypnosis was vivid – like a real-life dream. But he called himself Stanley 'Flash' Webster, not Jack Marwood. How could that be? Was he a time traveller? Even if time travel was possible, he was younger than Stanley. And what about his best friend, Carson? He looked and had the mannerisms of Mouse, from the dream. To make sense of this nightmare, he was going to need help.

'What happened?!' Jack exclaimed. 'Was it a dream? A nightmare? Who am I?'

The deafening silence in the room was eventually broken by the coach but, rather than answering Jack, he had questions of his own.

'Erik, what happened? Why did he wake up in such a state?'

'He had a panic attack, John. He woke up quickly because that is the point where he was killed. His journey was over.'

'So, did we get the information we needed?' the coach continued.

'The journey is complete. We have a full narrative. We need to collate and consider all the data accrued to find out how best to use the information. We will not know until the process is complete how successful we have been,' droned Erik.

'Hang on, hang on,' screamed Jack. 'I'm not dead; I'm right here. You'd realise that if you stopped ignoring me.' Turning to Poppi, he continued: 'Look, you did this to me. What exactly was that all about? Why did it seem so real?'

'Because it was real, Jack,' she replied. 'Everything you saw and felt was real. It wasn't a dream. It was cross-life memory recovery hypnosis.'

'What? How can it be real? How can I go back in time and be older than I am now? It doesn't make sense. And what about those two?' he screeched. 'He's John 'Lucky Cat' Carter. And he's Mouse. It's obvious. Pointing to the Coach and then Carson, he asked, 'So why is it that he has aged normally while he's got younger? As I see it John talks the same, looks the same and has aged accordingly. Carson looks a bit different but it's obviously him, and as well as being younger, he has a completely different accent.'

Looking toward his friends, he could sense they wanted to answer but yielded to an invisible, unspeakable force. Carson was about to reply but instead glanced towards Erik and Poppi before finally staring at his shoes.

Again, he pleaded: 'Poppi, you said if I did as I was told you'd give me all the answers I wanted.'

'Go ahead, Poppi,' boomed Erik from across the room. 'We have all the information we can get. He is of no further use to me.'

'OK, Jack. I'll keep my promise: you will have your answers,' she conceded.

The door slid open to reveal two large-set men in the standard white jumpsuit. As they marched towards him, she instructed them sternly.

'Gentlemen. Take him for Elucidation!'

PHASE 2 - ELUCIDATION

CHAPTER 15

Elucidation had not been what Jack was anticipating. After being frogmarched down endless corridors by two mute drones, he was left alone in a stark white room. He felt sure he would be accompanied by the rest of the coterie, or at least be reconciled with Poppi and Erik. To his annoyance, the only caller was a middle-aged man so devoid of personality he gave Erik a visage of excitement, and rather than offering insight, he simply explained that the first stage of Elucidation would be the reading of a manuscript entitled "The Preamble Manual of Elucidation".

'Would you like to receive this in electronic format or hard copy?' he was asked. 'You can have both, if you like.'

He had requested both, not that he was needy or wanted to create work but because he didn't understand the question: he had no idea what the difference was - and wasn't going to make himself look stupid by asking. The man had returned with a brown satchel strapped over his shoulder before taking him to his quarters. The impressive room caused a rare upward spike in his mood: an aquarium view running the entire length of one wall, or was it another TV screen? He couldn't tell the difference anymore. In the centre of the room was a large bed of crisp white covers, with the base, headboard and two side tables of walnut grain. In front of the aquarium window sat a reclining brown leather armchair and a coffee table. Between the bathroom door, to the left, and aquarium window was an office desk and captain's chair. On the coffee table was a rectangular electronic device, like the Heartbeat but bigger, a paper manuscript and a Concise Oxford English Dictionary. He realised the larger device was the "electronic" copy and the paper was the "hard" copy. He had detected sarcasm when informed that the dictionary was 'in case you don't understand any of the bigger words' but resisted the temptation to punch the man in the face. Besides, it had struck him while he was waiting that he wasn't sure what elucidation meant.

elucidation
/ɪˌl(j)uːsɪˈdeɪʃ(ə)n/
noun
noun: **elucidation**; plural noun: **elucidations**
explanation that makes something clear, clarification.

Sitting in the reclining chair, with his feet on the coffee table, he was hoping for elucidation as he poured a glass of wine. He had intended to relax while enjoying the aquarium and wine, but his gaze was inextricably drawn toward the small pile of paper next to his foot. Yielding to the inevitable, he placed the wine on a blue slate coaster and picked up the manuscript.

The Preamble Manual of Elucidation

Edition 27
August 1963
Commissioned by the Clover Council

The Doctrine of Elucidation.

An introduction to the history and genetics of the Clover Caste

INTRODUCTION
What is Clover Caste?

Clover Caste (CC) *is a somatic DNA mutation incumbent in 1 in every 10,000 people. If you are reading this document, you are CC.*

The cause of the mutation - and why individuals are chosen as Hosts - is not known. It does not discriminate against gender, race or creed and thus is present throughout the world. A somatic mutation is non-hereditary and does not pass through bloodlines. Once the mutation has run four life cycles, the Host dies.

Who are the Clover Council?

We are an advisory administrative body constituted from a mandate by CC throughout the world. The Council governs, advises and regulates on matters relating to all levels of Clover Caste worldwide. Matters of legislation and decision making are taken by the democratically elected Clover Senate.

This booklet has been compiled by the Clover Council as an introductory explanatory document for CC Hosts experiencing their first transition, which is the most difficult, causing high levels of disorientation, stress and confusion. Although each CC reacts differently during transition, this document will endeavour to explain the process generically.

It is, therefore, a preamble to the intensive residential training, mandatory for all CC to attend during this transitional period, which will augment the process and address personal idiosyncrasies.

THE HISTORY OF THE CLOVER CASTE
Relations with non CC (Normals)

The DNA mutation is the differentiation between CC and Non-Clover Caste. Non-Clover Caste are usually referred to as **"Normals"** *due to their traditional DNA structure and the ratio balance of 10,000:1 in their favour.*

CC have surreptitiously co-existed with Normals throughout history, although this relationship was altered following the introduction of the Clover Council. The Normals, however, are unaware of the existence of CC.

Traditionally, Non-Clovers were referred to as "Ants", derived from the Greek word Anthropos. The Clover Senate have now deemed the term Ants derogatory due to the potential comparison with the insect; the relationship of worker ants being subservient to the queen ant was considered comparable to Normals serving a CC. For this reason, the Council recommended the term "Normals" replace the term "Ants".

The Gammadion League (before the Clover Council)

Before the Clover Council, CC were governed by the Gammadion League. The Gammadion League had existed for many centuries, giving each CC (referred to as the Gammadion Admiral) command over his/her ratio of Normals (myriad army of 10,000 Normals). The Gammadions were highly secretive and shared none of their superior technology or knowledge with the Normals.

Over the centuries, it became clear this privilege was being abused by some CC who were either using the Normals as slaves for financial gain or were joining forces with other Gammadion Admirals to control large sections of the globe.

Although many Gammadions believed this to be the most effective way of cohabitating, many believed the Normals deserved to be treated equally. Eventually, a groundswell of progressive and liberal thinking forced the issue of a plebiscite, which took place in 1745.

Initially, the progressive thinkers pushed for a full plebiscite, where the Normals were equal to CC and the shroud of secrecy would be lifted. In the end, what was proposed became known as "Plebiscite Light", where the Normals were considered equal to CC and selected technology was made available, but secrecy was maintained.

The plebiscite of 1745

The decision to hold the plebiscite had evolved over a period of decades, beginning in what became known as "the Age of Enlightenment". During this period the traditional belief about a group of 10,000 Normals (a myriad army) serving one Gammadion Admiral (known as the Absolute Monarch) was questioned.

For the first time, this period gave semi-transparency to the Normals as many areas of thought previously limited to the Gammadions were shared, including the widely accepted principles of consequentialism and metaphysics. Whilst the Normals were included, they were kept unaware of the CC. Although many pro–Enlightenment CC pushed for full transparency, the Gammadion League resisted such pressure, opting to remain clandestine. As most of the Gammadion League were counter-Enlightenment this was to be expected, unlike the surprise decision to hold the plebiscite in the first place.

The repeated call for a plebiscite had been ignored for decades by the Gammadion League. The plebiscite was finally held to put an end to the question once and for all, with the League expecting the notion of the Clover Council to be defeated. The Gammadion League were accused of propaganda and scaremongering during campaigning to sway the vote; nevertheless, the majority voted in favour of a Clover Council.

Although the result of the plebiscite was conclusive, due to the reluctance of many CC to accept the result, it took five years before it was possible to complete the transition. The Gammadion League continued to claim that the Clover Council was too radical and would result in devastation for CC. But, despite the claims, democracy was finally upheld in 1750 with the creation of the Clover Council.

Although the results of the plebiscite were implemented centuries ago, the divisions created still exist among the Caste. Whilst the Clover Council has proven to be a success, there are still many progressives who feel the changes did not go far enough; conversely, there are also counter progressives resenting the changes made, who regularly push for a second plebiscite.

The formation of the Clover Council

Following the Plebiscite of 1745, the Clover Council and the Clover Senate were founded in 1750 in Waterville, County Kerry, south-west Ireland, replacing the Gammadion League. The Council was made accountable for the management of the general affairs of the Caste, with the Senate involved in issues of higher complexity. Elections took place to select the committee members for both the Council and Senate.

DNA MUTATION
What does the mutated DNA do?

The mutated DNA enables those affected to experience **metempsychosis**. The state of metempsychosis is finite and is repeated four times. It is not known why the process is limited to four cycles.

What is metempsychosis?

Metempsychosis is the transmigration of the soul from one mortal body to another after death. The ability of CC to experience metempsychosis is sacred to those within the Caste, as are all documents and eschatological properties pertaining to it. Any CC discovered to be in breach of this sacred knowledge will be imprisoned for the rest of their life, and any subsequent lives. Any normal in possession of edification will be humanely and discretely killed.

How does metempsychosis work?

The first process of metempsychosis is the fertilisation of the Host egg, resulting in the development and growth of the CC embryo. At this stage, it should be explained that as CC have a non-hereditary somatic DNA mutation, there is no direct maternal lineage. CC embryos are reproduced asexually within the womb. In simple terms, CC have no parents.

The natural type of asexual reproduction required for successful development of the CC foetus is known as **parthenogenesis**. Whilst uncommon in humans, parthenogenesis is a common method of reproduction for many crustaceans, amphibians, sharks and birds. Other than for CC, there have been no recorded cases of parthenogenesis in mammals in the wild. There have been several unsubstantiated claims of artificially induced parthenogenesis in both mice and frogs.

As the foetus develops its own parthenogenetic stem cell line independently of the Host, the mother is effectively an unwitting surrogate. Although sperm does not contribute to the genetic makeup of the foetus, it is required to stimulate the activation of the egg, making the father, too, an unwitting surrogate. This is a sub-strain of parthenogenesis known as **gynogenesis**. Due to the nature of the process it is often referred to by doctors as the "cuckoo conception". The CC strain will only be detected by the network of medical CC strategically located within hospital and medical facilities who regularly carry out DNA strand checks. It cannot be detected by non-CC doctors.

Cuckoo conception can only be carried out once in the Host, which is why CC do not have siblings. As the process is only activated when a CC requires to move to the next Leaf Level, the eggs can remain dormant for many years. The surrogate parents of CC are often older than the average aged first-time parents and believe they cannot have children.

BIRTH /CHILDHOOD AND TRANSITION TO ADULTHOOD

CC children appear to be identical to the offspring of Normals. Generally, those of the Caste are discovered by the network of medical CC during routine checks throughout childhood. However, due to increased detection methods in DNA technology, this is happening more often in the foetal stage during standard pre-natal scanning stages. Early detection within developed countries is close to 100% in the foetal stage; the percentage is much lower within less populated and less technologically advanced areas of the world.

Although the Host can be found anywhere in the world, and the foetus can develop in mothers of all nationalities and colours, there are often striking similarities over all four-Leaf Levels. It is believed by many progressive CC that this is due to an energy template within the soul of the person being passed down along each Leaf. However, it is more widely accepted from a scientific point of view that the similarities are due to the repetitive nature of the DNA strand.

Once identified, the progress of the CC will be monitored throughout childhood by a network of doctors, teachers, lecturers and various other mentors strategically located. As CC children develop at different rates, recently transitioned CC are often placed as "friends" to those about to go through transition.

Mentors and Greeters

As the Host approaches the first transition, the Council will assign Mentors and Greeters.

Mentor - The role of the Mentor is to secretly guide and support the Host and to identify the correct moment to instruct a Greeter to intervene.

Greeter - The role of the Greeter is to seamlessly remove the Host from his/her everyday life to enable The Council to conduct Elucidation. Upon completion of Elucidation the Greeter is responsible for sensitively reintegrating the Host back into society.

THE THREE STAGES OF TRANSITION

1. Awakening 2. Somnambulation 3. Elucidation

    STAGE 1 - The Awakening – *During adolescence the previous life cycle memories will begin to occur within the Host in the form of "flashbacks" or "déjà vu". It is the responsibility of the Mentors to recognise the early signs of the Awakening and identify the optimum point to assign a Greeter to transfer the Host to Elucidation. The Host will also experience significant muscle growth at a rate far superior to that a Normal is capable of, as the current body becomes advanced enough to accept 'muscle memory' from previous lives.*

    STAGE 2 - Somnambulation – *Following Awakening, the Host enters a brief stage of sub consciously reverting to the previous life. The Host is unaware of what is happening and enters a state of abstraction, often compared to sleep walking. It is the most vulnerable stage in the Host's transition, presenting significant risk and danger to both the Host and Caste. During this stage, if unsupervised the Host will become unstable and may resist Elucidation.*

    The previous life information contained within the memory map and extracted during Elucidation is often vital to the Caste. Once the Somnambulation stage is entered, this information becomes more difficult - sometimes impossible - to withdraw. Thus, it is vital for all stakeholders that the Host is placed with the Council for Elucidation before somnambulating begins.

    STAGE 3 - Elucidation – *During this stage, the Host is placed with the Council body that conducts the process of Elucidation. Any information and experience required by the Council is acquired using persuasive,* non-aggressive hypnotherapy. Upon completion of the hypnotherapy the Host is sent to the School of Enlightenment where the process of transition and the Clover Caste in general is explained.

You are currently in the first process of Elucidation (The Preamble Manual of Elucidation). You will shortly begin the second process of Elucidation (the School of Enlightenment).

THE FOUR CYCLES OF METEMPSYCHOSIS (LEAF LEVELS)

The four cycles of metempsychosis - more commonly referred to as Leaf Levels (LL) - all have differing characteristics and relevance to the CC. CC will experience four different but consecutive lives. The four cycles are shown in the diagram below:

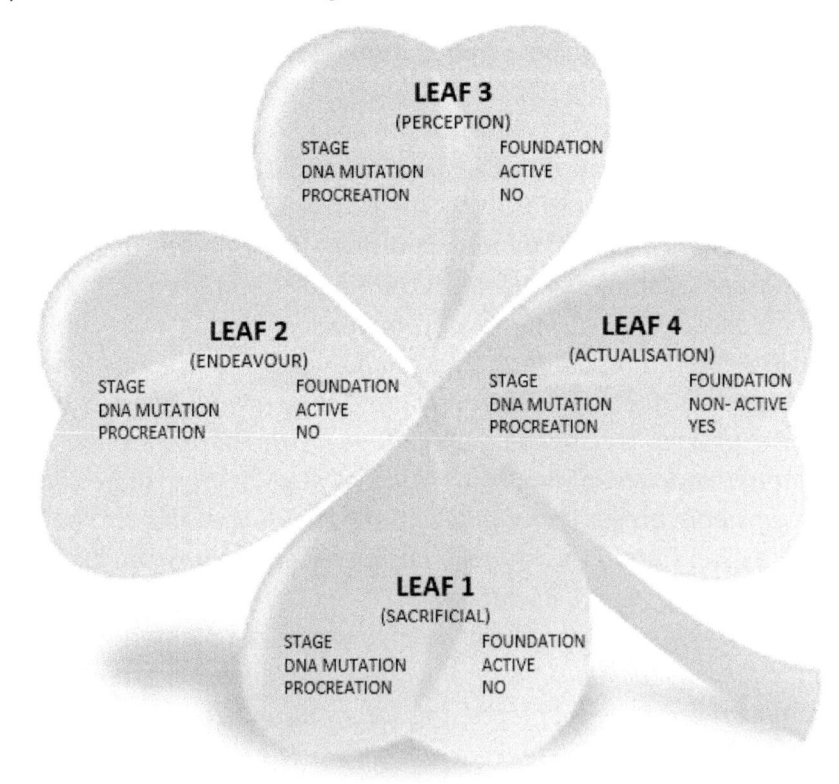

LEAF 3
(PERCEPTION)
STAGE	FOUNDATION
DNA MUTATION	ACTIVE
PROCREATION	NO

LEAF 2
(ENDEAVOUR)
STAGE	FOUNDATION
DNA MUTATION	ACTIVE
PROCREATION	NO

LEAF 4
(ACTUALISATION)
STAGE	FOUNDATION
DNA MUTATION	NON-ACTIVE
PROCREATION	YES

LEAF 1
(SACRIFICIAL)
STAGE	FOUNDATION
DNA MUTATION	ACTIVE
PROCREATION	NO

The DNA mutation associated with CC is only present during LL 1 to LL 3. Levels 1 to 3 are referred to as the "Foundation Levels". During the foundation levels the Host will have the health benefits of the active DNA mutation but are unable to procreate.

Due to the DNA mutation, CC will enjoy better health than Normals during the foundation stages; that is, when the DNA mutation is active (LL1 to LL3). At this stage the cells are highly effective in repairing faulty genes created within them; thus, there have been no reported cases of cancer in CC during the foundation stage. However, CC are still susceptible to virus-based illnesses such as colds and influenza.

Level 4, often referred to as "Self-Actualisation", is the most closely associated with the life of a Normal as the DNA structure is no longer mutated; thus, the CC is now susceptible to DNA related diseases such as cancer. However, in this final cycle procreation is possible. Although similar in DNA to the Normals, the CC will still benefit from the superior knowledge attained during the previous three life cycles, which is stored in the memory map. CC also benefit physically as muscle memory is transferred through all transition stages.

During the four life cycles of a CC, the Host will be expected to serve the Clover Council and Senate in ways beneficial to the development and longevity of the Caste. The more a Host can help the Caste, the more favourably he/she will be looked upon during the final cycle.

During all cycles, the Host will be expected to execute any tasks, missions or forms of employment requested by the Council. The nature of the tasks will vary depending on the level of the Host. The riskier tasks will usually be assigned to LL 1 as they still have three lives remaining after the first cycle. LL 1 will also be allocated the most mundane tasks as they are considered to have the least embodied intellect due to a shorter life cycle and sparsely populated memory map. Conversely, LL 4 will be allocated the least risky but most intellectually challenging tasks.

Leaf Level 1 (Sacrificial)

LL 1 is referred to as the "Sacrificial" level. This is not to say the Host is expected to die for the Caste (although this may ultimately transpire), more the need to sacrifice a significant amount of time during this level.

During LL 1 the child will not appear to benefit from the CC status and, unless identified by the CC network, can pass unnoticed. Although it is considered rare in the developed world, instances of undetected CC – particularly LL 1 - are more common in less developed areas of the world.

As the Host has no previous life experiences, he/she will not experience déjà vu, remaining unaware of CC status.

LL 1 - Role / tasks within the CC network:

After an assessment of the capabilities of each Host, LL 1 are split into two groups: "Lions" and "Donkeys". The most capable Hosts are classified as Lions and carry out the most dangerous tasks. They are often field operatives trained to help maintain the equilibrium within the Caste. The Donkeys are assigned easier tasks, often in administration.

Leaf Level 2 (Endeavour)

LL 2 is the first level during which the Host will experience past life recollections and is considered the most traumatic of the three transitions occurring within the four life cycles.

During the first transition, the Host is often disorientated, confused and panic stricken. It is not unusual for Hosts who are unaware of their status as Clover Caste to share their experiences with Normals, compromising both the Host and the Caste. To counter this, many centuries ago the Gammadions invented the doctrine of déjà vu. Although a concept manufactured by the Caste, it has been documented and publicised so successfully that even Normals believe to have been affected by it.

Despite the success in cloaking indiscretions, it is essential that the Host is carefully monitored during the transition period. Mentors are located strategically at levels within a Host's immediate social grid. The Mentors will track the Host's progress and inform the Greeter when the time has arrived for Elucidation.

LL 2 - Role /tasks within the CC network:

Because the transition from LL 1 to LL2 is delicate, it is considered prudent to have other LL 2 Hosts to act as Mentors and Greeters as they themselves have, relatively speaking, most recently been affected and can therefore offer the most sensitive approach.

LL 2 are generally inducted for higher level administration and research functions, whilst others are inducted in the field as Special Operatives.

Leaf Level 3 (Perception)

The move from LL 2 to LL 3 is straightforward in comparison to the previous transition as past life recollections have been previously experienced. The memories begin at an earlier age and continue to be recollected regularly throughout childhood. The LL 3 Host processes this information subconsciously and, once absorbed, the material intelligence forms a preceding life cycle outline. By early adulthood, the Host is aware of the status of CC, possessing sufficient data to contact the Caste at their will when ready. There is no requirement at this level, for the use of either Mentors or Greeters unless the Host is known to be volatile or high profile to the Caste.

LL 3 are the highest level of the Caste with the DNA mutation. This is reflected in the roles they fulfil within the Caste network, and they are appointed to high level jobs. The knowledge acquired during the previous two life cycles, along with an understanding of the Caste, makes LL 3 ideal for serving in positions that feed directly to the Clover Council. This involves serving within the higher echelons of governments, Councils and organisations within the Normals' society.

Working directly as subordinates, they act as conduits between national governments and the Clover Council. These are highly sensitive and responsible positions, held in great esteem within the Caste. An effective LL 3 will influence governments and organisations throughout the world to implement decisions already made by the Clover Council surreptitiously.

LL 3 - Role / Tasks within the CC network:

LL 3 often take up such roles as high-level politician, diplomat, and commander in the armed forces.

Leaf Level 4 (Self-Actualisation)

LL 4 is usually referred to as self-actualisation but is sometimes called the retirement level. This is the final life cycle of the Host and does not contain the mutated DNA strand associated with the previous three life cycles. The DNA makeup of the Host during level 4 closely resembles that of a normal.

Nevertheless, there are still many advantages for the Caste during LL 4. The energy template becomes influential at the foetal stage by releasing muscle memories within the Host, thereby creating *a healthier, stronger mortal body. Although the DNA has ceased to mutate, life expectancy is still significantly higher than that of a normal. Many factors contribute to the improved final cycle longevity: the superior physique and fitness levels passed on from the template, alongside regular health monitoring by the Council, achieve a long and healthy life. The monitoring is backed up by early-stage treatment for any illness which may occur utilising professional expertise and technology far superior to that available to the Normals. However, although the Host is now open to diseases such as cancer, it is uncommon for the Host to develop anything other than viral infections.*

Since the creation of the Clover Council, all members of both the Council and Senate have been LL 4. The embodied intelligence created by three lifetimes of experiential learning makes LL 4 Hosts ideal for jobs at the highest level. The experiences and knowledge acquired during the previous three life cycles are transferred to the Host by a congenital memory map that is accessible from an early age, making the LL 4 Host highly intelligent, even by comparison with other CC Levels.

The ability to procreate is the main differential between Level 4 and Levels 1 to 3, though it is not known why it is possible only in the final life cycle; however, as the DNA mutation occurs in the first three cycles, this is believed to be the root cause of the anomaly. The creation and nurturing of children is considered the pinnacle of the life cycles and is a significant factor in the directional approach taken by the Host in the initial three cycles.

The behaviour of the Host is monitored during the three cycles and is key to the options available during LL 4. Those who work hard for the Council will be rewarded for their efforts and loyalty in the final life cycle. Money accrued during each life will be commandeered by the Council and used as a "pension" in LL 4. The prominent level of political positions is available to Hosts who have excelled in their duties during the previous cycles – often as Lions at the Sacrificial level.

The pension funds, used for full retirement, must be redistributed in a manner that will not draw attention to the recipient. This is achieved by locating the LL 4 Host in traditionally high-paying jobs, such as CEOs of multinational corporations. If substantial funds need transferring, the Council may choose to coincide this with the release of technology into the domain of the Normals. This is commonplace in areas such as California, where technology is regularly being drip-fed into the mainstream.

LL 4 - Role / Tasks within the CC network:

There are many wide-ranging choices of lifestyle available to LL 4 CC, from high-level positions within the Council to a full life cycle retirement of choice.

Enhanced intelligence makes the LL 4 Host the ideal candidate for positions at the highest level within Normal society. Since the formation of the United States of America, every President has been CC LL 4 - selected, funded and lobbied by the Clover Council. However, CC may choose to live the final full life cycle in full retirement.

**The first process of Elucidation (The Preamble Manual of Elucidation) is concluded.
You will shortly begin the second process of Elucidation (the School of Enlightenment).
Good Luck.**

CHAPTER 16

He was awoken by a familiar voice, and a gentle shake of the shoulder.

'Wake up, Flash. We've got a busy day ahead!'

At first, he wasn't sure if he was dreaming. Did she call him Flash?

'Good morning, Mr Marwood,' announced a second, familiar voice. 'Would you like some breakfast?'

He was more interested in the food than the visitors; but with the contents of the silver platter hidden by an oval dome with an ebony finial, his gaze returned to Poppi and her companion. He recognised the voice as the 'Tuscany Guy' from their earlier encounter.

'So, you're the guy with the Maserati and a place in Tuscany. Payne is it?' Jack proclaimed, as he sat upright on the bed.

'Oh, so you were awake all the time, were you? What a hoot. You could have said something; it would have saved us all a lot of time, you know?' Payne complained, his whiny dialogue accentuating his New York twang.

Poppi placed the platter on Jack's lap. Payne, now facing the aquarium with his arms crossed behind his back, continued the sarcasm.

'I see Poppi is presenting you with your culinary delight. Those English sure now how to cook. Mmmmmm...'

Payne was younger than Jack had imagined; and taller and better looking than he had hoped. He was comfortably over six-foot-tall and well-built with good-conditioned, flowing blonde hair. Jack already disliked him, adding moaning and sarcasm to Payne's ever-increasing personality misdemeanours.

Poppi leaned forward to remove the oval dome and whispered, 'Ignore him. He's a prick!'

As Jack laughed, Poppi raised her voice, 'We've given you a classic English breakfast: bacon, eggs, sausage, tomato, beans, toast, fried bread – and even a nice cup of tea.'

With the dome removed the familiarity of the smell caught him by surprise.

'Have you missed the English breakfast?' Poppi quizzed.

'I've never had one before.'

'You have' Poppi laughed, 'It was your favourite meal in your first life. That and fish and chips.'

'In England?' Jack enquired hesitantly, as the memories of the previous day began to return.

'Yes, we try to shoehorn in happy memories from the first life to help during the process of elucidation. It's a lot to take in – being told that you've lived a life before. It's unbelievable at first, but as the memories flood back, you'll realise it's true. Having multiple lives is a blessing; one which should be embraced.'

'I've no recollection of this breakfast, but I do recognise the smell.'

'When you start eating it the flavours will become familiar. You'll begin to accept the truth, as unlikely as it may seem now.' Poppi confirmed. 'And later, you will have fish and chips, for dinner.'

'Oh, I can hear your arteries blocking up as we speak,' Payne interjected.

But before eating the food, he found himself re arranging his plate. The fried bread was put to the side and the toast pushed to the centre. On top of the toast he put the bacon and sausage, on top of which he placed the eggs, before spreading over a bean and tomato blanket. He looked up at Poppi, startled.

'You look like you've done that before,' she said as he devoured the breakfast, 'So, how far did you get with the manual. Did you manage to read it all?'

'Yeah. Yeah. Read it all,'

'How much did you understand?'

'All of it!' he replied.

'Really?' she laughed, 'you understood it all?'

'OK, not all of it.'

'How much?'

'Not much really. There were parts I understood, parts I didn't and some of it I just didn't believe.' he confessed.

'Well I can't blame you for that,' she consoled, 'but it *is* vital you understand what's in it – and even more important that you believe it. What do you remember?'

'Errr... We have a DNA mutation which gives us extra lives. People who don't have extra lives are called Normals. We're not allowed to call them Ants, for some reason; although I can't remember why we called them Ants in the first place. We are now governed by The Clover Council, but before that it was somebody else. The Gammons, I think.'

Poppi laughed, 'The Gammons! Must be because you're eating bacon. It's the Gammadions.' She was having difficulty regaining her composure and continued to laugh. It was the first time Jack had seen her human side.

Payne turned around, shot an angry glance at her, before interjecting, 'The Gammadions are the reason we cannot call them Ants, as they used the Normals as slaves, or cannon fodder in their armies. Each Gammadion Admiral used to control his or her ratio of 10000 Normals. They were supposed to use them for the greater good of the Caste. This was not the case, as some were using the Normals to line their own pockets- or worse still – teaming up with other Gammadion Admirals and controlling large sections of the globe. It's easy to see why the relationship between a queen ant and worker ants was compared to that of a Gammadion Admiral and the Normals.'

'Yes, that's why the Clover Council replaced the Gammadions, and why you had the plebiscite?' Jack asked, before gulping his tea.

'Yes, that's why *we* had the plebiscite' replied Poppi, having regained her composure, 'But it wasn't straight forward.'

'Why?' Jack enquired.

'Because,' Payne continued, 'Many of the Caste considered that Gammadion rule was the best way to co-exist with the Normals and were strongly against the plebiscite, refusing to accept the result; instead calling for a second plebiscite, immediately.'

'Mmph,' Jack grunted, 'Some people don't like democracy. That'll never change. Its arrogant to think, you're always right. If you live within any society; whether it be the Normals, the Gammadions, or the Clover Council, you should abide by democracy; otherwise it would be anarchy. Besides, what good would a second plebiscite have done; surely the result would have been the same so soon after."

'Indeed,' Payne affirmed, adopting an amicable demeanour. 'The plebiscite was conclusive, although far from unanimous. Still, if you want to live within any society you must, as you say, accept the mandate of the masses. At the time the Gammadions held all the power and were complacent about the result. It's believed that had a second vote taken place they would have made sure the outcome was different by altering the format of the vote to ensure victory; maybe giving three options, two of which would be designed to split the pro Council vote.'

'Sneaky,' Jack commented.

'Well, they are politicians after all. The plebiscite took place over 200 years ago, but to this day there are still people who want to return to the Gammadion style of rule. It took more than 5 years after the vote, before the Clover Council were formed; and there was still much squabbling between the two sides. Those on the side of forming the Council argued that the Normals should be equal and have access to our technology; those against wanted things to remain as they were. In the end a compromise was made and neither side were happy.'

Jack mused, 'that's about as much as I remember. The rest is fuzzy. I was tired when I read it; it just didn't sink in. For example, why do I have extra lives? I read something about a DNA mutation, but why am I different to a Normal?'

Payne explained, 'We have a non-hereditary DNA mutation which affects 1 in 10000 people. We don't know why it only affects certain people, but there are things we do understand.'

'Like what?'

'The way we're conceived plays a large part in our DNA make-up. We all know how humans are conceived, but for Clover, things are different.'

'How?'

'We're conceived with a type of asexual reproduction known as parthenogenesis. It's a natural form of reproduction common for many crustaceans, fishes and birds. Clover caste Hosts are the only mammals known to reproduce this way, although there have even been unsubstantiated claims of artificially induced parthenogenesis in both mice and frogs.'

'Perhaps that's why there were boxes of frogs in the freezer in Uruguay?' questioned Jack, 'But if we reproduce asexually, doesn't that mean we're conceived by only one parent?'

'No,' replied Payne, 'We actually reproduce using a sub strain of parthenogenesis, known as gynogenesis which requires sperm to fertilize the egg, so both parents are required.'

'You said the DNA mutation was non-hereditary, but now you're saying it comes from our parents.'

Poppi explained, 'With gynogenesis the foetus develops its own stem cell line independently of the Host, so the mother is an unwitting surrogate. Although sperm doesn't contribute to the genetic makeup of the foetus, it is required to stimulate the activation of the egg, so the father, is also an unwitting surrogate.'

'I don't understand. Do we have our mother's DNA, our father's or both?'

'We have neither parents' DNA,' she continued, 'the mother is just an incubator and the father's sperm activates conception. Forget about parthenogenesis and gynogenesis, it's usually referred to as "cuckoo conception". If you think about it like in those terms, then it's easier to understand.'

'But, why are we different?'

'Nobody knows, Jack,' proclaimed Payne, 'One in 10000 are conceived like this but we don't know why. Nature is nature.'

'But we haven't got to the complicated part yet,' laughed Poppi. 'Metempsychosis is the tricky part to get your head around.'

'Metempsychosis?'

'Metempsychosis is the transmigration of the soul from one mortal body to another after death,' explained Payne.

'What!' Jack exclaimed, 'You mean like reincarnation?'

'No, well yes, but no. I mean no. Re incarnation is a bit like metempsychosis, but completely different. But reincarnation is made up of course.' stuttered Payne.

'What Payne is trying to articulate,' Poppi interrupted observing the confusion on Jack's face, 'Is that, although they are the same thing, they have a different literal meaning. We made up the word reincarnation to confuse the Normals'

'Why?' Jack enquired.

'Because metempsychosis is the very root of our existence, it's vital the Normals don't find out about it. The fact we've introduced a fake word into the Normals dictionary indicates, at some point, they have found out. Perhaps they've been told by a Clover Caste Host in a relationship, or maybe they've somehow stumbled across the Preamble Manual of Elucidation'

'How do you know they've found out?'

'Sometimes,' continued Poppi,' despite our best efforts information about us is discovered and published in some format: maybe a magazine or book. We deal with the source of the problem, so it doesn't happen again...'

'Deal with them?'

'Kill them discretely. A little accident here, untraceable poisons there; maybe some nerve gas on a door handle. It depends on the Agent. But the most difficult part is dealing with the information out there. So, what we do is make up similar things to muddy the water. We then flood the libraries and magazines with articles about the similar, but made up, occurrence so that description is more easily found. It's a fake word, but we call it "borrowed diction"'

'I'm not sure what you mean, Poppi'

'OK. Let me use the differences between metempsychosis and reincarnation as a demonstration. Metempsychosis is the transmigration of the soul; a straight migration which embodies all the characteristics of the Host body to a new body. When we transmigrate, we take with us the memory map for the previous life, or lives. All the knowledge we have accrued, we keep. All our experiences and memories, we keep. We also maintain muscle memory from the previous physical bodies. Both the memory map and muscle memory lay dormant until the new physical body, and brain, has developed sufficiently to cope.'

'But how does that differ to reincarnation?'

'Reincarnation is a rebirth of the soul, which would result in the soul starting from the beginning. Metempsychosis exists but reincarnation doesn't. We made it up. But if you were to investigate transmigration of the soul, you would probably end up reading about reincarnation. But there's no such thing as reincarnation.'

'So, any Normal who finds out about us is killed? Why?' gasped Jack.

'Why! Why!' exclaimed Payne, 'Because it would be a disaster, that's why. Every society needs to be led by a ruling class. It's not politically correct, I realise this, but it *is* true. And who better to do it than a supra society of people such as the Clover Caste?'

'Supra society' laughed Jack, 'have you heard yourself? Why are we a supra society?'

'Because of the memory map, obviously,' snapped Payne.

'Payne's right,' Poppi interrupted, 'it sounds arrogant, but we are a supra society because of the memory map. By the time we reach our final life we could, theoretically, have lived for over 400 years. I believe there's a final life Clover, whose combined total lifespans are almost 500 years. How do most societies learn and develop?'

'Er, through experiences and reading books and education, I suppose,' Jack replied hastily.

'Exactly Jack. The books and education, you mentioned are snapshots of history which, combined with our own personal experiences, form the basis of society. We learn everything from the mistakes of history and improve together by embracing previous societies successes such as technology, philosophy and experiences. Having 400 years of personal experience makes us more suitable for taking society forward compassionately; even if some of our methods may – at first – appear barbaric.'

'OK Poppi, I admit it's more compelling from you than Payne, but It's still arrogant.'

'It's not arrogant. We've more embodied knowledge than the Normals because we live longer. That's an undisputable fact. Maybe spending so much of your first life in England has rubbed off on you. The English, like most nations, lack confidence. If you are better than somebody else, just admit it. When you were in England – did you ever try to compliment anybody? If you did, I bet, they nearly had a nervous breakdown. It's no coincidence that Americans are more confident and come across as arrogant to other nations. We are the base for the Clover Caste, resulting in a high concentration of Clover Hosts; this confidence often rubs off on the Normals,' continued Poppi.

'If we're so great, why do we need to hide ourselves from the Normals? Why don't we reveal our true identities?'

'They wouldn't accept us,' Payne interjected, 'or to be more specific, they wouldn't accept us as a ruling society. They would want to help run society. They wouldn't accept we are more capable of doing so and out vote us.'

'But why should they accept us? Why shouldn't they be part of the ruling classes.'

'Oh, grow up, will you? Do you think with our superior memory map, we should allow important decisions to be made by Normals? Are you suggesting we allow direct democracy?' Payne asked.

'We already do,' Jack countered, 'the Normals can vote.'

Payne laughed, 'you really are naïve. The vote Normals have don't count; they're a pig circus. The only direct democracy we have is similar to that used by the Greeks thousands of years ago whereby only a small percentage of the population could vote. These were Clover, of course. Quite rightly so, in my opinion, as each member of the Senate and Council will have lived for hundreds of years. Their experience far outweighs that of a Normal. You've got a lot to learn'

'Which is why he's undertaking elucidation,' offered Poppi, sensing the mounting tensions. 'We aren't here to discuss the merits of the Council and the Senate. We're here to help Jack cope with his transition from life 1 to life 2 which, as you know Payne, is the most traumatic and confusing of all the transitions. The structure of the Caste will be covered in detail during the school of enlightenment. I think this is a good time for a break.'

The impact of Payne's stomp out of the room was diluted as he slowed down to wait for Poppi, who in return gestured for him to leave, which he duly did with a grunt.

'He's not as bad as you think,' Poppi explained.

'Well it was you who called him a prick.'

'Well he is, but a harmless one and his heart's in the right place.'

'Really?' protested Jack, 'I thought it was in his trousers after the conversation he had with you earlier, when he asked you to go to Italy with him. You weren't interested. Even I could see that, and I had my eyes closed!'

'I can handle people like him all day long. He doesn't mean anything. Its' just his way. I can't imagine his chat up technique is often successful; but then he is a Lion, and some women like that about him. It can be a career leg up to know a Lion. Maybe he thinks that's enough to be able to get away with lazy chat up lines.'

'A Lion,' quizzed Jack.

'During the first life, all Hosts are assessed based on their capabilities and split into two groups: "Lions" and "Donkeys". The most capable Hosts are classified as Lions and carry out the most dangerous tasks. They are often field operatives trained to help maintain the equilibrium within the Caste; the Donkeys are assigned easier tasks. Being a Lion is prestigious and, barring any major incidents, the Host will be classed as a Lion throughout the four lives. You see Jack, even within a supra society, there is still a higher class. Only around 1 in 100 are Lions. It is possible to work up from a Donkey to a Lion; but it's difficult. Being a Lion almost guarantees a favourable outcome in the final life. Payne's a Lion, which some women find attractive.'

'1 in 100 isn't rare though?'

'It is if you work the numbers. 1 in 100 Clover Caste equates to one in a 1 000 000 people on the planet when you factor the Normals in. There's 325 million people living in the USA today – that's only 325 Lions pro rata, although in reality, there are many more due to the high concentration of Clover in the USA. They are powerful.'

'So, I take it you're a Lion, Poppi?'

'No, I'm a Donkey; Payne's my boss.'

'Really? I would have put my life on you being the Lion and him being the Donkey. You're the one in control; the one who doesn't panic at the first sign of pressure. How did he become a Lion and you a Donkey?'

'I'm not sure. Maybe if I work hard enough and impress the right people, I'll be a Lion one day. But Payne is a Lion – and so are you.'

'Me?'

'Yeah, and being a Lion is a great advantage even within the already privileged Clover Caste; as you'll find out, Jack. Like I say, some women are *very* attracted to Lions.'

'What about you, Poppi? Are you attracted to Lions?' Jack coaxed.

'Well that depends.' She teased.

'On what?' he replied.

'On how sharp his teeth are!'

CHAPTER 17

Payne was the first to re-enter the room, followed closely by Poppi. It had been a couple of hours since they left, during which time Jack had occupied himself by eating his lunch and relaxing. He felt he should have been reading the manual but opted instead to relax on the bed and gaze into the aquarium.

'I take it you didn't enjoy the fish and chips?' Payne sneered, observing the half-eaten food on the table.'

'It was OK, I just wasn't hungry after the breakfast.' Jack replied.

'Well, quite.' Payne continued scooping up the plate, 'I'll get rid of this, before it stinks the place out.'

As the door closed behind Payne, Poppi turned to Jack, 'I forgot to mention the break was to allow you time to read the manual again. Did you read it?'

'No,' I haven't,' he replied, before changing the subject. 'It seems important to you to be a Lion. Why?'

Poppi sighed, 'We have four lives; the first three we work hard to make a legacy for our final life, which is a retirement life. Lions always get the best final lives. They can do anything they want. I want that life. Everybody wants that life. Who wouldn't?'

'You work hard for three lives for material gain in the final life. So, you are sacrificing 3 lives for one good one. Doesn't sound a great deal to me. What about living in the moment?'

'That's alright for you to say, you're a lion. And after what you did in your first life, you're guaranteed a fantastic final leaf. I'd do anything to be in your position,' she replied, the desperation in her voice catching him off guard.

'In that case, why don't you take Payne up on his offer and tour Tuscany in his Maserati?' he asked.

'Well, almost anything,' she laughed as Payne, right on cue, returned to the room.

'Jack, did the manual make more sense this time? After our one to one session we find the manual begins to make more sense. It also makes this next session easier. You have read it again haven't you?' he enquired.

'No, he hasn't,' Poppi interrupted.

'What? Why?' Payne snapped, 'That's great. You did tell him to read it didn't you Poppi. That was the whole point of having the break!'

'Yes, she did tell me,' Jack quickly responded,' But I couldn't be bothered. I was tired, so I decided to relax and eat my lunch and watch the fishes in the aquarium. I was so busy apologising to each fish in there for eating their brother that I forgot to read the manual. Sorry to be a pain, Payne.'

Payne's look of disgust was eclipsed by Poppi's expression of appreciation. Despite not fully understanding the manual, he knew enough to recognise the hierarchy within the room. Both he and Payne were Lions which put them higher on the food chain than Poppi, however unfair that may be. Taking the fall for not reading the manual would have less consequences for him than Poppi; indeed, the success of his first life may even give him the edge over Payne, he pondered, remembering the panic in Payne's voice when he originally found out who Jack was. Jack stared directly at Payne whose expression changed from disgust to resignation as the balance of power within the room was transformed.

Payne continued, 'As children we're identical to the offspring of Normals – so detection occurs during routine medical checks throughout childhood, often during pre-natal scanning stages. Early detection within developed countries is high, but much lower in less populated and less advanced parts of the world. Normals cannot detect the mutated DNA; only we have the technology. That said, even we can miss a Host in an underdeveloped part of the world.'

'Can we go through a life undetected?' Jack asked.

'In theory, but it's unlikely.' Poppi explained. 'You see, although the Host can be found anywhere in the world, and the foetus develops in mothers of all nationalities and colours, there are striking similarities over all four-Leaf Levels. It's believed by some that this is due to an energy template within the soul of the person being passed down along each Leaf; but, the general belief is that the similarities are due to the repetitive nature of the DNA strand.'

'Once the Host has been identified' Payne interjected, 'progress is monitored throughout childhood by doctors, teachers, and Mentors placed as "friends" to those going through transition.'

'Carson!' exclaimed Jack, 'was Carson one of these "friends"?'

'Yes, he was,' soothed Poppi, who was obviously the one primed to deliver shocking news to him, 'and the Coach.'

'So, he isn't really my friend. He's just doing a job!'

'No, they are both your friends.' said Poppi continuing her compassionate narrative, 'They are very good friends from your first life. They volunteered for this mission to make sure you had the best outcome during this, the most difficult transition.'

'The Coach? But he's much older than me?'

'Yes 18 years older – you were the same age in the first life. You and Carson died before him that's all. It's common for Clover Caste to have friends of differing ages as there is often a time disconnect between transitions.'

The sensitive nature of the conversation had rendered Payne's role temporarily defunct; even Jack was lost for words. Payne took the pause as his opportunity to continue the conversation in a less emotive tone.

'As the Host approaches the first transition, the Council will assign Mentors and Greeters. Carson and the coach were Mentors. The role of Mentor is to secretly guide and support the Host until it is time to instruct a Greeter to intervene. Which is what they did.'

'What's a Greeter?' grunted Jack.

'The role of a Greeter is to remove the Host from everyday life for the Council to conduct Elucidation. After Elucidation the Greeter reintegrates the Host back into society.'

'Is that why I heard the Doc and the coach arguing about not sending for a Greeter earlier?'

'That's right,' Payne continued, 'there are 3 stages during transition and it's the responsibility of the mentor to correctly identify the first stage – the awakening – before informing the Greeter.'

'The awakening?'

'During adolescence the previous life cycle memories will begin to occur within the Host in the form of "flashbacks" or *"déjà vu"*. This can be disorientating and scary during the first transition and, if not identified correctly, will result in extreme reactions.'

'Like what?'

'Like violence or, in your case, fleeing into the direction of places you were familiar with during a previous life. Fortunately, we had Carson and the Coach looking out for you, so we caught you early in stage 2; Somnambulation'

'Somnambulation?'

'Yes,' replied Payne, in full flow, 'After the Awakening, the Host sub consciously reverts to their previous life in a state of abstraction.'

'Abstraction?'

'A bit like sleep walking. The Host is vulnerable at this stage; and so is the Caste. The Host may resist elucidation and lose previous life information contained within the memory map. Worse still, in a state of panic and confusion the Host may divulge sensitive information to a Normal. This could have dire consequences – particularly for the Normal. Once in the somnambulation stage, this information is difficult - sometimes impossible - to obtain; so, it's vital the Host is safely scooped up by the Greeters before somnambulation begins.'

'And you are currently in the third phase of transition – elucidation,' Poppi continued, 'where any information and experience required by the Council is extracted via hypnotherapy. After hypnotherapy, the Host is sent to read the Preamble Manual of Elucidation – If he doesn't find it too boring that is! After which you will be sent to the School of Enlightenment where the process of transition and other aspects of the Clover Caste are explained. But before you are ready for the School of Enlightenment, you need to understand the Four Cycles of Metempsychosis.'

'We call the four cycles of metempsychosis Leaf Levels. We experience four different but consecutive lives,' explained Payne.

'Different? What do you mean different?' quizzed Jack, 'surely, we just have four lives, one after the other?'

'Yes, but each life has different significance to the Caste, part of which is because of the strain of DNA mutation, which differs in the final life, or leaf, as we call them.' Payne continued, 'The mutated DNA is present in leaf 1 through to leaf 3; but is not for the final leaf. For this reason, Leaves 1 to 3 are referred to as the foundation levels and Leaf 4 the actualisation level. '

'Why does it change? What happens to the mutated DNA?'

'We don't know Jack; it just dies out. There are many theories, but no conclusive evidence. This will be discussed in more detail during the School of Enlightenment. But the outshot is there are significant differences to the Clover Host from the foundation stage to the self-actualisation stage.'

'Firstly,' Poppi said, 'during the foundation level we have all the health benefits of the active DNA mutation but are unable to have children. The DNA mutation means we enjoy better health than Normals during the foundation stage, because the mutation is effective in repairing faulty genes created within them. There have never been any reported cases of cancer in Hosts during the foundation stage. However, we are still susceptible to virus-based illnesses such as colds and the 'flu.'

'Level 4, or "Self-Actualisation", 'Payne continued in unison, 'is the life most like the life of a Normal as the DNA structure is no longer mutated. The two main differences are that the Host is susceptible to DNA related diseases such as cancer, and we can reproduce. But we still benefit from the superior knowledge attained during the previous three life cycles, which is stored in the memory map. We also benefit physically as muscle memory is transferred through all transition stages. But the biggest change is the ability to have children, which makes Leaf 4 sacred to Clover Hosts, and is why we call it self-actualisation.'

'So that's why working towards Leaf 4 is so important, because we can have kids? But why is being a Lion is important?'

Payne explained, 'during the foundation stage the Host serves the Clover Council and Senate in ways beneficial to the the Caste. The more a Host helps the Caste, the more favourably he/she will be looked upon during the final cycle. Being a Lion means it's easier to impress the Council as they hold the most high-profile jobs; although the job will also depend upon which leaf level you are on.'

'Why?'

Payne continued,' During the foundation level, the Host will take up employment recommended by the Council. The type of employment will depend on leaf level and statue – ie whether Donkey or Lion, and which life you are on. The riskier tasks are assigned to Leaf 1 as they have the most lives remaining. Leaf 1 will also be allocated the boring and less brain taxing jobs as they have the least intelligence because their memory map is smaller. On the other hand, Leaf 3 will be allocated the least risky but most intellectually challenging tasks. Upon reaching Leaf 4 the Host can decide to continue to work for the Council or retire from work altogether.'

'Each Leaf Level has a title with expectations as to the roles required from the Host.' Poppi pronounced, 'For example Leaf 1 is referred to as the "Sacrificial" level. That's not to say you are expected to die for the Caste - although this could happen - more the need to sacrifice time. It is during Leaf 1 the Host is assessed and split into two groups: "Lions" and "Donkeys". Leaf 1 Lions are often field operatives trained to help maintain the equilibrium within the Caste. The Donkeys are assigned easier tasks, often in administration.'

'So, what about me. I'm on Leaf 2 – what's Leaf 2?'

It was Payne's turn to explain, 'We call Leaf 2 *"Endeavour"*. It's the first leaf when the Host will experience past life recollections and is the most traumatic of the three transitions. '

'What will be my job in Leaf 2?'

'It's difficult to say. Typically, a Leaf 2 will carry out similar task to those which they did during the first leaf. Quite often a Host who has just completed Elucidation themselves and has the complexity and sensitivity of the first transition fresh in their mind will become a Mentor or Greeter. With you I'm not sure. You're high profile after your first leaf. The Council will have something big planned for you!'

'Oh right,' replied Jack, taken back by Payne's comment.

'How does that make you feel, Jack? Knowing your status within the Caste, and the expectations we have for you?' enquired Poppi.

'No problem,' boasted Jack defiantly, 'it is what it is.'

The reply was instinctive. Could it have been a stock male response to appear strong in front Poppi and Payne? Or was it instinct pulling through from his previous life, where he was well respected for his achievements. Maybe his memory map was re-populating? It was an impressive show of bravado; but who was he trying to impress? He barely knew Poppi, but what he did know he liked. He would like to know more about her but, it would appear, so would Payne. Payne was a rival and his reply was akin to beating his chest Neanderthal style. But below the façade, he wasn't comfortable with the expectations. He was 18 years old for god's sake; he still had difficulty talking to girls - hardly an ideal trait for a hero. He had the broad shoulders, but did he have the mental fortitude?

'That's what I thought,' beamed Poppi.

Her enthusiastic response irritated Payne who continued, 'Your next life will be Leaf 3 – or "Perception". The transition from Leaf 2 to Leaf 3 is straightforward compared to the first transition. The memories begin at an earlier age and continue to be recollected regularly throughout childhood. The Leaf 3 Host will process this information at an earlier age than in Leaf 2 and form the life cycle outline without the confusion or distress you are going through now. There's no requirement at this level, for the use of Mentors or Greeters unless the Host is known to be volatile or high profile to the Caste. But usually the Host knows what is going on by early adulthood and has the intelligence to contact the Council when they are ready.'

Poppi re-joined the conversation, 'Leaf 3 are the highest Leaf level with the DNA mutation, which is reflected in the roles they fulfil within the Caste network and are appointed to high level jobs. The knowledge acquired during the previous two life cycles, makes Leaf 3 ideal for serving in positions that feed directly to the Clover Council, such as the higher echelons of governments, Councils and other important organisations within the Normals' society. They are conduits connecting the national governments and the Clover Council. These are highly sensitive and responsible positions, held in great esteem within the Caste. An effective Leaf 3 will influence governments and organisations throughout the world to implement decisions already made by the Clover Council surreptitiously.'

'You mean we place Clover Caste people within governments and Councils to interfere with the decision-making process?' asked Jack.

'Of course, we do,' laughed Payne, 'We can't allow them to make their own decisions. Could you imagine that; with their puny memory map from just one lifetime? No, Leaf 3 have an extensive memory map making them ideal to take up roles as high-level politicians, diplomats, and commanders in the armed forces. If they like, they can carry on with these high-profile careers in Leaf 4!'

'Or...' interrupted Poppi, 'They can enjoy retirement. Although we call Leaf 4 self-actualisation it's also known as the retirement level. This is our final life, but it doesn't contain the mutated DNA strand like the first three lives. Our DNA during level 4 is the same as a Normal: but there are still advantages being Clover Caste during Leaf 4. The energy template still stores muscle memories, so we have a stronger mortal body. Although the DNA doesn't mutate, life expectancy is still significantly higher than a normal because of our superior physique passed on by muscle memory, and the health monitoring and treatments provided by the Council. Our Doctors and their medical equipment are far superior to those available to the Normals.'

'In our final life we can decide whether to carry on working, or to retire,' mused Jack. 'That's interesting. I imagine most people choose to retire. Why carry on working?'

'Most people do retire. Of those who continue to work, very few do it out of necessity. We have 3 lives to build up our funds; even those who are on the lower end of the pay grade, as it were, have a better-quality retirement than a Normal can dream of,' Poppi responded.

'But, what if, say, a Clover had 3 short lives and there wasn't time to receive many credits from the Council?' questioned Jack.

'That can't happen,' interrupted Payne, 'we're immune to DNA based diseases in the first 3 lives. The most likely way we would have short lives would be to be killed on dangerous assignments for the Council. But, if that was the case, then you would be rewarded handsomely for it. Besides the Council try not to put a Host in dangerous situations in more than one or two lives. This goes back to why the first life is referred to as the sacrificial life.'

'That's right,' Poppi confirmed, 'Most Clover Caste choose to continue to work because they want too as the work is interesting and rewarding. All the best jobs are available to Clover Caste Hosts in their final life.'

'Example,' probed Jack.

'President of the United States of America. Prime Minister of the UK...well Head of State in any developed country' Payne spluttered, hardly able to contain his excitement. 'You name it. All the best jobs. Oh and of course there's the possibility of working on the Senate, which is more powerful than the President and Prime Minister rolled into one and multiplied by a million. You could be given the franchise to a football team – or in your case a soccer team.'

'And supposing you're not a megalomaniac,' groaned Jack, 'and you just wanted to retire and enjoy the fruits of your labour. How does that work? How do you know how many credits you have, and what you can do with it?'

'During your first 3 lives,' answered Poppi, 'your services to the Council are monitored and this is the key to your options during Self Actualisation. The harder you work, and the more loyal you are – the greater will be your rewards. Should your efforts result in sacrificing one, or more of your lives; you will be greatly rewarded. As Lions are given the best jobs, they are likely to accrue the most credits. Assets gained during the three lives will be commandeered by the Council at the end of each of the foundation lives and put into what we call a "pension pot" This pot will be gradually distributed to the Host during early adulthood, during Leaf 4'.

'Gradually redistributed? Is that so the Council can hang onto it for as long as possible to collect the interest?' Jack enquired.

'The Council don't need interest!' scoffed Payne, 'can you imagine how odd it would look if a random 16-year-old appeared onto the scene with a huge mansion, flash car and millions in the bank? The funds are introduced gradually, so as not to draw attention to the Host.'

'How?'

'Many final Leaf Clovers play small parts in large companies – such as CEO or chairman. Others are fortunate enough to win money in lotteries and game shows. Others may be accredited with inventions which make them appear rich,' Payne continued.

'Inventions? Like what?'

'Pretty much everything,' offered Poppi, 'like the mattress on the treatment table you laid on earlier. We have had this high viscosity mattress for years, but only recently released this technology to the Normals and marketed it as a "waterbed". The invention has been credited to a successful final leaf Host in San Francisco, who is now living it up as a millionaire. An innocuous invention, on the face of it, but perfect to release funds into a Leaf 4 bank account!'

'So, you release technology to launder money, rather than to benefit the Normals?'

'No,' said Poppi, 'we do it to release funds, killing two birds with one stone. It's complex deciding how to do it though. We have an entire department which specialises in making those decisions – mostly Leaf 3, I think. Much of the investment takes place in the USA and California, where technology is regularly drip fed into the mainstream.'

'Why can we only have children in the final life?'

Poppi replied, 'We don't know for sure, but as the DNA mutation occurs in the first three lives and not the last then this must be reason. In a way it's a blessing. Can you imagine having children, then dying and coming back to life younger than them?'

'That would be one messed up family tree!' Jack observed.

'You're not kidding,' agreed Poppi. 'But you can see why the final life is important. Your child is not going to be Clover Caste, like us; so, you need to make sure you leave a legacy for them, so they don't spend their only life working their fingers to the bone. What's the point saving up money if you can only spend it when you're old. Enjoy it when you're young and enjoy your children while they're young.'

'Ok,' Jack mused, 'I'm beginning to understand, but I've more questions. Like how we transmigrate?'

'Good question, Jack.' Payne added, 'It shows you're ready for the next stage of Elucidation.'

'Next stage?'

'Yes,' Payne continued, 'this is stage 1 – the Preamble Manual of Elucidation. It's just a taster; an introduction to the Caste. The next stage is the School of Enlightenment, an intensive residential course dealing with the more complicated idiosyncrasies of being Clover Caste. Transmigration of the Soul – or metempsychosis – will be dealt with there. And lots of other things, including things we have touched on today, but in more detail. Good luck.'

'Yes,' repeated Poppi, 'Good luck, Jack.'

'Will I see either of you again?' asked Jack with platitude, despite being interested only in one reply.

'Perhaps,' Payne replied first, 'but it may not be in this life.'

'Possibly,' replied Poppi before hesitating. 'Probably. I hope so.'

PHASE 3 - DOMINION

CHAPTER 18
8th December 1980

It had been sixteen years since elucidation. Those fortunate enough to be identified as Lions during the First Leaf were expected to progress steadily through the Clover hierarchy. Even for a Lion, Jack had exceeded expectations by tracking down and killing the Caste's number one enemy. Since the assassination, he had become the hero of a fluid, ever evolving fable that had grown wings and flown away from him. He played down the event only to discover his modesty added more fuel to the flames, and now the story was out of control; he was a legend, whether he liked it or not. Recalling his fears and how anger had propelled him to kill a dying man, he felt like an imposter; he was scared and lost his temper. Hardly the act of a heroic man.

Of course, the Council and Senate gratefully ingested it, spoon-feeding propaganda throughout the Caste. In a time of weaponry so advanced you could shoot a fly from half a mile away, the notion that the greatest threat to the Caste was killed by the bare hands of one of their own was delicious. This absurdly implied romanticism was not lost on Jack, who had lived the much less impressive real-life experience. Still, there was a period where cynicism was forgotten as he enjoyed the spoils of victory, masquerading through the higher levels of society with a beautiful woman on his arm. The level of hospitality extended to successful Caste members left him breathless and not without pangs of guilt. But remorse was put to one side while the opulence of the Caste was laid before him.

Unfortunately, this happy chapter was short lived and now an even more distant stranger than elucidation. Recently, he found himself musing on the simplicity of his old life and hankering for the pre-déjà vu days. His status within the Caste had taken a turn for the worse. It was anticipated that he would hold a strategic military role in keeping with that of a high-profile second leafer. Instead, he opted for the less stressful role of Mentor, to the widespread disappointment of the upper echelons. He also changed his name back to Stanley Webster, which was lesser known despite it being the moniker he used when performing the dastardly deed which had come to define him as Jack Marwood. This had not gone down well with the Council as they did not approve of those within the Caste using their names in a non-chronological order. Even his friends were uncomfortable calling him Stanley, usually opting for his nickname, Flash. Still, despite their protests, there was nothing they could do about it; he was Stanley Webster, not Jack Marwood, whether they liked it or not. But perhaps that was why he did it? He had detached himself from the Council and, though he still possessed his Heartbeat and Skin, they sat gathering dust in his wardrobe.

Despite flying below the radar, he was well provided for by the Council, smiling wryly as he looked through the window of his Manhattan apartment overlooking Central Park. It would take a Normal many years to be able to afford such a view, yet it was gifted to him for free. What kind of view would he have, if he had travelled the expected route?

Observing a mother playing with her young daughter, he told himself he had made the right career choice. Walking innocently through the park, she would be unaware of the existence of the Caste, let alone the privileges bestowed upon them. Maybe she was Clover Caste? No, of course not: she has a child. Unless she was Leaf 4. But what is the likelihood of that? The odds of her being Clover are already 1 in 10,000 so the odds of being Level 4 Clover are even more remote. He sat, trying to work out the mathematical probability. Is it four multiplied by 10,000 or is it 10,000 multiplied by 10,000 four times? He convinced himself that if she was a Leaf 4 living in New York he would know who she was, thus saving himself a difficult calculation.

He was uncomfortable with the relationships between the Caste and the Normals and had developed a progressive attitude. Did he think the Caste should reveal themselves to the Normals? Well, that's a tough question, a multi-layered conundrum he was unable to decide upon. But he was a strong believer that they should have access to more technology and equal access to healthcare and medicines. And although there were no official restrictions, he felt an awkwardness about romantic liaisons with a Normal: it was unfair as it was unbeknown to the Normal, that procreation could not happen. The surreptitious nature of the Caste required the relationship to be built upon a foundation of deceit. Most Clover were not adversely affected by this, but he considered it morally wrong, rather than a necessary evil. He had heard the cautionary tales of Clover Caste being honest with Normals, resulting in both the Normal and Clover disappearing from the face of the earth.

He was in an emotional juxtaposition. His admiration and respect for the Normals was far greater than for the Caste. Theoretically, the Caste were more advanced physically, mentally and technologically but, still, he envied the Normals. Despite having only one life, they stumbled through it with gay abandon, with little concern for the future, and though they didn't enjoy the self-healing DNA mutation, they continued to drink and smoke to their hearts' content. The Caste, on the other hand, planned their lives meticulously in preparation for the coveted final life of 'self-actualisation'. All three foundation levels were spent in servitude to ensure a final leaf of wealth and power. In comparison, many Normals made no plans for their retirement, spending their money frivolously. But, to him, they seemed the happier of the two.

To avoid deceit, his only relationship could be with another Clover. Although this was the righteous thing to do, he had to continually reassure himself to keep his sanity. It was difficult enough to meet a girl without having the odds reduced by a ratio of 10,000 to 1, a statistic further exacerbated by his choice to turn his back on the high society of the Caste.

He was still in touch with Carson and John, although the frequency had diminished with the passing of the years. John was still on his first leaf and in his sixties, an age which suited him. Even when they were the same age, he felt the conversations with John were a lecture from an elder rather than bilateral exchanges with a peer. As the only survivor of the Uruguay mission, John had milked his notoriety to the full, using it to finally shoehorn the nickname Lucky into the equation. Unlike Stanley, he had fully accepted the generosity and acclaim handed to him by the Clover Council. Stanley had no problem with this as John was a man of good heart and tireless dedication to the Caste.

He deserved the accolades. He was still a good friend and tried to persuade him to switch roles and become more involved within the Council. He had even disrupted his rapid career rise to take up the guise of 'Coach Carter' to help him through the difficult first transition. He was also responsible for the completion of the mission after his own demise: John had held off the attackers until the rescue squad arrived, ensuring the DNA information was passed on to the Council.

Carson chose to stay within the military, accepting a high-level strategic role. He was doing well, but his relationship with John was still frosty. Stanley had always been closer to Carson than John and the new age gap had added to this. Carson's military role provided him with many anecdotes, making Stanley's life even less interesting. But the one which amused him the most was Carson's continual insistence that one of the Beatles had stolen his Leaf 4 retirement plan. True, he had mentioned, around the campfire in Uruguay, his intention to start a band with some friends to tour the world, but this must be a coincidence. He was convinced either that John had shared this information with a Leaf 4 to spoil his plan, or he had been overheard back in Liverpool discussing the idea. It was a theory he had become obsessed with. There was no way of knowing if the Beatles were Clover Caste let alone if they had stolen his plan, but Carson claimed he had heard through his military connections that one of them was Clover, probably either John or Paul.

The Beatles story was always a good pick-me-up for Stanley. At least until today, when a couple of quick fire events had hit him in the face faster than a left-right combination from a feather weight: he had awoken to the shocking news of the death of John Lennon, which had happened only a couple of blocks away from his apartment. The indirect part the Beatles had played in his awakening, and Carson's frequent rantings, had left him with an obscure attachment to John Lennon and the band. He was also alarmed at the nature of his death. The style of assassination was evocative of the Clover Caste, leading him to ponder whether Carson's theories were more than pure bluster. Maybe John Lennon was Level 4 Caste and was going to use his worldwide platform to blow the lid on the Caste to the Normals? From what he had seen of him, over the years, he did appear to be progressive by nature. Usually such people just disappeared. But maybe he was so high profile he couldn't simply vanish into thin air?

Before having too long to pontificate, the telephone rang, causing him to jump. A stinging endorsement of his social popularity. He picked it up, unaware that the assassination news was merely a left jab, lining him up for the right hook he was about to receive.

'Hello, Jack,' beckoned the voice.

Stanley froze. It had been years since he had been called Jack; it had been years since he had heard her voice.

'Jack ... Jack, I know you're there.'

'Yes, yes, I'm here,' he stammered, regaining his composure. 'Long time no speak.'

'We don't have much time,' came the terse response. 'Have you seen the news?'

'Er, yes.'

'Then you'll realise you're in danger. We'll call round for you when it's safe.'

Click. The line was dead.

CHAPTER 19

It had been two hours since the phone call and Stanley's mind was in overdrive. He couldn't recall how long it had been, since he had heard Poppi's voice, but it was more than ten years; for sure. Irrespective of timescale, one thing was clear: she still had the same effect on him. He was racked with self-loathing for being so weak, having previously convinced himself that she was in the past and could no longer provoke a response within him. He was psychologically puny back then but was now much stronger and intellectually mature. He told himself that should their paths cross again there would be no fluctuations in his heartbeat or throbbing of the pulse; moreover, she could not induce the stomach-churning, heart-breaking feelings of despair he had experienced before. He had done such a comprehensive job of convincing himself of this that he had not expected to find himself glued to the armchair, in a state of emotional turmoil. He longed to return to his self-imposed emotional vacuum. To say the relationship had ended abruptly was an understatement. He still didn't understand what had happened, how their perfect alliance was quickly and unexpectedly dismantled until all that remained was a pile of broken dreams and expectations.

She was the girl on his arm as he sauntered through the early stages of Leaf 2, the Leaf 1 sacrifice having left him riding the crest of a seemingly endless wave. He was popular back then, a sought-after commodity, and who could have chosen any of the eligible Clover Caste females, never having to worry about the complexities of dating a Normal. But to him the choice was simple. From the moment they met, he knew it was more than a crush. She was the one. He thought about her constantly; she dominated his thoughts. It was strange and overwhelming yet reassuringly comfortable. Having never been in love before, he was terrified; so, while a new door had opened in his brain, he wanted to both run through it and slam it shut in equal measures. He wasn't in control. He cherished the idea of embracing another soul but recoiled at the thought of his own vulnerability - if she told him to jump off a cliff, would he? He wasn't sure, which was the worrying thing.

It was perfect in the beginning. He was a hero, and she a well-respected psychoanalyst, and for a while they were the golden couple - until, completely out of the blue, she ended it. She wasn't ready for commitment choosing to focus on her work to gain as many credits as she could towards the all-important final Leaf. At first, he didn't believe she was ending it; he thought there was somebody else and he thought that somebody was Carson. He found out the hard way it wasn't, escaping the accusations with their friendship barely intact.

He descended into what he referred to as his "free fall" period and took time off to travel. It was during these travels he decided to change his career path from the military to becoming a Mentor. He was disillusioned with the Caste. The rewards for servitude during the foundation levels had increased to a level he was uncomfortable with. Many Final Leafers had chosen high-profile celebrity status as the prize for their serfdom. President of the United States had always been a favourite but being an A-list actor was now on the increase, and the presidential elections, a month earlier, suggested that the extremely privileged could do both!

He blamed the Caste for the end of his relationship with Poppi. The fascination with the Final Leaf stopped people having fun and enjoying their lives, instead of living in the moment as the Normals did. He disagreed with the power available during Leaf 4, as many of the presidents entrusted with this entitlement were unsuitable for office. Even when proven to be inadequate they would remain in office with the support of the Council. He wondered how the Normals didn't suss them out, considering some of the idiotic decisions they made. But mostly he blamed the Council for Poppi leaving him.

Sat in his armchair, the past was the least of his worries. The trepidation of the reunion allied with the dialogue of the brief tete-a-tete formed a greater reason for concern. What did they mean by "you'll realise you're in danger"? What danger? And why would he know about any danger? He had spent the last ten years keeping himself out of danger; or at least he thought he had. As far as he was aware, his life was quintessentially mundane. That's what he'd planned and that's how he liked it.

His heart raced as the doorbell rang. He knew it was them. He had not buzzed any visitors through the main entrance door, a formality their training would bypass. Besides, few people ever visited. As he opened the door, standing before him were Poppi and John.

Poppi was in early middle age, but time had been her friend, her flawless, porcelain-like complexion the consummate backdrop to her flowing black locks and efflorescent eyes. He was momentarily distracted before tearing his gaze towards John. Time had been less benevolent to him. In his early sixties, he had aged disproportionately since their previous meeting. The remainder of his hair was grey, his eyes accentuated with well-established crow's feet. Maybe their last meeting had been longer ago than he remembered? Despite his surprise at the haggard exterior, he envied John. Would he himself ever live long enough to offer time the chance to ravage him? As they entered the apartment, he noticed John's attire was unusually free of his trademark cat motifs. He must be keeping a low profile.

'We have to leave quickly; we haven't got much of a head start, if any,' Poppi announced stoically without feeling the need to exchange pleasantries.

'What's going on?' Stanley quizzed.

'You've no idea?' she replied.

'Not a clue,' he answered in the direction of John despite the question belonging to Poppi.

Although Poppi shaped her mouth to speak, it was John- having no time for social awkwardness - who answered.

'You really have no idea?' he asked.

'No!' snapped Stanley, irritated by the question and the insinuation he was naive for not knowing the answer. He had often been on the receiving end of John's condescendence, something time failed to make less annoying.

'Look', he continued, 'I don't see what I have to do with the assassination other than it was a few blocks away. Maybe the guy was one of us, like Carson thought. Even so, it has nothing to do with me.'

'Mmmm,' John muttered in a rare moment of reflection. 'I'm aware that you'd stayed in touch with him and, of course, we monitored your meetings in this apartment, but I thought he must've told you more than his conspiracy theory. What did he tell you when you weren't in this room? Can you remember exactly what he said?'

'What do you mean "monitored our meetings"?'

'This is a Council apartment. You must realise it's covered by surveillance. You're not that naive, surely?'

Stanley was fuming at the idea of his every move being followed and the return of John's arrogance.

'You never saw him use one of these while he was here, did you?' John continued, nodding toward a small electronic device in the palm of his right hand.

'No. What is it?'

'It's a blocker. Blocks all surveillance equipment with the press of a button. These old apartments have low specification equipment, which is easily blocked. The green light indicates it's active. I turned it on the moment we got here.'

'No. Anyway, why would you need to block it? You're here on behalf of the Council, aren't you?'

John and Poppi glanced at each other. Stanley chortled, 'No, surely not, John? Are you turning your back on the Council? I can't believe it. That's made my day!'

Poppi cast him a bitter glance. 'No, he hasn't. How dare you question his commitment? We can't take anything for granted. There's a cancer within the Council. How malignant we don't know, but it's there. We must be careful. We don't know who's listening. Chances are there are only a few rotten apples, but until we find out more, we have to be vigilant.'

'But what's this got to do with me? And why are you so keen to know about my conversations with Carson? You don't think he had anything to do with what happened yesterday? You can't think Carson shot John Lennon?'

Once again, they looked at each other.

'No way,' Stanley sniggered. 'Not a chance in hell did Carson kill John Lennon. That's ludicrous. And for what reason? Because he "thinks" he stole his idea? We were both laughing about it the last time he was here.'

Poppi stepped towards him, rested her hand on his shoulder. 'He's not who you think he is.'

'He's not a killer, I know that much,' he protested. 'And where do I fit into all this? He hasn't told me anything you don't already know.'

'Look, pal, we need to go. We can tell you more on the way. We need to get you out of here or you could be next,' John ordered.

'Next! Next! Next for what? For assassination? But why? I have no connection to John Lennon. Even if you maintain this ridiculous theory that Carson has something to do with it, why would he kill me now? He's had plenty of opportunity in the past.'

'Because things have changed recently. Something's happened which makes you, and other high-profile operatives, dangerous to certain parties. Dangerous enough to be silenced. You're a walking liability.' Poppi had reverted to her soft, reassuring voice. He had fallen for it on their first meeting before elucidation; but during their relationship, he had acquired the ability to notice when it was turned on. It became transparent and annoying at the time but, for now, was oddly comforting. It proved she cared about his welfare. Well, kind of.

'You're going to need this,' she said, taking a small plastic bag from her pocket and tossing it onto the table.

He knew it was a Skin, vacuum packed to a size that seemed impossible for him to fit into. It had been a long time since he felt the need to wear one, and he knew that she wasn't giving it to him, so he could keep warm or excel at sports.

'Do you still have your Heartbeat?' asked John.

'Yes,' replied an exasperated Stanley. 'It's not charged though; it's been in my wardrobe for years.'

'Perfect. That's great.'

'Why?'

'Because you've one of the older Heartbeats that haven't been upgraded. They still work off the old network. If you don't log onto the new network, your calls can't be traced, and the GPS isn't activated. They can be used covertly with other unlocked devices. They're illegal and are like gold dust to get your hands on. When the charge is back on it will prompt you to update. Press NO. That is extremely important. Do you understand?'

'Yes.'

'Do *not* call the numbers in the contact list, send electronic letters or log onto the Councils network. The only people you are to call are me and Poppi. We both have unlocked devices. Do not log on! Do you understand?'

Blowing away the dust from the Heartbeat, he was surprised to see a small amount of charge in the battery. Stanley retorted, 'But what if I want to scan a fish or something?'

'We haven't got time for jokes,' John growled. 'We don't have to be here, you know. We've come for your safety, at risk to ourselves. We can go now if you fancy your chances alone?'

Stanley realised he was serious; the situation was real, and he had no choice but to do as John said. He had always been there for him in the past and to risk the wrath of his beloved Council, it must be important. He was less sure of Poppi's motivation for helping him. Was it guilt for leaving, or did she still have feelings for him? Maybe she had to leave him? Maybe she had no choice? Whatever the reasons, it was time to leave self-pity city. He just hoped they had a good plan.

CHAPTER 20

From the rear window of the car he could see the New York skyline fading into the distance. As the darkness of night began to fall, he guessed it was around 4pm. Sitting in the front of the Chevrolet Chevette were Poppi and John. The popularity of the entry level four-door hatchback made it the perfect car to steal. He could see from the condition of the cream mock leather seating, which matched the cream exterior, that it was only a couple of years old.

Stanley was surprised by how quickly he had reverted to his training. The shackles of his self-styled stagnation were cast aside as he returned to his high-level skill sets. It would have been easy to stand aside while the vehicle was commandeered; but he was a little rusty - not in an obvious way, he'd just forgotten the more refined aspects of auto theft. Without hesitation, he gained entry to a maroon AMC Spirit. The sleek hatchback, a new model, boasted the latest anti-theft locks, yet he was in like a shot. The fast car would have made good time on their long journey, but as John explained it was too new, distinctive and only had two doors; they needed a common model with four doors to aid a speedy exit. John targeted the Chevvy, which had been rolling off the production lines for years and for the last two was the bestselling car in America. It used to be second nature for him to know stuff like this. It was only a small detail that he had forgotten, but it was the sort of detail that could prevent you from being killed. By the time John had explained this and got into the car, Poppi had already changed the plates.

John was in the driving seat as they left the city. John was usually in the driving seat, one way or another. Glancing towards Poppi, Stanley wondered whether becoming a Mentor had been the right decision. It was worthwhile, and he had helped many confused young souls over the years, which, he had told himself, was why he chose to do it. But looking at Poppi he knew the real reason.

Who knows what may have happened had he not changed roles? He could have kept an eye on Carson for a start. He had always been the glue keeping the trio together and he was disappointed at how disconnected John and Carson had become. Back in the apartment he had asked what any of this had to do with him. John had changed the subject, and the thrill of grand larceny had distracted him further, but the question remained.

'You never answered my question. What has any of this got to do with me?'

Much to his chagrin, they both sniggered. Maybe it was relief at the elephant in the car finally introducing itself or perhaps something sinister. Either way, he was getting angry at being belittled.

'What's so funny?'

'I'm sorry', smirked Poppi, 'but you're not going to like the answer.'

'It can't be worse than being laughed at!'

'Well', Poppi continued, 'you have some information in your head that's vital to the Council.'

'What?' he exclaimed. 'We've already done this. Erik said you'd got all the information required, and I remember him saying it could only be done once before the information was gone forever. That's why the Council went into meltdown when I went on my little somnambulation walk about.'

'That was a few years ago,' explained John. 'Like I said, back in the apartment, things have changed. Things that put you back in the firing line.'

'Like what?'

'Over the past ten years, the Council have developed new technology, with Poppi being at the forefront.'

'That's right, Flash. Can we call you Flash? I never cared much for Stanley.'

'Fine, fine, just carry on.'

'Well', she continued, 'we've developed a "Brain Decoder" device. It works out your thoughts and hacks into your memory bank using algorithms to decode neuronal activity. As usual, most of the donkey work was done by the Normals, who believe they're working on a mechanism of communication for people who can't speak. Indeed, it could be used for such a purpose but it's far too important for us to release to the Normals.'

'But how's a brain decoder going to work on me? You have all the information I know.'

'The technology to access thoughts has been available for a while.' She continued: 'When people have a thought, it appears as a voice inside the head. We are able to access those thoughts.'

'But isn't that illegal? You're stealing people's thoughts,' Stanley responded.

'The technology requires large hardware for it to be effective, so the person has to be taken to the machine. It's used as a method of lie detection. We ask them a question and steal the answer before they have time to lie! In the future, it could be used as surveillance to read people's minds, but I doubt that will ever be possible,' said Poppi.

'But why's it not possible?'

'Because it works via a specifically created medical prosthesis.' Noting the blank expression, she explained further: 'A prosthesis is a device placed in contact with the subject to enable the process to work. Without this contact it can't be effective and obviously nobody with anything to hide will voluntarily wear one.'

'OK. But, what does this have to do with me?'

'Because we've discovered a way for the brain decoder to display the memory images.'

'But I told you everything I know. So how will this help?'

'Don't you see? We can re-access memories more than once, which makes it easier and more accurate. But, most importantly, we're presented with a visual image of the memory, which we can record,' Poppi oozed.

'But it's only the same information.'

'Maybe, but we can study the images and see things which were not picked up the first time around, in the narrative. Or zoom in on things in the peripheral vision to catch something vital in a reflection.'

'So, you can see everything in the memory. But how?'

'It's all down to a really clever piece of hardware', Poppi boasted with pride, 'a medical prosthesis which fits over the eyes and displays the images onto a screen. That's what I've been working on. That's why I've been so busy and have had to put the rest of my life on hold. That's why ...'

'Poppi has been at the forefront of this development,' John said, hastily jumping in. 'This is a game changer and I'm proud of her.'

Poppi stared bashfully out of the window. Stanley stared intently at her. He was trying to gauge her reaction and noticed a faint blush appear on her cheeks. She continued to stare into the distance as though something of great interest was in progress. There was nothing: the night was drawing in, leaving a meagre landscape of no discerning interest. She was avoiding eye contact. Regrouping.

Stanley paid no attention to the magnitude of Poppi's achievement as John elaborated, with the conversation floating away into the ether. He wasn't interested in the technicalities of her invention, he wanted to know what was she going to say? He wanted to lean forward and throw a right hook into the side of John's head, for interrupting. Why did he always have to stick his oar in? She *must* have been about to admit that this was the reason they broke up. It would make perfect sense, why it all happened so quickly. This *must* be the project she sees as her way to a glorious self-actualisation.

He had not felt like this in a long time: the knot in his stomach had disappeared. He felt relaxed. Happy? Is this what happiness feels like? He couldn't remember. All the while, her eyes remained focussed on the desolate landscape rushing past them. John remained silent.

The more he thought about it, the more convinced he became that he was right. It had to be true; if it wasn't true then why were they both silent? The window, backdropped by darkness, showed her reflection. He wanted to see her eyes. He needed to what was in them, but her eyes remained static, her horizontal lips hinting at neither happiness nor sadness. He stared at her reflection, hoping for a chink in the statuesque poise, but the dazzling headlights of a passing truck broke his focus.

'So, what did you and Carson speak about when you weren't in the apartment?' John enquired.

Stanley emerged startled from his reflections as his mind came back to the car journey. He had forgotten John was there.

'Er, well, nothing really. He told me a few stories about his missions. Nothing specific though. He was always professional. He knows the importance of not burdening people with information. And, of course, we talked about what our plans were for the rest of our lives,' Stanley relayed without emotion. After regaining his focus, he continued: 'So what makes you think he's such a menace to the Caste? If you think he shot John Lennon, you must have a low opinion of him.'

'I never said that,' John jostled defensively. 'You made that assumption from what I said. He is a prime suspect though.'

'But why?'

'There are lots of reasons, which I can't discuss. But come on, you must remember how against the Council he was? Can't you remember the conversations we had around the campfire, in Uruguay? Even back then he was against the Council.'

'The way I remember it, most of the things he was asking were reasonable questions about the status quo. I don't remember anything treacherous. I think you may have missed the fact that he was winding you up a fair amount. You were too involved to notice but I could tell.'

'Rubbish. You remember it how you want. I'll remember it how it actually happened. Besides, there's a lot more to this than you know. I wouldn't trust him as far as I could throw him. I'm not sure if he's seduced by money or has turned progressive but he's not the person you think he is. He's dangerous. You may think he's your friend, but he isn't. No doubt he kept visiting you to gather information and keep an eye on you. He wouldn't give a second thought to killing you.'

'So, tell me some of the things he's done?'

'You don't need to know, Flash. All you need to know is that for the time being the only people you can trust are sitting in this car,' John informed him with his usual authority.

'Well I've only got your word for that!'

Poppi emerged from her trance-like demeanour, turning swiftly to glance at him.

'You don't believe us?' she screeched with indignation. 'You don't believe us. How can you doubt me after what I've ... er, we've risked helping you? We've done this out of friendship. More than friendship.'

They fell silent. Seated in the back he felt scolded, like a naughty child, but he didn't feel guilty; he was overjoyed: Poppi's Freudian 'I/we' slip further confirmed his suspicions. Once again, his gaze fixed upon her reflection, his mind wandering towards the future. Perhaps they could pick up where they left off? Now she had finished her thought-stealing machine there would be more time for him; after all, that was the wedge which had driven them apart.

He had fallen out of favour with the Council, but they would have him back; his status and skillsets outranked his recent negative behaviour. In fact, the Council would do well to take him back as he could act as a conduit to get Carson back on track - if it wasn't too late.

He still had many questions to ask: even with the new technology, why would he be in danger? What could he have in his head that would put him in the firing line? And who could be after him? But they could wait for another day. His new future could be laden with opportunities, with Poppi at the forefront. The possibilities stretched before him like the open road passing beneath. As the burden of his thoughts which had weighed down his mind disappeared, and the adrenalin began to subside, he drifted off to sleep.

CHAPTER 21

He awoke, unsure of how long his catnap had been. It was dark and Poppi was at the steering wheel.

'So, what now?' he enquired groggily. 'Where are you taking me?'

'We need to get you hooked up to one of Poppi's machines, to see if you missed anything on the last mission.' John replied.

'And then what? Spend the rest of my life on the run, hiding in the shadows like The Phantom of the Opera?'

John laughed. 'You are a drama queen, Flash. The Phantom of the Opera? Anyway, he's better looking than you!'

'Well, it's OK for you to laugh but it's me who's walking around with a target on my back! I might as well be wearing a Who T-Shirt.'

As John and Poppi laughed, he realised he was returning to his old self. He used to crack jokes all the time. He used to do lots of things he no longer did. He had taken Poppi to see The Who, in San Francisco, back in the '60s. He couldn't remember if it was '66 or '67 but he did remember after the show he had bought her a T-shirt with The Who and MoD target on the back. The joke was aimed at her; she was laughing. Mission accomplished.

'Which is why we need to get you to this machine as soon as we can. Once we have the information, you're no longer a target - there's no point shooting you in the head again after we've downloaded your memory from the Uruguay mission,' John reassured.

'Oh, thanks for being so subtle,' he replied. 'So how long before we get to this thought-stealing contraption then? Have we got time for a beer on the way?'

'I'm afraid there's no beer until we've sorted this out.'

'So, are we close?'

'Well', John began hesitantly, 'there's a slight problem with that.'

'Let me guess,' he interrupted. 'Because you don't trust anyone at the Council, you are going to have to sneak me into the building. Am I right?'

'Yes.'

'So where is the machine? Please tell me it isn't on the space station.'

To his annoyance, in a routine which was now becoming habitual, they looked at each other.

'Brilliant. But how are we going to do this? There's no way you can sneak aboard that thing!' he exclaimed.

'"Right but we do have a plan B!' John beamed with pride.

When it came to acts of sheer big-headed pomposity, John Carter was difficult to eclipse. He knew how to build the part and ingratiate himself with an audience.

He continued: 'Poppi did most of her work on this machine in the research centre in Montana. Over the years, there were dozens of prototypes created. Some were close, some not so close.'

'But', interrupted Poppi, 'the final prototype was perfect. OK, it lacks the aesthetics and finesse of the finished product, but it works.'

'You have a functioning prototype in Montana?'

'Yes. Would you believe it's sitting in the bottom drawer of one of the cabinets? There's no lock on the cabinet door or on the door to the room. As far as anyone is aware, it's just another pile of useless junk! Of course, to anybody else it is a pile of useless junk. But not if you know what you're doing – and you have this.' She gesticulated towards a silver cross hanging from her necklace.

He had noticed the crucifix on the chain around her neck when she entered the apartment. It was unusual as she only wore jewellery on special occasions. It occurred to him that she had either found God or had been given it by a "friend". As neither of those options appealed to him, he was pleased to hear it had a practical function.

'This is the missing link in the algorithm, a piece of computer coding completing the jigsaw. Using the information on this memory stick, with the program in the computer on my office desk, we can access your memory. It's perfect. We have access to all the hardware and software required. I have programmed a little glitch into the coding on the space station in case they got to you first. Still, without my help, I doubt they could composite the individual pieces anyway. I've been careful to involve different people in different aspects, so only I understand the sum of the parts. Each operative only has access to a small part of random information. Only I can get the machine to work. I have information power. And nobody knows about the prototype. For the moment, neither of us are undercover. At some point, we will need to break cover and we must have the information by then,' Poppi rattled out before pausing for breath.

'OK. But how are you going to get me into the building?'

'I have duplicated an access pass belonging to one of my subordinates. He's about the same build as you but quite a bit younger. It should be straightforward. My office isn't in the high security section and is isolated and they usually don't check the pass. We shouldn't be disturbed.'

'We'll go through that in more detail later,' John interjected. 'But now we need to stop for the night. Just in case they are on the lookout for the three of us, we need to split up into two. We'll drop you off first, dispose of the car and return to the motel.'

'Here's your new identity,' Poppi said, passing over an envelope. 'There's enough cash to cover the cost of the room - it's not the best motel; the kind where people pay cash.'

Stanley opened the envelope. There was the expected bundle of used banknotes in various denominations. He had been in similar situations before, all over the world. American bank notes were uniform in size regardless of value; European notes differed in size depending on their value. He preferred different sizes - Dollars looked too similar. There was a California driver's licence complete with his photograph. He was Eugene James Anderson, 74 Hollywood Court, Los Angeles. That's all he needed to know.

'Eugene,' he said. 'Really?'

'Don't worry about it. You can use the middle name if you don't like it but you make a good Eugene,' John jested.

'Well you aren't in a position to laugh with your track record of names.'

'Why?' Stanley asked, 'What names has he been given?'

'It's not the names he's been given but the names he's chosen himself,' Poppi announced. 'He called himself John Smith, before he realised it was such a common name that lots of people use it. Then one time we were in Ireland, on business for the Council. We were watching television and there was a local singer called Johnny Logan, which he thought would be a good pseudonym. Unfortunately for John, this guy went on to win the Eurovision Song Contest, so whenever he used this name people would look at him to see if he was the singer. Not exactly keeping a low profile!'

Stanley sniggered, 'Nice one, John!'

'But that's not the best. A couple of months ago he was asked for his name. Realising he couldn't use John Smith or Johnny Logan, he made one up off the top of his head, but he panicked and came up with the best name yet.'

'What was it?' asked Stanley.

She was laughing so hard she could barely speak. 'Christian...'

'Christian what?'

'Ha, ha, ha! Christian Surname.'

'Christian Surname?!' howled Stanley. 'Seriously, John, you really said that? What were you thinking?'

'I wasn't, I panicked. It's hardly a big deal. You don't think as quickly when you get older. Somehow, your brain isn't as sharp. And anyway, I got away with it. But will I ever hear the last of this?'

'No, you won't, you plank!' Stanley replied in hysterics.

As the laughter subsided, he felt a sense of relief. Beneath the facade, John was human. He had always appeared superhuman, but silly mistakes were endearing. He was more likeable, somehow less intimidating: for the first time, he was flawed. His grey hair and crow's feet, allied with dubious decision-making, exposed chinks in his previously impregnable armour. But why was this? Why did Stanley like him more because he was fallible?

John's self-assurance had played a part in Stanley's inability to accept his friendship as readily as Mouse's; an assurance which was more than verbal posturing. In Uruguay, he had conducted himself with uncompromising confidence, ability and humility. John was as assured in performance as he was in theory: he talked the talk and walked the walk. His execution couldn't be questioned either. It was he who held off the attack and completed the mission. He delivered the end product. He was the complete package. Perhaps, subconsciously, Stanley resented him for surviving the mission and still being on his first Leaf. But what kind of person did that make him? He should be proud to have such a man as a friend, a man always supportive and helpful. John's consistency and solidity may not be as exciting as Mouse's sharp, observational wit but, surely, they are still good foundations for friendship? So, if he found the hand of friendship hard to accept because it had been offered by somebody, he considered better than himself – who were his friends? Did he surround himself with people he considered his equals in order not to feel inadequate? Worse still, did he collect lesser mortals to feel superior? The problem clearly lay at his feet. John had been a good friend for many years, but Stanley had not appreciated this friendship. It had taken John's frailties as an older man for him to realise this.

With John and Poppi coming to his rescue, and Mouse on the run, he was beginning to think: maybe he had been backing the wrong horse?

CHAPTER 22

The A1 Budget Motel was definitely budget but whether it was A1 remained to be seen. From the exterior, it seemed a long shot. It was dark and dimly lit; the number of cars in the forecourt suggesting it wasn't close to full occupation. He counted four in total. The fewer cars the better: fewer people to identify him.

The white L-shaped one storey accommodation block had no more than a dozen rooms sprawled around the car park. Each room had a window and door set back from the roof, forming a canopy under which was a timber chair. It was hard to imagine anybody sitting outside to soak up the atmosphere. In the centre of the car park was a large timber cable spool converted into a picnic table, with two blue perforated metal benches opposite each other. This curious "al fresco" dining area being separated from the parking bays by half section wooden logs painted white.

The reception area was detached with a flat roof and even less aesthetically pleasing than the accommodation block. There was a large white plastic sign with "Office" in bright red letters on the fascia and a "vacancy" sign on the glazed entrance door. On one side of the door was a letter box below a faded orange plaster moulding of a sea horse, oddly in keeping with its eclectic surroundings. To the other side sat a soda and ice machine. The step into the reception area was painted yellow leading inside to a grey tiled floor and white walls littered with signs. A sliding reception window was next to a white timber panelled door. To the left of the window were two orange plastic chairs, one each side of a large but empty leaflet stand. To the right was a pale blue waggon wheel, hung in the centre of the wall, above a gumball machine, which completed the internal ensemble.

Approaching the reception window, he caught his solitary reflection: John and Poppi were disposing of the automobile and would check-in later, for safe distance. He was pale, even by his own standards. A man in his thirties appeared at the window and, considering the lateness of the hour, was in a chipper mood.

'Greetings!' he exclaimed with a large smile. 'How can I be of help to you, young man? Do you want shelter from the storm?' he quipped before breaking into an effeminate giggle.

He was wearing a white t-shirt emblazoned with the word New York, with a navy-blue neck and arm cuffs, and faded jeans. He wore small round rimmed orange tinted glasses, and with a flowing shoulder length brown mane, he bore more than a passing resemblance to John Lennon.

'Er, a single room for me, please,' he replied. 'I'm on my own,' he continued unnecessarily.

'Well, we have no single rooms available, but I can do you a twin for the same price,' he replied, tapping a price list on the counter.

'Yes, that's fine, thanks. Shame about John Lennon,' he found himself saying to break the silence as the booking was added to the register. John had told him to keep conversations short and not to engage in unnecessary dialogue - the shorter the better - but, so far, he had managed to needlessly reaffirm that he was alone and instigate small talk.

'Yeah, yeah. A real bummer that was. Strange as well. Who'd wanna do something like that? Still, can't say I was a big fan of the Beatles, or John Lennon for that matter. Too twee and obvious for me.'

'What do you mean, obvious?'

'Well, take that song "Imagine", for example. "Imagine no possessions". Well, that's easy to say if you're a millionaire who lives in the Dakota, isn't it? If he was that bothered about money, he would have given it all away to the needy. If you ask me, he was just showing off; don't you think?'

'Well, I can't say I'd thought about it like that,' he stammered. '"Imagine" is not about money, though. It's more about peace, I'd have said.'

'Well maybe, but I've always been a bit suspicious of him to be honest.'

Stanley, who had been looking at the gum ball machine, spun around to gauge the stranger's expression. He had said a similar thing sixteen years ago to Carson in the park, the night the Beatles had appeared on the Ed Sullivan show. It couldn't be a coincidence? But there was no mischievous glint suggesting a subversive password had been offered; the man's expression remained constant and he continued without so much as a facial flinch.

'I'm more of a Bob Dylan fan myself. Hence the joke when you came in!' he continued before giggling again.

'Joke? Sorry, what joke was that?'

The guy looked over his glasses. 'Shelter from the storm. It's a classic - you must have heard it. The joke still works even though it's not raining it's very cold so it's shelter from the cold. But it still works.'

'No,' he replied glumly. 'I'm more of a Beatles man myself. I'm surprised you aren't, to be honest. Has anybody ever told you that you bear a striking resemblance to John Lennon?'

'No, man, you're the first,' was the curt response. 'Room five. Enjoy your stay,' he continued, sliding the key across the counter. He disappeared as quickly as he had appeared.

Stanley was relieved to leave the reception. He couldn't believe the John Lennon resemblance hadn't been mentioned before. If he doesn't like him, then why dress like him? Why wear those glasses? Still, it must take an unusual personality to survive the nightshift at the A1 Budget Motel.

He entered the room, disappointed at how he had allowed himself to engage in conversation - his old skills were returning too slowly. The room was better than he had expected although the turquoise wall was an odd colour combination with the two burgundy bed covers. He threw his bag onto one of the beds and slumped onto the other, kicking off his shoes and relaxing.

CHAPTER 23

He was vigorously awoken by John shaking him by the shoulder. Looking out of the window, he saw it was still dark, the clock on the wall confirming that he had only been in the room for twenty minutes.

'I see you picked the lock then?' he observed drowsily. 'I suppose cheap motel rooms are easy pickings for you?'

'They are when the doors are open!' came the response.

An ocean of disappointment washed over him; once again, he had made a schoolboy error in John's presence.

'Don't beat yourself up about it,' John reassured. 'You're just out of practice.'

He would have preferred a telling-off. The fact that he didn't get one indicating John didn't think he would benefit from it: he was so far off the pace such formalities were futile. He was being treated like a civilian - a Normal, even - but still he sought John's approval.

'Look, I know I'm rusty, but things are coming back to me. I know it's no excuse but I'm tired. I wasn't expecting any of this when I got out of bed this morning. I'm OK when I'm not tired – I proved that earlier when we stole the car, didn't I? I just need to remember to think the same way when I'm tired. Like I used to.'

'I'm not criticising, but I am concerned. We need to work quickly and don't have time for a learning curve. Our chances of success would improve if you could rediscover your A game. But that's why Poppi and I are here, to help you along the way. But you do need rest. Clarity of thought whilst tired is a mindset we train for. Poppi is in Room four, next door. I'm taking the first watch, which I can do from here, so you go next door and sleep. Poppi will take the second shift but you won't take any. We need you fully refreshed.'

He wasn't even trustworthy enough to take a shift as lookout; this was the ultimate humiliation. He was a Lion, the hero of Uruguay, but how the mighty had fallen. He considered arguing – but based on what? He had no credibility left after falling asleep with the door open. His gradual but enduring emasculation was an issue he would have to address in isolation without putting his friends at risk.

Room four was identical to his room in all but three ways: the layout was a mirror image; it was a double room and Poppi was in it. The change in orientation was easier to process than Poppi and the bed. Noticing the concern on his face, Poppi, who was lying on the bed, began to laugh.

'Don't worry about the double bed. John and I booking into a twin room would have looked suspicious as we must pretend we are a couple. Although it would have been better had we pretended to be together - I think it would have been more believable, don't you?' she added, laughing.

'Er ...,' he stuttered, unsure if she was complimenting or teasing him. 'Perhaps you should have got a twin room and said he was your dad. That would have been believable!'

'Oh, I don't know,' she replied, winking. 'He's hot stuff for his age!'

'Well, technically, he's the same age as me and I think I look much better!' he joked.

'That's more like it, Flash. Where have you been? Do you remember the time we went to watch the Who and you bought me a t-shirt? We stopped in that hotel near the train station. After the concert, we went back to the hotel and you put on an English accent and told everyone you were Pete Townsend's brother.'

'Yeah, I remember. They believed me, as well, and were buying us drinks all night. You had so much you slipped over in the lobby!'

'Yeah, it was a good night, that. I often think about it. 1967, wasn't it?'

'I think so.'

There was a pause in the conversation before Poppi reignited the dialogue with 'So what happened to you, Flash? Why did you decide to quit as a front-line operative? Surely, it can't have been down to me? You can see now why I did what I did. Why it was so important?'

'It's difficult to say, but yes, part of it was to do with you leaving. It hurt and I resented the Council as you saw them as more important than me. You put your career ahead of me.'

'But I thought you understood. I'm on Leaf 2 and I'm not a Lion, so I don't have credits with the Council, like you. You're the Lion of Uruguay. That on its own virtually guarantees a good self-actualisation.

I don't have that – I'm working hard to climb the ladder and have managed to work my way up to where I am now. Do you have any idea how intimidating it was going out with the Lion of Uruguay? I had to find my own way and be a success in my own right, otherwise people would have thought I was with you for the prestige and fame. I could have done that and milked your status for all it was worth; instead, I chose to step out of your shadow, which wasn't easy – but you should have understood this as we talked about it often enough. It was no reflection of how I felt about you. You know it's not as simple for us as it is for the Normals. Having four lives complicates things, and sometimes you must compromise in the short term to get what you want in the long term. You've made me sad now, because I've done this to you,' Poppi confided, her voice cracking with emotion.

'Look, it wasn't all down to you. It was also because of what I saw in Uruguay. It was terrifying. And strangling somebody doesn't make me a hero. The things I saw shook me to my core: there were bodies sucked dry of their blood and people frozen alive in ice baths to preserve their bodies for sick experiments, which nobody seems able to explain. I wasn't far off freezing to death myself. I didn't want to go through that again and I used your leaving as a convenient excuse. Or maybe it was a bit of both. Either way, it's not your fault. I understand why you value your career and work so hard to achieve your goals.'

His bid for conciliation had not had the desired effect. She was sitting on the edge of the bed, stooped forward with her head in her hands. The attempt to disguise her feelings was betrayed as a tear ran between her fingers and fell to the floor.

'I'm jealous of the Normals sometimes, that's all,' he added, attempting to rectify the situation.

'Why? Why should you envy them?' she sobbed. 'They're unfortunate. They only get one bite of the cherry and, because of their DNA breakdown, sometimes it's only a small bite. We have more chances to get things right, to plan our future. We have access to technology they can only dream of. I watched a TV program, when I was in England, called Tomorrow's World. It was a program by the Normals about how technology of the future may look? Every item on it already exists for us; in fact, most of what we already have exceeds their future expectations. Have you seen their attempt at the Heartbeat? It's a wireless phone about the size of a cinder block attached to a battery the size of two cinder blocks. And, despite its size, the battery only lasts a couple of hours! Yet they're happy with it!'

'Exactly. They're happy with it. We have technology far in advance of theirs but we're never happy. And does this technology improve our lives or make us dependent on it? I stopped using my Heartbeat years ago because I was fed up being reliant on it. I would go to Clover only clubs and people would be sitting around with their faces glued to their Heartbeat, not talking to each other. What's the point of going out only to spend your time ignoring the person you're sitting next to? We're turning into anti-social creatures of habit and losing our basic interpersonal skills. Yes, it's great technology but we don't know when to stop using it. Technology should make life easier not take it over completely. That's what I love about the Normals, one of the things I envy: they don't have such distractions. If you go out with a Normal, they're focused on you not a little lump of aluminium with a glass front. And, they aren't reliant on it for their entertainment, they make their own, with other people. That's why they're more social than us – why they're more interesting. Not only that, but I resent the Council knowing my every movement. All your personal information ends up on their data base; they know everything about you. The Normals are lucky they don't have to put up with such a violation. No wonder they're so happy.'

'Happy? Are you sure they're happy? They run around like headless chicken's half of the time. They plan little for retirement, which happens at a stage in life when their bodies are too worn out to enjoy it - that's if they haven't already destroyed themselves with all the drinking and smoking, they've done along the way. And when they die, they leave little, if anything, to their children – so the whole wretched cycle begins again! No money, no memory map, nothing!'

'There's plenty of Clover who smoke and drink,' he countered.

'Yes, at the foundation levels, when the DNA mutation counters the effects. But there are few who do it during self-actualisation. And what makes you think they're happier than us anyway? What makes you think that Clover aren't happy?'

'I'm not saying we aren't happy, but I am saying that the Normals show us a different way. From Leaf 1 we're indoctrinated into the work ethic. It's like a triple life treadmill. Anyone not towing the line is ostracised, told they aren't good enough, not pulling their weight. The carrot dangling from the stick is high-level remuneration in the Final Leaf. But even that isn't guaranteed. You could work hard for hundreds of years, then upset the Council at the end of Leaf 3 and lose the lot! These promises are nothing more than golden handcuffs to make us do as they say. The USA was founded by the Clover as a land of freedom and opportunity, yet the Clover aren't free - not really, there are too many constraints and expectations. The Normals show us a life of freedom, where they make their own decisions and mistakes. The Council have made us sterile by putting us in a safe environment where everybody thinks the same. There are no freethinkers anymore. Or if there are, they are too intimidated to speak up. The Normals say what they like. Sometimes it sounds stupid to us, but it's freethinking: free speech.'

'I never realised you thought about it so deeply - though you always did think too much.'

'No,' he snapped. 'I don't think too much. There's no such thing: we're too reliant on the Council doing the thinking for us. We expect them to sort out our problems rather than having the gumption to do it ourselves. The senate of so-called "experts" repeatedly get things wrong, but nobody questions them. They're a bunch of self-appointed autocrats. Of course, I don't agree with the Gammadions, but I do agree with some of the things Mouse says. I agree with the idea of the Council and, if we had a second Plebiscite tomorrow, I would vote for them over the Gammadions. So, while the Council is great in theory, in practice they've become a collection of elitist academics who've formed an oligarchy. Too much power in too few places only puts a smile on particular faces! At least the Gammadions would argue with and question each other. The Council have become arrogant and self-serving, and anyone who disagrees with them is intellectually mocked:

how can they know better than these well-educated "experts"? They are subversive for daring to seek an alternative way.'

'So, what do you think we should do?'

'The structure needs to be larger: a subsidiary of Clover from all walks of life – and even a few Normals - should feed into the senate. As it is, the senate is too small to represent such a diverse cross section of people from all over the world. I'm not saying it's corrupt, just out of touch and elitist, which can breed corruption. We concentrate the decision making into one small pocket of experts, but we should have "mini senates" dotted throughout the world, in touch with local needs. And considering the communication technology we have; it seems ridiculous to centre all the decision making in one location. It's imperialism, Poppi – and history has proven that it doesn't work. Look at the Gammadions and their constant quest to form a hegemony, which, in the end, is what we've done; we've formed a hegemony - the one thing we were trying so hard to stop them doing in the first place! But instead of using force, we've used a less abrasive technique: anyone who stands in the way isn't shot, not with bullets, anyway. They're shot down with something worse: putative intelligence - it's not as loud or obvious as a war but more effective. We have an environment built on reliance upon a small number of high-profile, strategically placed "experts" which has created a utopia of human virtue. So Poppi, as the only benchmark to compare with this utopia is the non-inclusive reign of the Gammadions, those who question the Council's tactics are defined as having the same beliefs. Thus, any person daring to question the virtues of the intellectuals is made to feel stupid and discriminatory. I believe, this is a default processed into the mindset of the Clover population from an early age, and, as a result, Clover sit in a safe environment, discussing safe topics with people of the same safe opinions - that's when they can drag themselves away from their Heartbeats for long enough! God have mercy on anyone who points out that this utopia is formed by surreptitiously making ordinary people afraid to express an opinion, and it doesn't matter if an opinion is forced upon you by a Nazi, or one of the intellectual elite, the result is the same: freedom of speech denied. I don't agree with Mouse going rogue, but I can understand where he's coming from. That said, I don't care for the alternative he's opted for - I've seen it first-hand, remember – and it's not the future; it's sick – whatever the hell it is they're up to.'

'Wow, you *have* given this a lot of thought.'

'Since I switched to becoming a Mentor the days have bled into years; so, I've had lots of opportunities to ponder.'

'Well, if you think things need changing, why did you become a Mentor? You were in a better position before, when you were the Lion of Uruguay. It sounds to me like you've been talking to Mouse too much.'

'No. Mouse doesn't talk about the Council. We talked about sports, life in general and, of course, the Beatles. John seems to think that we talked about espionage and top-secret Council issues, but we didn't. That's why I'm surprised at the way things have turned out for him: he didn't have an appetite for anything like that. He was more like you; I would have said: super focused on his career.'

As they lay on the bed, facing each other, Poppi gently brushed his fringe to one side, which soon returned to its original arrangement. Again, she brushed his fringe, this time to the other side.

'I'm sorry for the pain I've caused you, Flash. Without wishing to sound dramatic, I feel I've banished you to the wilderness.'

'No, you didn't,' he replied, his tone now elevated toward a mildly triumphant crescendo. 'Things have changed today; the fog is lifting. You don't owe me an apology, quite the opposite: I should be thanking you.'

As Poppi caressed his hair, his mind occupied the no man's land between sleep and consciousness. Her lips were soft and tender, and for his heart and soul it was a seamless transition; their relationship had never ended. Since they were last together, time had marched forward relentlessly but, for a fleeting moment, even time yielded to a higher force of nature. He experienced a glorious sensation of returning to the past. Time disappeared.

When he awoke Poppi was gone. John was asleep next to the window, his body slumped in one armchair, his feet on another. He was unsure of how much of the intimacy with Poppi he had dreamed and how much was real.

With an acute sixth sense, John opened his eyes: 'Morning, Flash. Did you sleep well?'

CHAPTER 24

The journey continued in another Chevy, this one in immaculate condition, although Jack quickly made his mark on its interior by littering the back seat with crumbs and potato chips from the makeshift breakfast Poppi had delivered with the car. Their departure was uneventful, with the John Lennon lookalike replaced by a girl of mousey appearance in her early twenties.

Once again, Stanley found his gaze inextricably drawn towards Poppi. Their brief liaison offered hope, with her explanations and guilt as genuine as they were welcome. The break in their relationship had created a lengthy detachment, which afforded him a clarity of mind he had not achieved before; he had been too involved during their time together, too submersed to think objectively. Empowered by this, a clear direction now replaced the rudderless flow of the previous decade: he was alive with excitement, his future brimming with hope. Her career focus would be a tough nut to crack, but she was right about one thing: he would be better placed to improve life for the Normals if he was working on the front line; and his co-operation with the well-respected John Carter would not go unnoticed.

But what could he do about the Mouse situation? Had he travelled too far down the wrong path and beyond the point of no return? Whilst John had inferred his betrayal of the Council, how much was fact and how much surmised? John and Mouse had never enjoyed the best relationship, but surely, *he* could keep Mouse on the straight and narrow? Stanley was the glue who held the three together – a human sticking plaster. Mouse had been like a brother, and he would have carried Mouse's body to the meeting point but for the protestation of John. Still, he felt guilty about the adoration he received after the mission because Mouse had sacrificed just as much as him but was not regarded with equal reverence. OK, he had killed the mark, but Mouse had incapacitated him, and as he had drawn first blood, he should be held in higher esteem. He had often wondered if John had anything to do with this. Had he played down Mouse's involvement? But now it was he who was surmising.

Unexpectedly, the car, driven by John, veered from the main road onto a single-lane dirt track. The track was uneven and bumpy, with occasional lengths of wire fencing along each side interrupted by small trees and broken fence poles. The twin concave undulations on the track - suggesting that it was used infrequently - held small pools of water within them, the water now temporarily displaced by the slow-moving Chevy. Pangs of concern filled his mind. Why had they turned off the road; they couldn't have even been halfway to Montana?

At the end of the track was an ad hoc rubbish tip created by the locals, to dump trash they couldn't dump legally. The doubts multiplied in his brain as John and Poppi turned and gave a cursory glance. The obvious thing to do was to ask but he didn't want to alert them to his doubts. He needed to play his cards close to his chest; he needed time to think. But would it be odder not to ask why they had taken the detour? Maybe his silence was more conspicuous. Had he been foolish to trust them? Had he been tricked? Should he make a bolt for it? He could easily outrun John – and probably Poppi. As they pulled up alongside the tip, he knew his chance was now.

'You're not thinking of making a run for it are you, Flash?' laughed Poppi.

'Well not now,' he thought.

'Er, no. What do you mean?'

'You don't trust us', she continued, 'which is disappointing and insulting after what we've risked for you.'

'What do you mean?' he enquired, the shallow pitch of his voice betraying him. 'I do trust you. I haven't said anything. What are you? A mind reader? I'm not plugged into one of your machines yet!'

'I'm not a mind reader, but I am an expert in human behaviour. I can smell lies a mile away. Even the most accomplished con artists have difficulty getting one over on me. And trust me, Flash, you're not a good liar. I saw the look of terror on your face, as we left the track. If you trusted us, you'd have asked why we had left the main road, so far from Montana; instead, you just sat there, planning your escape. What were you going to do? You'd have no chance in direct combat, and I could outrun you - I noticed last night how out of shape you are.'

She had stopped him in his tracks - literally. He considered protesting but what was the point? She was on the money and they all knew it. He felt guilty about doubting them but wasn't going to apologise. Why should he? Trust him to have had a relationship with a human polygraph.

'So why have we come down here?' he asked, sweeping the situation under the carpet.

'Well, you didn't think we were going to drive all the way to Montana, did you?' she replied, agitated. 'This is where we dump the car and take to the air.'

'But there's nowhere around here to land a plane.'

'There's a big field the other side of those trees,' she nodded.

'Well why didn't you tell me that instead of disappearing down a dirt track?'

'Because', John interrupted, 'the less you know, the better for us all. Let's face it, you're not equipped to keep quiet about our plan, should you be caught. We've gone out on a limb and don't need to be implicated.' The jovial John of yesterday had disappeared, his voice indicating his seriousness.

'Are you sure a plane can land over there? It's just a grassy field.'

'Who said anything about a plane? We're being picked up by a helicopter and flown to a nearby private airstrip.'

'By who? I thought you were doing this without the permission of the Council.'

'We are.' John explained, 'So far, nobody knows what we're up to. The guy who's picking us up thinks you're just a prisoner.'

'But won't he recognise me? I've been out of the game for a while, but I used to be high profile – possibly the most famous Clover on the Planet at one time,' he added, with an equal touch of boastfulness and enquiry, the doubt in his voice creating ambiguity. Was he telling them or fishing for compliments?

'Don't worry, my darling,' beamed Poppi, with reassurance. 'You're still famous within the Caste, which is a problem resolved by putting this over your head.'

Poppi revealed a black cloth bag, which she dangled in front of him, it was standard issue for blindfolding prisoners; thin and breathable but impossible to see through. Like the Skin, it was designed to be a snug fit. He knew inside would be plastic wrist restraints and a gag, which were issued together.

'Is that *really* necessary?' he groaned. 'I thought nobody suspected you yet. And do you have to take so much pleasure in it?'

'There's no way around it, I'm afraid. Some may argue it's an improvement,' John mocked. 'You said you felt like The Phantom of the Opera, well now you can look like him. We can't risk anything. We think we can trust this guy but can never be 100% sure. Besides, it'll be fun being tied up and having a bag on your head. You'll have to trust us – won't you?'

John and Poppi was both laughing. Stanley was still in a state of consternation; this was his worst fear, the nightmare scenario. If he didn't let them tie him up, he would be betraying their trust. But did he trust them? Their recent actions implied that they were on Team Flash. John had always been a straight shooter and nothing he had done so far had been a contradiction. He knew Poppi well and over the past decade had loved and hated her in abundance, but like John, she was a good person; too Council-centric for his liking but that wasn't a crime. Unfortunately.

If the eyes are the windows to the soul when he had looked deeply into them in the cheap motel room - everything had been A1, after all. Besides, what choice did he have? They were highly trained armed operatives. He was outnumbered and outclassed, and he knew that if they had wanted him dead, he wouldn't have seen them coming. They had nothing to gain but everything to lose, so it was time to stop being ungrateful and yield to the inevitable.

'So how many are coming?' he enquired.

'Just two. One will stay here to lose the car. The other will fly us to the plane, then on to Montana.'

'I'm surprised you aren't flying the plane yourself, John.'

'Well, the thought had crossed my mind. But that would break protocol and may look suspicious. I would prefer to be in the cockpit, to be honest.'

'Look, we need to get this done - they'll be here in ten minutes,' Poppi said, looking at her watch. 'Hands behind your back, darling, I need to cuff you.'

The expandable blindfold allowed him to breathe and was comfortable, except for his eyelashes being pushed into his eyes. The restraining cuffs were soft and malleable, stretching to give way with gentle persuasion, but locking at sudden movement. He sat quietly, with trepidation, awaiting his ride.

CHAPTER 25

The transition from car to helicopter was seamless and, with no words spoken, they were soon air bound. It was typical Clover Caste: ruthlessly efficient and discreet to the point of invisibility.

'Am I OK to talk?' boomed a voice loud enough to be heard over the noise of the engines and rotor blades.

'Yes, it's fine. He won't be with us much longer - if you know what I mean.' John laughed malevolently.

Stanley rocked in his seat indignantly, producing a muffled tirade, forcing the cuffs to tighten. He wasn't concerned with John's comment, he wanted to augment the masquerade; the reassuring stroke of Poppi's finger across the palm of his hand was as out of character as it was risky. What if the pilot had seen it? She was usually more careful. Perhaps his presence was having the same disorientating effect on her? He smiled beneath his mask.

'Oh, I see,' the mystery voice snorted with equal malevolence. 'Is he anyone I might have heard of?'

'No, just another Normal who's found out about us. No one of importance.'

'And to think, if we listened to the progressives, we'd let them back into society to blab about us. How did he find out about us? No doubt from a progressive who couldn't keep their mouth shut,' the mystery voice added.

Stanley was alarmed at how little respect he had for the Normals, seeming both irreverent and happy at the impending doom facing the supposed prisoner. If this was the attitude of high-level site operatives, the sooner he could get back into action the better. It's 1980, for God's sake, not the dark days of the Gammadions. He wanted to rip of his mask in defiance, just to see the look on his face. It would also scratch a nagging itch at the back of his mind: had he heard the voice before?

'I'm not sure,' John replied. 'We weren't informed of the full details. Probably was though. Perhaps his girlfriend? You know how risky mixed relationships are.'

'Too right, pal. They're OK for a bit of fun and practice for when we reach Actualisation but that's all. They've got no right knowing our business, so hat's off to the Council, I say, for getting rid of him! After all, when we switched from the Gammadions to the Council it was supposed to help the Normals. We don't command individual armies, like the myriad days, yet we now have much more power over them. The Senate's command is absolute, and our position is getting stronger and nobody will ever question it because it's done so politely. Sometimes I wonder who actually won the plebiscite!'

'Yes,' John replied. 'Sometimes I question the sense in having a small Senate making such big decisions. I trust them implicitly, but is it any fairer than the old ways?'

'Don't question it, pal, just go along with the ride. We've never had it so good!'

Stanley's mock discontent entered a new phase, with the comments of the pilot making it easy for him to show displeasure. He was surprised to hear that John was beginning to doubt the Council and the Senate. Perhaps they were corrupt? It wouldn't take much to gain advantage within such a small hierarchy, with the potential rewards available providing the necessary temptation.

'So, have you heard from your mate Mouse, then? He's in it up to his neck, you know, so the Council are after him big time now – he's public enemy number one.'

'But they just want him for questioning?' John asked.

'Where have you been for the last twenty-four hours, man? Haven't you had your Heartbeat on? The Council have CCTV footage of him killing Lennon. Apparently, Lennon was a high-level Caste in previous lives, which is why he landed the job of being in the Beatles. All those stories Mouse used to tell about Lennon stealing his idea was a smokescreen. He and Lennon went on a mission, years ago. It was a sensitive mission which didn't quite go to plan and nobody knew why. They had the intel and training, but it all went wrong. Mouse survived and went through the usual hypnosis, but nothing was found out. It remained a mystery how they'd been ambushed. Then it happened again, as I'm sure you'll remember.'

'You mean in Uruguay?' John chimed.

'Exactly!'

'But he was killed in Uruguay.'

'Yes, but he was still on Leaf 1 and it would have looked super suspicious had he survived, again.'

'So why did he kill Lennon?'

'Because he thought the new memory retrieval technique would implicate him, sentencing him to his remaining lives behind bars.'

'But that technology is new and under a veil of security. I'm surprised you even know about it,' gasped Poppi.

'Everybody knows about it now. They had to explain the reasons why Mouse is dangerous, especially as he has a good reputation and plenty of friends. They need to understand why he must be captured by any means possible, which won't be easy. He's as good as you in the field, isn't he, John?'

'Well, I don't know if he's that good, but he is exceptional.'

'He's had the same training as you and occupies a younger body, so my money would be on him if you held a gun to my head,' the mystery man taunted.

'Well, age isn't everything.'

'I'm surprised you haven't asked about your other mate – Flash.'

'Wh ... what do you mean?' John stuttered.

'Well, he's already killed Lennon and your mate Flash also went on a mission with him, which went wrong. It's obvious he'll be after him next and, by all accounts, he lives around the corner from where Lennon was killed. That's not him under the mask, is it?' he joked.

Stanley paused, unsure of whether to carry on his protests, or perhaps increase them. How would a genuine prisoner react to such an accusation?

'Yeah, you're right,' John replied, with all the conviction of a man for whom lying formed an integral part of his job. 'I hadn't arrived there yet but, now I think about it, you're spot on. Maybe he'll come for me?' he concluded, his confident dismissal of the question signalling it was too ridiculous to dignify an answer.

As Stanley had been on the receiving end of John's rebuttals, he knew how difficult they were to resist. A brief pause gave him time to process what he had heard. So, it was true about Mouse: his best friend was a murdering traitor. He tried resisting the idea, but the evidence was irrefutable; besides, deep down he knew it was true, and as much as he favoured Mouse over John, he couldn't doubt John's integrity. Mouse was different. He had an awkward relationship with the Council, his support often wavering. It was no surprise he had chosen a different direction.

Still, Stanley was shocked at the path he had taken to reach this new direction. Why didn't he choose to change things from within - as he himself had now chosen to do? As the mystery man had said, Mouse had a great reputation and many friends, which he could have used to effect a positive change. But he had always been impetuous, preferring brawn over brain, and now his reputation was gone. Killing people in cold blood had been second nature to him but to do it without direct orders - that wasn't his decision to take. He must have been worried about the contents of Lennon's subconscious to have gone to such extremes. But what could have been in there? What had he done during the mission that was bad enough for him to risk everything? Mouse had been on many missions but never spoken of them. He understood why – he himself could barely think about the horrors of Uruguay. But still, Mouse had never mentioned Lennon directly, just his Beatles conspiracy theory, which was arbitrary and could have involved any of the band members.

So, will he be coming for him next? John seemed to think so and he was usually right. If John and Poppi hadn't warned him, he may already be dead. But what could he have seen in Uruguay that he hadn't already revealed? By the time he got to Mouse he was already dead, and the mark was on his last legs. When he was put under hypnosis, Mouse was in the room; and must have heard something which, using the new techniques, would incriminate him.

The more he thought about it the more sense it made. Back on the day of the Ed Sullivan Show, he opened up to him about the déjà vu, but this was never brought to the attention of the Council. As an experienced Mentor, he himself now understood the importance of instructing the Council to assign a Greeter when the first signs of the awakening occur: the chances of memory retrieval are reduced with each passing day and drastically during the somnambulation stage. As a Mentor, Mouse knew this but deliberately ignored the signs to reduce the probability of a successful retrieval. Maybe his plan had worked; maybe he hadn't remembered everything that had happened on that fateful day.

When Stanley began the Awakening, he was confused and vulnerable. He had no idea that Carson was Mouse. It was the responsibility of Mouse as the Mentor to ensure the Awakening was managed effectively to protect both Stanley and the Caste. Mouse had abused this responsibility for his own benefit. If he hadn't been his friend during Awakening, had he ever been his friend? Stanley began to think about recent conversations in the apartment and in Central Park. Had they been as innocent as he had thought? Had he been periodically assessing him to see if he remembered anymore from Uruguay? Did he see Stanley as a threat? Were his impromptu visits no more than risk management?

'I would imagine the Council have it in hand,' John conjectured. 'They'll have seen the CCTV footage and ring-fenced Flash and other vulnerable targets. I'm surprised they haven't contacted me, but, then again, I've been on a mission with this fella. I haven't had my Heartbeat logged onto the network; it's been on mission mode. I bet when I log on there will be a red flag warning - as if I need a red flag warning. If he fancies his chances against me, then I'm ready. I was born ready!"

John had Stanley's admiration: his story was so good, even he believed him.

'That's what I like to hear!' boomed the mystery man in agreement. 'Bring it on!'

'Is that our airstrip?' Poppi enquired.

'Yes. Sit tight and I'll put her down here. It's all ready and good to go so we'll get straight off. No point hanging around.'

CHAPTER 26

Relief washed over him as the mask was finally pulled off, rubbing his eyes to ease the itching sensation in his lashes. It wasn't the only irritation he had been subjected to during the journey. The constant pro-Council rhetoric and anti-Normals diatribe had taken its toll. The journey, although only a few hours long, had seemed endless. After parting company with the pilot, the mask remained over his head until they reached the destination.

The house was surrounded by trees and John was outside, on a large timber decked area, puffing on a cigar. Stanley joined him, leaning against the glazed balcony before gazing across the dense woodland. The Caste had many hideaway lodges, built with carefully selected materials and were designed to morph into the surroundings. These were indigenous structures at one with nature, using vast areas of reflective glazing to create privacy from the outside and transparency from inside.

John held his arms horizontally to his torso, slowly bending his knees until at a full squat. With equal deliberation, he returned to an upright position. He often broke into random bouts of exercise, and Stanley sniggered as the jerking motion of his fitness regime caused the ash to paradoxically fall from the cigar in his outstretched right hand.

'You must see the irony of smoking a cigar whilst exercising?' teased Stanley.

'It's not exercise. I'm warming down, loosening my muscles after a day of sitting in cars and planes. It's vital at my age. I need to stay on top, especially now. Besides, you know we can't get cancer.'

'Even so, filling your lungs with smoke will reduce your aerobic capacity. It's got to, hasn't it?'

'Huh,' John grunted dismissively, the cigar now in his mouth. 'Maybe.' His tone suggested a reluctant acceptance of the obvious. 'You're the only one who was surprised. You do know that?'

'What do you mean?' asked Stanley.

'You know what I mean.'

'No, I don't!'

'About Mouse killing Lennon. We all knew it, except you, but deep down you must have realised the truth of it. You've always been too soft. Trust is important but common sense more so. You place friendship further up your hierarchy than truth. It's your main failing as an operative - giving people the benefit of the doubt. Facts first, friends second!'

'Second!' he snapped, with the passion of a man scorned. 'I'm amazed you rate friendship so highly. I'd have thought the Council and those stupid cigars came higher!'

'Now you come to mention it ...' John mocked, with Stanley's wounded reply indicating the verbal battle was won.

Gazing over the vast expanse, Stanley noticed the decking was higher than the surrounding landscape. Looking across the smaller tree canopies, recollections of his first childhood in England began to flood his brain. These memories were formed in a previous lifetime, and in country thousands of miles away, but the terrain was so familiar he could still be there.

He was brought up by his surrogate parents, on the outskirts of Sheffield, and although the city was built on industry, he had lived in a rural area. The City was one of the main steel manufacturers in the world, his father one of the tens of thousands of men who paid their way with its wages. He would happily spend any spare time with his father, watching the local football team or exploring the nearby woodland. He lived near a place called Greno Woods which was home to a group of pine trees they would pass on their wanderings. It became a tradition for Stanley to climb as high as he could in one of the trees – until it began to bend – with his father shaking the tree at the bottom. This became known as the "coconut game" and although Stanley was shaken rigorously, he never fell out of the tree. He called his favourite tree the "danger pine".

His father was a kind man who, under different circumstances, would have earned a living by means of brain over brawn. Or would he? Maybe the simplicity of this life suited him: he was always happy. This life suited Stanley, too, and during his New York solitude, he often mused about those good times, back in England, and what had become of his surrogate parents. He once looked at his old home via a satellite image, noticing a large motorway had been built through the middle of the woodland. Maybe the danger pine was no more? If so, it was reassuring to see its doppelganger sitting below the lodge, although it was unlikely, he could talk John into playing the coconut game. It wouldn't be the same anyway: his father was a strong but gentle man and always knew when to stop shaking the trunk; John was an ultra-competitive alpha male who would end up snapping the tree in half. Without realising it, he began to tell John about his childhood and the danger pine.

'Sounds like you had a great first childhood,' commented John, who had now joined him, leaning against the glass balustrading.

'Yes. It was simple and straightforward. It was my first life. The Normals are so different to us. Very little is planned, and they live in what we would see as an unconventional and illogical way, but I loved it. We lived in an area called Low Green, which was at the top of a hill, and the local football team were called Sheffield Wednesday, even though they played on a Saturday. Our house was tiny; we hardly had enough money, and the toilet was at the bottom of the garden – *and it gets cold over there in winter* – but we were all happy. We had everything we needed and wanted nothing. Or was it that we wanted nothing because we had everything we needed? When you think about it, we don't need much to be happy. I often wonder what happened to my first parents. I wonder if they're still alive. I once thought about going over to see them, you know?'

'No,' John snapped. 'You can't do things like that. It's not fair on them either. Besides, you are on your second Leaf now; the age gap would freak them out, plus they have probably passed away.'

'It wasn't recently,' Stanley countered. 'While I was still on Leaf 1, when it wouldn't have been too much for them, I just wanted to let them know I was OK. They were good people and didn't deserved to be abandoned. They brought me up only for me to be whisked away by the Council and taken to the School of Enlightenment. I wonder what story the Council gave my parents about why I never returned?'

'Which is why you could never have returned,' John explained. 'If you compromised the Council's story, both you and your family would have been at risk. Surely you know this?'

'Of course, I know this,' Stanley retorted. 'But I still wonder. Don't you ever wonder? Doesn't anybody ever wonder what happened to their surrogates? I've never heard a single Clover discuss it.'

'No, they don't,' John muttered. 'It's just you. You must realise you're different?'

'What do you mean different?'

John was uncharacteristically quiet, avoiding eye contact, choosing to look at the danger pine instead. 'You're more sensitive than most, that's all I mean.'

Stanley was perturbed by John's behaviour, sensing he was on the cusp of revealing something deeper; but instead remained silent. He considered asking him what he had meant; but it was too late, the moment had passed.

Stanley opted for a change of tack. 'So, do you think he's out there now, looking for me?'

'No, I don't.'

'But what about the information I have which may incriminate him? Won't he try to make sure I can't point the finger in his direction?'

'Think about it logically,' John replied tersely. 'You heard the pilot: the word is out - he's on the run. He's no idiot - he'll realise you're with me. Do you know how many hideaway lodges we have in the woodlands surrounding Montana? Well do you?'

'No.'

'There are over a hundred. And what about sanctuary pods? You must remember the sanctuary pods? You ended up in one when you went walkabout during somnambulation? How many of those do you think there are?'

'Er, I don't know.'

'Well neither do I but there are more pods than lodges. Do you think he'll be hunting you out, with all those options? He'll be expecting you to be safely hidden away in one of the pods. They are secure, covered by CCTV and dotted around the countryside in areas accessible only by foot. Don't you remember how long it took you to get there on foot? Do you think he will do that over a hundred times?'

'Well, perhaps not.'

'And he knows you're with me. So, he must find you, breach the security and then get past me. But, of course, all this is irrelevant because we're not even in a pod. I decided to put you in a lodge to reduce the odds further. He'll no longer have access to the network for information so everything he does will be solitary: he's on his own, with no one to help him and no technology either. And, on top of that, you may not even have anything relevant in your head. Like I said, he's no idiot. He won't be looking. He's hiding.'

'OK, so what's the plan? You haven't told me anything.'

'To have a couple of drinks and relax,' Poppi replied, joining them on the decking, carrying a tray of drinks.

'But ... I thought we needed to focus? I thought there was no time for relaxing?' Stanley quizzed.

'There's been a change of plan,' Poppi informed him. 'It's Wednesday today, but Friday's the best day to go to my office because it's always less busy on Fridays. So less risky. Consider tomorrow your day off - for good behaviour.'

'Oh. OK'

'And how better to start your day off than with a nice drink? I take it you still like your gin and tonic over ice and with a slice of orange?' she continued, with a cheeky smile.

'Yes, I do, thanks,' he enthused, returning the smile.

Toasting the future, Stanley felt a wave of optimism envelop him. The last few days had been mentally gruelling but had awoken him. He knew what he wanted to do - what he had to do. He knew who he wanted to do it with and who he could trust along the way.

The clinking of glasses signalled the coming together of individual epiphanies over a short but life changing chapter. Although recent events were pivotal, this clarity was over a decade in the forging. He had been lost since Elucidation. Unable to cope with the sickening legacy of Uruguay, he had ringfenced his emotions and had become an island. An island with only one inhabitant and infrequent visitors. But not anymore, his future was brighter.

'No more than two drinks each,' John stated with typical authority.

It was a timely reminder that there was still work to be done and that John would make sure it was.

CHAPTER 27

The Caste had a high concentration of facilities in the Montana area. Many, such as the woodland lodges and refuge pods, were discretely located and painstakingly camouflaged. Others were hidden in plain view. Often, they were unremarkable buildings, with a liberal assortment of Normals employed within to validate their existence. There were similar "business parks" located the length and breadth of the USA - but none was as strategically important as the one Stanley, John and Poppi were approaching. Headrock Business Park was named after the large rock formation looming over it, which vaguely resembled a face. The spurious nature of the name was questioned as from most angles it appeared to be just a large rock, but it was claimed that from certain angles, when the light began to fall at dusk, a face was formed by the shadow lines.

The origin and location of the units were well documented during elucidation. With the formation of the USA, and the transition from the Gammadions, the Caste had relocated from their original base in Ireland. With an increase in the surrounding population, they had outgrown their bases in the Emerald Isle which, despite their remoteness, had become increasingly easy to stumble across. Eventually the decision to relocate was expedited by an event which became written into Clover Caste folklore. *The Curious Tale of Fergus Leahy* was intrinsically intertwined into Clover Caste culture. It was taught during the School of enlightenment, recited during elucidation and deemed by the Caste as a multi layered symbolic tale. To many, it was a demonstration of the power the Caste held over Normals, but to others it highlighted the consequences of uncovering knowledge of the Caste

THE CURIOUS TALE OF FERGUS LEAHY (as taught to Clover Caste Students during the School of Enlightenment)
In the early 19th Century, Fergus Leahy was a resident of Waterville County, South West Ireland. Fergus, in his mid-twenties, was a well-

known local character and respected hunter who worked as a farm hand on a nearby homestead, giving him regular, but low paid work. To subsidise his meagre wage, he would take to the countryside to hunt. Whatever was left over, after he had provided for his family and the family of his childhood sweetheart, he would sell.

    Despite his lowly position in life, he was a man of considerable intelligence and ingenuity. He was the only non-educated man in the village who could read and would occasionally swap his spoils for books, with a local man of education. Although the books came with a few fragmented reading lessons, he was largely self-taught.

    He had considered moving to a city and attempting a route into education, but such opportunities were difficult for someone of his background, although not impossible. He was sufficiently confident in his intellectual capabilities and work ethic, not to be dissuaded by the traditional barriers of entry. He was, however, twice in love and could not envisage anything in the City to replace the respective voids which would be left in his heart and soul by the absence of his beloved Orla, and the beautiful rolling countryside. The simple pleasure of hunting his own food and seeing the warm smiles of gratitude from his loved ones, were education enough.

    His skills as a farm hand elevated him above those of his cohort. His strong physical shape was backed up by natural practical skills, making him the first port of call for the farmer in the event of broken machinery. These skills were used for hunting, where he made weapons and traps, which were lauded throughout the village. His solitary outline was often seen disappearing into the countryside, early in the morning, donning traditional woodsman's clothing, and weighed down by all manner of timber and metal curiosities, which would be transformed into traps. When he returned, often days later, the raw materials had been replaced with a bounty of food.

    Whereas other hunters were to be seen with muskets and gunpowder flasks, Fergus was traditional. He used only his traps and bow and arrows – which he made himself using sheep intestines, from the farm. Although his catch varied, his preferred game was hare, which was plentiful, and easily carried.

If a long winter was predicted, he would hunt Deer. Hunting deer was the only occasion he would invite another hunter along to help him carry home the heavy bounty. There was never a shortage of volunteers, as a trip with Fergus was almost a guarantee of deer and on only one occasion did, he return empty handed. He had a deer in his sights but refused to kill it. When his frustrated companion demanded to know why, he explained, he wasn't sure if it was a Deer or an Elk. This further annoyed the man who pointed out that an Elk was bigger than a deer and would have produced more precious meat. Fergus explained that he would not kill an Elk which he saw as a mystical, historical figure, hunted to extinction. Nobody knew if it was an Elk, which had not been seen in Ireland for hundreds of years, but each time the story was told in the local Tavern the antlers grew bigger until eventually they were so huge, only an Elk could possess them. That hunting trip had been the final one of the season, two winters past, and he had never hunted deer since. The lack of meat resulted in a long, hard winter for his family, with little hunting possible and work on the farm scarce. Yet, despite the hardship placed upon herself, and her family, Orla's feelings for him grew after this act of compassion.

It was with a glorious inevitability that he and Orla were betrothed soon after, in an arrangement suiting all parties and bringing great happiness to both families. With the arrangements for the union under way, and his life heading towards this favourable chapter, he headed out to the countryside.

To save enough money for the wedding, and begin married life, he was hunting more. He was inventing newer, more ingenious ways of catching his prey, and returning home with bounties, so heavy he could scarcely carry home.

His main weapon, the bow and arrow, was replaced with a spade. He discovered the best way to catch hares was to dig a large pit in the ground and coax them in with bait. He constructed a large timber box to place over the hole, which was disguised with strips of turf, giving the appearance of a small mound. The camouflage was as much to hide it from other hunters as it was to trick his prey. The location of his traps was often discussed in the village, but none had ever been discovered. At each side of the box were small, hare sized square tunnels leading to the bait, dangling from the roof of the wooden box. A small access panel enabled the trap to be emptied, and the bait replaced. The trap would catch many prey and, alongside his other traps dotted around the countryside, ensured a swift bounty.

    Due to the success of his new technique, he decided to build a larger underground trap. The location was vital; it had to be remote enough to elude other hunters, but close enough to a hare's trail to ensure potential foot traffic from his furry prey. He decided to go further into the countryside than ever before. Whilst surveying the surrounding area, he noticed something unusual in the distance. It was a speck of red on the top of a mound, which appeared to be moving. It looked like a person. Could it be another hunter? Why would he be dressed in red? Nobody in the village wore such extravagantly coloured clothing. Suspiciously he approached the red dot. There were two people, dressed in full body suits and masks. He had noticed the red suit from afar, but the green suit was less conspicuous against the landscape. They were walking around the giant grassy mound carrying a box and long stick, which was being waved in the air. The mound was obscured by a row of trees which, unusually, had grown in a straight line equidistant from each other. They were detached from other clumps of surrounding trees, standing ominously to attention.

    He had to get closer. Slowly creeping on all fours, he crouched behind a tree. The brightly attired figures were now walking up the mound waving the sticks in the air. From the end of the sticks came clouds of smoke. Were they sticks, or magic wands? Arriving at the summit, they separated until at opposite ends of the mound. Simultaneously reaching down, they pulled a circular metal lid until it flipped open and began climbing into the mound. As they disappeared down the hole, the lid closed with a loud bang, echoing across the fields.

    Fergus lay on the floor behind the tree, unable to make sense of what he had seen. He pondered a giant rabbit trap, dwarfing anything he had constructed; but it was too big- such an explanation was preposterous. Sensing his safety was at risk, he headed back to the village with a headful of theories, and a handful of ideas, until he approached the village convinced, he had discovered the purpose of the mysterious mound. Alongside the books, his learned friend had given him a selection of periodicals. One article, from a publication in England, discussed the emergence of leper colonies. The infectious nature, and disturbing appearance of sufferers, resulting in many colonies being clandestine; outside the knowledge of local inhabitants.

This must be it, he concluded. The more he thought about it, the clearer it became. One of the treatments for leprosy was to drink lambs' blood. Lambs were plentiful, in the fields and around the farms. There had been recent cases of lambs mysteriously missing from fields, probably to be sacrificed for their blood. Lepers carried clappers and bells to warn people of their disease. The people he saw carried a stick which they waved around, producing a cloud of smoke. The smoke must kill airborne germs and prevent the disease spreading further. Leper colonies were supervised by men of religion. He had read of the Order of Saint Lazarus Monks, who looked after lepers throughout the world. That would explain the clothes. The green suits were the monk's robes with red robes to identify the infected.

But, what could he do? He was the only person in the village who knew about this. Only hunters ventured to places of such isolation and, despite being the best, even he had never been this far before. He was the only hunter who could read and would be able to make such a connection. The villagers were in danger. They must be warned. Now on the main road, the burden of knowledge and responsibility weighed heavily upon him. What should he do? Who should he tell? It was an unusual set of circumstances, requiring the attention of a man with an equally unusual skillset.

Thomas Evans was one of the few scholars in the village. He was educated, financially buoyant and well-travelled. He was often away on business trips, visiting exciting locations including Paris and London. His wealth, education, glamorous lifestyle and good looks making him the most eligible Batchelor in the County. It was through Thomas that Fergus had obtained his reading literature and basic reading tuition.

Despite their differing backgrounds, Thomas and Fergus had formed a convivial alliance. His admiration for Thomas extended beyond gratification for the part played in his recent education. He felt a personal affinity with a man who, alike himself, projected a unique image within a small village. Although no words were exchanged on the matter, this appreciation appeared mutual. They stood out as characters in an otherwise unremarkable backdrop.

Thomas's dexterity signalled him as the man to approach. It was a sensitive matter on many levels. He needed to speak to an educated man, who could offer a balanced opinion, as what he had seen was as unbelievable as it was startling. It was possible many of the villagers would not believe him. He hoped he wasn't away on one of his frequent business trips.

Arriving at the house, he was in luck. A small light emanating from the library indicated he was home. He was greeted with the usual courtesy and before long was nestled on a rocking chair next to the fireplace.

'Would you like a whiskey?' Thomas asked with a friendly smile, pleased with the surprise visit, 'I was thinking of having one myself. I've had a touch of writer's block. I'm writing an article for a London periodical.'

'Thank you. That's very kind,' he replied, returning the smile.

Looking around, he began to relax with the contentment of a man having made the correct decision. He had been in the house many times before. It had an aura of relaxation. Despite his obvious financial means, he had not succumbed to the temptation of opulence. It had a feeling of simple elegance and warmth. The library was the largest room in the house – and Fergus's favourite. He had never seen so many books in one place, causing him to speculate whether there were more books in this one room than the rest of the village. He would wager a week's pay there were.

'So, my friend, what brings you here? I saw you heading out hunting this morning, but I can't see any prey. Is it a social visit, or are you on the lookout for more literature? I'll lend you a book or two. You don't have to pay me with game, you know?'

'I like to pay my way. I don't expect anything for free. But that's not the reason I have come.'

Fergus proceeded to tell his confidant the story of his hunting experience, down to minutest detail. Throughout the tale, he gauged his fascial expressions, hoping to catch a glimmer of his friend's reaction. Would he believe him? What would he suggest?

'mmm,' Thomas mused as the end of the story was reached, 'That's unusual, but from what you have described, it does sound like a leper colony. I haven't seen one myself, but I have heard them described that way before. What do you think we should do?'

'I'm not sure. That's why I came straight here to talk about it. I don't know why, but you seemed the best person to talk too. The one most likely to offer an explanation'

'Have you discussed this with anybody else?'

'No, but I was thinking we should tell the Villagers, round up a party of the best Hunters and go back together. Do you agree?'

'Well,' Thomas replied, 'You need to be careful. You have no idea what these people are capable of. If they are Lazarus Monks, as you think, I have heard some unsavoury stories about their behaviour. They do not take kindly to having their privacy threatened.'

'You've heard of them?'

'Yes, on my travels, and in books and magazine articles. One article I read was of particular interest. It concluded that if you were to come across one of the secret colonies you would be recommended to leave it alone. The Monks keep themselves and their patients isolated, to the point where no harm can come to anyone outside of the colony walls. They do good, necessary work, but react aggressively if disturbed. The writer gave an excellent analogy. Think of the colonies like beehives. If you leave them alone, you will benefit over time, but if you poke it with a stick, you will immediately regret it. My initial reaction is to follow the chap's advice.'

On his way to the house he had tried anticipating his mentor's reaction. He thought he had run through all the possible answers, but this suggestion had taken him by surprise.

After a short pause Thomas continued, 'Am I to deduce from your silence, you are unsure what you want to do. It is a big decision. A life changing decision. You need to think it through. My advice would be to forget about it and carry on with your life. Somebody else will discover it one day and they can carry the burden. You are getting wed soon? Do you need this right now? And the villagers won't thank you if the

Monk's turn nasty and somebody gets hurt, or even killed. Are they harming anybody?'

Fergus sat in his chair contemplating his decision. Thomas had considered possibilities which would not have entered is mind. He knew he had come to the right place. The decision was simple.

'We need to tell the villages,' he replied concisely, with the confidence of a man blessed with decisiveness. 'It's evening. The local tavern will be full. I will tell them in there and we can make a plan.'

'Are you sure,' Thomas spluttered, 'Do you really wish to unleash a torch carrying mob of drunks upon them? Because that's what will happen. There will be no plan. These people aren't like us. They lack intelligence and aforethought. They act now and think later. And that's when they're sober. Imagine the state of them after a night in the Tavern.'

The desperation within his voice caught Fergus off guard. His voice had cracked, his accent deviating from his usual soft Irish dialect to English. Suddenly he wasn't as intimidating or self-assured. He was a man of words, not action, but some things could not be resolved with words. Thomas had helped him many times. Now it was time to return the favour. He would thank him in the long term.

'Look Thomas, it needs doing - but you must stay here. We need somebody to document what has happened. We can't risk exposing you.' Fergus exclaimed with a matter of fact. He had said this to spare him any guilt or accusations of cowardice, but as the words articulated, he realised they were also true.

'OK,' he replied, 'But I will come to the Tavern with you. I must keep a record of what is said in the meeting. Are you sure this is what you want to do?'

'Yes'

'In which case, I will get my coat.... And one more glass of whiskey for us both.'

As Fergus reached for the bottle, Thomas advised, 'No, not that one. I have a special peaty whisky I picked up in Scotland. I've been waiting for a worthy occasion '

It was dusk as they stood outside the Tavern. The plentiful farm work available during the springtime guaranteed a good trade in beer.

This was advocated by the noise emanating from inside. Fergus stumbled as he approached the door.

'Wait', he said, leaning forward, using the frame of the door as support. He was lightheaded and weak. He didn't drink often and had consumed 2 large glasses of Whiskey on an empty stomach. He tried to recall when he last ate.

'Are you OK?' Thomas enquired.

'Yes, yes, I'm fine. Drinking on an empty stomach doesn't agree with me. The Scotch Whisky must have been too strong for me. I'm not used to it. It tasted unusual - like medicine.'

'It's supposed to taste like that. It's the peat they use to dry the malt, which flavours the whisky. It's an acquired taste, but I like it. Are you OK to go in. Shall we go back?'

'No. There's no time to waste. I'll be fine.'

The cloud of smoke which engulfed him, exasperated his sickly gait. He had anticipated the inhabitants of the cacophonous den of pollution. He could recognise their voices, each louder than the last, but were a mass of random, unfocused shapes. His fatigue was winning over his senses. He leaned against an upturned barrel to avoid collapse.

'Listen here, listen here,' yelled Thomas, uncharacteristically loud, 'Fergus Leahy has information he would like to share.'

Clinging to the barrel, Fergus could barely stand.

'Go on, Fergus.' Thomas prompted.

'I can't, I feel weak' he protested.

'Tell them about the men in the suits. I will furnish them with the details,' Thomas whispered into his ear.

Pointing towards the countryside he proclaimed, his slurred words barely audible, 'I've shheen them. Men in red and green shhuits. On the fieldsh. A lepersh colonish'

His legs lost the battle with gravity as he tumbled to the floor, conscious, but paralysed. He could no longer make out the blurred shapes, only sound remained. The Tavern fell silent, before the inquisition began.

'What's wrong with him?' shouted one voice.

'Did he say leper colony?' asked another.

'People, people, there's no need to worry,' Thomas reassured. 'I'm afraid my friend here has been helping himself to my exquisite Scottish whisky. It must be too exotic for him as he is indeed, intoxicated.'

Amidst a backdrop of laughter and mockery, he continued, 'He did not say leper colony, he said Leprechaun.'

'What's a leprechaun?' screamed a voice.

'Have you never heard of the leprechaun?' Thomas shouted, the silence and blank expressions answering his question.

'My father is from the North and he used to tell me stories of Leprechauns,' he continued 'They are little fairies who live in the woods around Ireland. They aren't real, it's folklore. If he thinks he has seen Leprechauns, he has lost his mind'

The Tavern erupted with hoots of derision. For some this was too good to be true. Although Fergus was a humble man, his quiet serenity and general aptitude, ensured he was a target for envy. Many claimed a farm hand who could read had ideas above his station, with his upcoming wedding to the most beautiful girl in the village, spawning more jealousy. Laying on the floor, drifting out of consciousness, he tried to grasp why his friend would tell such devastating lies.

He was laying across a pew in the local church when he awoke. The 12th Century building was small, but beautifully simple in form. He awoke facing the three large lancet windows, which defined its character and poured light onto the alter. What the windows lacked in delicacy, compared to the fashionable sculptured traceries, they replaced with honest reliability. The hardwood pulpit was intricately decorated with 3 steps elevating its prominence and complimenting the minimalistic stone surroundings.

His head was thick and cloudy, his right-hand ice cold, having rested on the stone floor. As he shuffled himself into a seating position, his visual lucidity contradicted his mental confusion. Before he had an opportunity to absorb his situation he was confronted by an enraged Orla.

'Why have you done this to us Fergus? Why? I thought you were different to the others. But you are just the same. A drunk - and a thief!' she exclaimed.

'W.w..what, what do you mean?' he stuttered in bewilderment. She had never been so volatile. He had no idea she possessed such venom.

'Don't lie to me Fergus, Thomas has told me everything. How you have been stealing books and whisky from him.'

'No, no, I haven't,' he protested. 'I don't understand why he is saying such things. He gave me the books and the whisky. I only had a couple of glasses of whisky'

'A couple of glasses! A couple of glasses!' she repeated for effect, 'Half of the village saw what a state you were in. You could hardly speak and when you did you were talking nonsense about little red and green fairies.'

'Leprechauns,' he exclaimed, recalling the conversation in the tavern before he passed out 'Yes, I remember the leprechauns.'

'So, it's true what they're saying. You've been seeing fairies?'

'No, no that's not what I meant….'

'You're not the man I thought you were. It's over,' she screeched, unable to control her rage.

'No, please,' he pleaded in vain.

The ring hit him in the face, landing on the pew. He frantically scrambled across to retrieve the handmade token of commitment. The very hand which made it, shook so violently with cold and shock, it laboured to clutch it. By the time his trembling fingers held the ring aloft, she was gone.

The story was untrue, but his fate was sealed. Fergus dealt in actualities. Nobody would believe the word of a mere farm hand with illusions of grandeur, against the articulate man of mystery. Only he knew the man was a charlatan and had experienced his truly disingenuous nature. He could no more make sense of it than he could argue his corner. A man publicly decried for seeing tiny fairies is destined for one place. The only reason he wasn't already on his way to an Asylum was the isolated nature of the village. His freedom was disappearing with the passing sands of time.

When they arrived to take him away, he was gone. Nobody knew how he left the church as there was only one door, which was guarded, and the windows remained intact.

Over the subsequent years, there were many theories on his escape and even more tales of what became of the fugitive. There were sightings of him, in the surrounding villages, and throughout Ireland. Stories were told of his attempts to settle in nearby villages being blighted by ridicule – the curse of 'the Leprechaun Man'. There were even reports he had been seen in London. None of the sightings were substantiated and, as the populations of the towns and cities increased, the sightings decreased. A few short years later, Fergus Leahy was forgotten, his memory occasionally resurrected in the minds of the people he touched, but his name was no longer spoken. His parents forgot they had a son, his job at the farm was filled and Orla married one of her many suitors. Life continued without him. He became the stranger nobody saw. But, the legend of his nemesis, the Leprechaun, went from strength to strength. Suddenly tales and sightings became common, eventually becoming part of Irish culture.

Some years later, the body of a man was found behind a Tavern on the outskirts of Dublin. He was known locally as a drunk who slept rough, often disappearing into the countryside for days on end. Although insular in nature, he had formed a small friendship with a local teacher from whom he used to borrow books and other reading literature. Upon his death, amongst the meagre contents within his pocket, was a crudely made ring with a small inset peridot gem. Out of respect for his friend, the teacher kindly volunteered to meet the cost of the cheapest burial, much to the chagrin of his wife. He was offered the ring in return for the kind gesture. Although an object full of charm and simple beauty, its only value was intrinsically linked to its owner. It was buried, with its owner in a small graveyard on the edge of the village. It was 15 years to the day of Fergus and Orla's proposed wedding.

~

Despite being a favourite tale of students during enlightenment, it had an uncomfortable place in Stanley's psyche. On one hand, he viewed the very nature of the story to be dubious. Was it true, exaggerated, or entirely manufactured? Given the death sentences handed out to unfortunate Normals, for knowing too much, why would they have kept him alive and gone to such extremes to discredit him? On the other hand, if the story was true, he was even more uncomfortable with the cynicism required within the Caste to carry out such an unsavoury exercise.

'Flash are you ready?' prompted Poppi as they edged nearer the security gate.

He had been to this facility on many occasions and knew the protocol. At the first security gate was a single guard responsible for low-level security checks. To the outside world Headrock Business Park was a mixture of office and industrial units. The first zone was accessible to anybody with a basic-level pass, including Normals, and consisted of small-scale office units. Buildings in Zone 1 ran parallel to the main road, providing a visual barrier to the outside world whilst presenting a façade of the ordinary. The siting of the buildings seemed random but, their position was planned by urban design specialists, who ingeniously used the terrain and natural constraints of the site for their clandestine purposes. The size, mass and angle of the buildings in relation to the road tricked the eye into believing what could be seen from the road was the extent of the estate. Behind Zone 1 was a large three-storey mirror clad industrial unit with a parking forecourt to the front. The industrial unit was fake, acting as a buffer to intercept unauthorised personnel having accidentally strayed from Zone 1. It was a gateway into Zone 2, accessible only to the Clover Caste.

'Hello Chip. How's the family?' Poppi enquired chirpily as they reached the first check point.

'Can't complain, darling,' Chip replied. 'Well who'd listen if I did, anyway?' he laughed. As Poppi held up the identity cards, without glancing at them he opened the barrier. 'Have a nice day sweetheart!'

It was over ten years since Stanley had been in Zone 1, but it had changed little and was still occupied by a series of two-storey brick buildings fronted with car parking spaces. Along the perimeter fence were more parking bays.

'It's just how I remember it. Some of the companies have changed but generally it's the same,' Stanley observed, as they approached the large industrial unit forming the gateway into the secretive Zone 2.

Although industrial in appearance, the three-storey mirror clad building was not as it appeared. The centrally located reception area was deliberately elaborate and well signposted to draw in visitors. The offices were, a decoy, with only the reception area functional and accessible from the front of the building. The remainder of the building was a shallow 'C' shaped enclosure wrapping around a high-tech car storage warehouse. Each car was driven into a steel mesh container, and stacked on a shelf mechanically, with such efficiency that hundreds of cars could be stored at any time and retrieved in less than 4 minutes. The warehouse hid the volume of cars required to serve Headrock; a facility which didn't officially exist.

To the right was an access road signposted 'deliveries only', screened by a uniform planting of trees. This barely noticeable single lane of tarmac was the link to Zone 2.

'Look away from the building, Flash,' snapped John, as they headed down the access road.

It was narrow, with a series of speed bumps and speed limit signs, designed to slow vehicles sufficiently for guards in the security bays to inspect and photograph the occupants of the vehicle. It was intended to intercept Normals taking a wrong turn; but under the circumstances, it was wise for Stanley to show the back of his head. Poppi and John's presence would be enough to convince the guards there were no unwanted Normals in the car.

The Caste were trained in methods of subterfuge and mimicry, with architects, designers, engineers and artists, referred to as the "magicians", dedicated to protecting the veil of secrecy. As the magician's department occupied buildings within Zone 2 of the facility, no expense, or ounce of genius, had been spared in showcasing their skills.

The entrance to Zone 2 was located at the far side of a large car park to the rear of the industrial building. Although sparsely populated, the few vehicles present were carefully distributed to screen the entrance from observation. To maintain the chicanery, the vehicles were replaced daily and the pattern of occupation within the car park changed accordingly – but certain spaces were always filled.

The vehicles used for the charade were in stored the car warehouse and regularly replaced, causing Stanley to muse as to the cost of the operation. He had never heard of a Normal straying to the rear of the mock office block, so was it even necessary? Still, it summed up the Clover Council's meticulous level of detailing.

The entrance to Zone 2 was beautiful in its simplicity. It was situated at the far corner of the car park and set within a ten-foot-high red brick wall, angled to deceive the eye, from distance, into believing there was no opening. It appeared to be set beyond the boundary of the car park, cordoned off by black and white striped bollards, but five of the bollards were an optical illusion, painted onto the ground – disappearing from vision upon approach.

'You'll be impressed with Zone 2; there's been a few change since you were last here,' Poppi informed him as they glided over the painted bollards.

'Like what?' he replied.

As the entered Zone 2 she replied, 'You see the two buildings on either side of the road, the round concrete ones?'

'Yes, but they were here the last time I came.'

'Maybe', she replied, 'but the building on top wasn't.'

'There isn't one.'

'Yes, there is! It's covered in reflective cladding curved at all the edges, so you don't see a shadow line. But the cladding is a huge screen onto which filmed images are displayed,' Poppi explained.

'What do you mean?' Stanley quizzed.

Poppi continued: 'It's a prototype. Images from the surrounding landscape are filmed and displayed on the screen so the building blends into the surroundings. When we look up now, what we see is not the sky but film of the sky in real time being played on the cladding screens. When you get closer, you'll be able to see the bottom of the building and the edges of the screen, but from a distance they can't be seen. There are no screens on the bottom as their purpose is to make the buildings invisible from above. A plane or helicopter flying over will see the screen on the roof displaying images from the surrounding landscape, so the building simply blends in. That's why it's been built on top of the two existing buildings – to cover them. Before, there was a large mural painted on each roof, but they didn't change to reflect the weather. In summer, the roof over reflected and the paint became faint and had to be reapplied every year. Of course, when it was repainted the operatives carrying out the work could be seen from above. In the winter, because of the heat generated within the buildings, the snow melted, and they stuck out like a sore thumb.'

'That's impressive. But what's it like inside, without any windows? I once stayed on a ship without windows and it depressed the hell out of me!' Stanley countered.

'Not here,' Poppi laughed. 'You see, the building is open plan, with the walls and ceiling made of the same cladding screen that's on the exterior, showing real-time filmed images of what's outside, so it's as if there are no walls or ceilings. The air conditioning not only regulates the temperature but also emits a subtle odour to replicate the passing seasons.'

Leaning back and peering through the rear window, he saw the bright blue sky interrupted by the underside of the structure as the car drove beneath.

'Put your game face on, we're here,' she announced. 'It shouldn't be a problem because we're not going into a highly-restricted area - there's no real security. We just need to get to my office with as little fuss as possible. John and I are often here so you'll barely be noticed. They'll think you're one of our staff, so just keep your head down and try not to flash that face of yours around while I use the pass to get us in. You remember where my office is, don't you? You may want to casually walk in the right direction as I'm signing you in; the sooner you're out of sight the better,' Poppi suggested.

'Yes. Level -4 isn't it? The untidiest office in the building if I remember, right?'

'It may look untidy but everything's where it should be. It's all filed in my head,' she defended.

The entrance was carved into the face of the giant headrock that led to the main headquarters below the surface, with only members of the Senate knowing how many levels were below. The rock section of

Zone 2 was the first to be constructed, with the smaller ground-level ancillary buildings added when it became difficult to excavate new levels below. It was rumoured that they had gone so far down that the Headquarters were in danger of reaching the earth's core, but Stanley had been given a more believable explanation by an engineer working on the air conditioning. He was informed that underground facilities of such magnitude needed complex systems to maintain the air quality, which were overseen by a team of specialist safety engineers. Ironically, the engineers charged with the maintenance and servicing were split into two colour-coded groups, each responsible for the incoming and outgoing air. The parallel between the engineers and those in the tale of Fergus Leahy was impossible to miss and the source of much amusement to everyone except the engineers themselves; the constant 'top of the morning' greeting and leprechaun taunts being a source of irritation. Stanley, who was not convinced by the leprechaun story anyway, had become friends with an engineer called Roger, with whom he often had his lunch.

Roger, an air conditioning safety engineer responsible for the expulsion of exhaust, explained the reason for not being able to excavate further down was because they had reached the maximum distance at which the air conditioning ducts could safely extract the air. He also told him that the lowest facility served was level -42. As only the first 4 levels were accessible to Stanley, and most people using the facility, there were another 38 levels below. There were rumours of escape tunnels from the lower floors that led to other facilities deep in the vast landscape of Montana. There were also rumours of a space shuttle launch area on the other side of the mountain ranges, accessible from Headrock HQ.

The entrance within the rock face was disproportionately small compared to the size of the rock itself and camouflaged from view by a wall made from materials excavated from the rock face. The glass entrance façade with a thin grey aluminium frame and double doors, opened automatically as they approached. Poppi took the passes to the reception counter while John and Stanley nonchalantly hung back, close to the stair door. After a brief conversation with the receptionist, she re-joined the pair and led them into the stairwell.

The grey concrete staircase with painted black handrails was the epitome of blandness; but still they held a special place in Stanley's heart. Whilst working there, they had acted as an important conduit for him between the contrast of the public reception areas and the shared work zones. The privacy of the stairwell empowered smaller, private snippets of conversations to take place out of earshot of the many. Subgroups were formed, surreptitiously timing their movements to take advantage of the opportunity for clandestine dialogue. Important issues were discussed in the brief time it took to walk the stairs between the four floors: from intimate details of work to sensitive relationship rumours. It reminded him of the happy days with Poppi, particularly the landing on level -2, where they kissed for the first time.

Poppi's office hadn't changed; files were spread randomly over desks with shelving used to store items that would have been better placed on the desk. She began wrenching open drawers with the ferocity of a thief ransacking the office. John and Stanley knew their place; there was no point attempting to help decipher the crazy puzzle, no more than there was criticising her techniques. For all the chaos, she was the only one who understood how to assemble and work this machine. Her appearance, articulation and all-round occupational thoroughness was contrary to this messy working environment. Even her apartment was spotless. Still, despite the disorder, her disarming self-confidence and consistently good results made it difficult to doubt her methods. By the time she had finished, her desk was a flurry of wires and circuit boards sprawled alongside a battered red motorcycle helmet. Incredibly, she had managed to make the room even more untidy, an achievement which had looked impossible.

'Here it is,' she announced, her voice brimming with pride.

Stanley and John looked at each other in disbelief.

'That's it! Seriously?! You've brought us all this way for that contraption? It's just a pile of junk. It looks like a robot has seen the state of your office and blown its own head off!'

One of them had to say it and it was always going to be John, who had a reputation for bluntness which he delighted in enhancing whenever possible. Stanley's heart sank at the crudity of the prototype, his unflinching confidence in her methods dissipating into the atmosphere, which could now be cut with the proverbial knife.

'I'm disappointed you don't trust me,' she replied.

Stanley was familiar with her demeanour. She wasn't disappointed, she was angry.

'This is our best shot. But if you don't believe me, we could attempt to sneak you aboard the space station?'

If Stanley was a country, he would be Switzerland; always the arbitrator, forever the diplomat, and, as John paced around the office, mumbling and kicking random debris on the floor, he knew his delicate touch was required.

'Look, we've come this far. It's too late to turn back, we've nothing to lose. Besides, if Poppi thinks it'll work, I trust her. If not, we'll have to figure out the space station option - and that won't be easy.'

'Thanks, Flash, I knew I could rely on you.'

John glanced across and scowled. He knew Stanley had no more confidence in the plan than him but had chosen to play the peacemaker. John didn't like appeasement; it was an easy, cowardly option as far as he was concerned.

They moved to another room on the same level, which was large, uncluttered and well-lit. A centrally placed aluminium treatment table was adjusted to an upright position by a tense looking Poppi. She was setting-up for the memory retrieval procedure, and the burden of expectation was starting to register; this was the moment of truth. It would be understandable if such a complex process could not be executed by a solitary soul using basic equipment - understandable but unacceptable.

'We call this room the Dream Academy,' Poppi said. 'Sit on here please, Flash. I'll explain how it works. Now, you've been through a similar procedure before, but this is different. As you know, instead of being a narrating observer, we'll be using you as a real-life movie projector. The images from your brain will be translated into real-time images projected onto that wall over there,' she explained, pointing towards a plain white wall directly in front of the table. 'I'll put you into a state of hypnosis, like last time, but a milder strand so you'll be semi-conscious. You'll see everything and because the hypnosis is milder, you won't be disoriented when you awaken. As it's not connected to the network, I will record everything on your Heartbeat for evidence. So, to begin, will you put the helmet on please?'

Stanley picked up the old motorcycle helmet. Inside were circular green rubber plungers with a series of blue lines running within, like micro-thin veins.

'So, these little suckers, I guess they stick to my head to transmit signals from my brain? ' Stanley enquired.

'Yes' she replied, attaching the helmet to his head.

'We know you're compliant by nature and have been through a similar process before, so you've nothing to be concerned about.'

Poppi's assured, repetitive narrative continued in a similar manner to the hypnosis he had undergone almost two decades earlier. This time he was older, wiser and more relaxed. But this time it didn't work.

He had sensed Poppi's early frustration, tempered by her painstakingly methodical attempts to breakthrough into his inner thoughts. Finally, her resolve broken, she admitted defeat. He must have become too strong willed. He wasn't the scared, weak-willed child of before. It wasn't her fault she had underestimated him. Expecting her to confirm the inconvenience of his new-found fortitude, what she said next took him by surprise.

'I'm sorry, Flash,' Poppi apologised, with her trademark tone of reassurance. 'I need to shave your head.'

'What?' he exclaimed.

'I thought this might happen, so I've put the shaver on charge, and I've got a razor in my drawer. We need to shave down to the skin to provide the optimum contact required for enhanced effectiveness.'

'Are you serious? Shave my head? But you know I have a thing about my hair. Why?'

'Because we need to fit the thought leeches, or suckers as you call them, directly onto your skin. That's how we did it on the test subjects. I know how much you love your hair, so I thought I'd try it this way first. But your thick hair is the reason it isn't working. I tried to put a couple on your forehead, but they didn't seem to stick. Maybe you have a funny shaped head?' she continued.

'Funny shaped head! You're enjoying this, aren't you? I don't have a funny shaped head!'

'Well, we'll soon see when you are as bald as a baby, won't we?' she replied.

'Surely you can't be serious? Is this really necessary?'

'I don't see what the big problem is. It's only hair. After what we've risked so far, you're being petty,' John interrupted.

Of course, John couldn't see what the problem was, having kept the same haircut for the whole of his adult life; shaven all over - number 2. He didn't deserve to still have hair at his age. As Clover Caste kept the same DNA for the first three cycles, so those who lose their hair during the first Leaf suffer the same fate in the next two. And despite their advanced technology and medicines, they were no nearer to finding a cure for baldness than the Normals. Still, he had a point. In the great scheme of things, it was no big deal.

'Say cheese,' Poppi said, taking a photograph of the newly shaven Stanley sitting forlornly on the table. It had not taken her long to shave his head, a task she had clearly performed before.

'Why on earth are you taking a photo?' he protested. 'I thought we were supposed to be incognito?'

'We are. But when this is over, I'm going to add this photo to the Circle.'

The Circle of Lives – or the Circle - was a global network of interconnected computers within the Clover community. Their computers were so far in advance of those used by the Normals that the standard issue Heartbeat, which would fit into a pocket, was superior to the most advanced government mainframes occupying several storeys within a building. Originally, the network was developed by the military, and only those with high-level clearance were allowed access. It was launched in the 1940s and Stanley had used it during the Uruguay mission. In the 1960s, the Senate introduced a public access network known as the Circle of Lives. Although an encrypted strand of the network known as "Mili-Net" was still used by the military, the universally accessible Circle was the most widely used network amongst the Caste.

Although Stanley was an advocate of Mili-Net, he hated the Circle. He understood from field experience the power of the network in providing covert communications and essential information but despaired at the frivolous use of this technology within the public domain. It had been developed by the Senate for communication between the Caste and as a conduit connecting the four levels. In reality, it was used for less noble causes, such as posting embarrassing photographs of people with shaven heads.

'You still using that load of rubbish?' Stanley sighed.

'Or course,' she replied. 'I can't understand your problem with it.'

'Because', he added with exasperation, 'it's an amazing piece of technology if used right, but the Circle has turned it into a forum for idiots!'

'It's not that bad,' she laughed.

'Oh yes, it is!' he exclaimed. 'If someone you hadn't seen for a couple of lifetimes came up to you in the street and showed you a picture of their dog and then told you what they were having for their dinner you'd run a mile. But that's all they do on the Circle and everyone thinks it's great.'

John and Poppi were familiar with Stanley's opinions on the subject and found it amusing and reassuring to see their usually laid-back friend lose his cool. John knew which button to press next.

'But you're forgetting', John coaxed, 'the Senate gave us this technology to help communication.'

'And that's another thing,' Stanley spluttered, barely able to get his words out fast enough. 'You don't believe that rubbish about the Senate doing this for our benefit, surely? They're doing it to keep an eye on us all and we're all stupid enough to do their job for them. It's self-surveillance – you must be able to see it? Haven't you read 1984? Big brother is here. Four years early!'

'Oh, shut up moaning and get the helmet on,' Poppi laughed.

With the helmet on his head, the thought-leeches felt cool against his bare skin. As the images of John and Mouse running towards him carrying a dinghy projected onto the wall, he realised Poppi's makeshift thought-stealing machine actually worked.

CHAPTER 28

Staring at the wall in disbelief, Stanley barely noticed the door being kicked open with such venom the top hinge tore away from its frame. He was in a state of shock, the Dream Academy had become a room of nightmares; but he had to hand it to Poppi, her makeshift thought-stealing machine had worked better than he could have imagined.

He had watched the Uruguay mission back in '45 unfold, climaxing with him running through the trees, followed closely by John, in search of the refuge pod. Despite the pursuer's bullets, whizzing above their heads, he managed to open the door to the mirror clad refuge pod, which popped ajar just before a bullet hit the back of his head, ending his first life. Swinging open ever so slightly its reflection revealed the identity of his killer. It was his friend - John Carter.

The shock of betrayal released him from the hypnotherapy, and he returned from the Uruguayan forest back to the table in the middle of the large white room, on Level -4, in the heart of Clover Caste Headquarters.

'Hold it right there, Carter. Put your hands where I can seem them!' a familiar voice cried, snapping Stanley from his stupor.

It was Carson, standing assured and confident, with a revolver pointing at John. John stood in the corner of the room, arms aloft.

'Did you get all of that, Poppi?' Carson asked.

'Yes,' She mumbled. 'Did you know about this? Did you know that John killed Flash in Uruguay?'

'I couldn't prove it until now, but I knew he had something to do with our deaths. It's a shame Flash couldn't have got to me sooner in Uruguay, so we could see for sure he killed me as well. But it doesn't matter. We have all the proof we need that he killed Flash,' Carson explained.

'What?' Stanley exclaimed. 'This can't be true. John's the most honest and reliable person I know. He lives and breathes the Council. He's my friend. There must be some mistake.'

'Wake up!' snapped Carson. 'You've just seen it with your own eyes.'

'Don't believe him, Flash,' pleaded John. 'I don't know what's going off- he's trying to frame me. Why are you doing this to me, Carson? Poppi, you must be in on it too. You've added that bit at the end to make me look guilty. Yes, that's it. With all your technology it must have been easy.'

'No, John, I haven't done anything to the dream sequence. Everything we saw came straight from his memory,' replied Poppi, who was now pointing her gun at John. 'Now, slowly take your weapon out and lay it on the floor.'

'This is a set-up, Flash,' John claimed, laying his gun down. 'What was on that external disk in the crucifix around your neck, Poppi? You put that into your contraption before strapping it onto his head. I bet it was an extra image or a scene - or something that superimposed my face onto the reflection on the door.'

'No, John, it was an algorithm that enabled the machine to work,' Poppi snapped with indignance.' Anyway, Carson, it's great to see you, but how did you know we were here? How did you know what was happening?'

'You mean you two weren't in this together?' gasped John. 'And you expect us to believe that? He just happens to walk through the door at this exact moment by coincidence? You've got to admit, Flash, this looks dodgy?'

Stanley's brain was in free fall. What was going on? Who could he trust? Only moments ago, he was convinced of John's guilt but now he wasn't sure. He looked guilty but maybe his image could have been added? But how? It had come directly from his own memory; he would have known if it had been altered. Whether he could trust Poppi was anybody's guess, but Carson was on rockier ground. Why else would he have killed John Lennon, other than to protect himself from any secrets he may have stored in his brain from the mission they were on together? And how did he appear so conveniently?

'He's right, Carson. How did you even know we were here?' Stanley quizzed.

'I can't believe you're doubting me after what you've just seen,' Carson replied angrily. 'The images you saw are based on neuronal activity transposed from your brain. Of course, they can't be altered.

They were displayed in real time. Don't let him trick you, Flash. Don't let him play mind games.'

'You haven't answered my question.' Stanley repeated: '*How* did you know we were here?'

'I tracked you from your Heartbeat' he replied. 'I realise you're rusty, but didn't you wonder why you still had a charge after ten years? They're good, but not that good.'

Stanley felt stupid as John laughed. Even with two guns pointed at him he was still able to make Stanley crawl with inadequacy.

'When I went into your apartment, I put a slight charge on, so I could track it. I had to scrape dust from the shelf above and put it onto the screen - I thought you would notice, but I guess you picked it up in a rush. I knew he would ask you to take it. No doubt he put a track on it too, just in case you got wise to him. I've been following you the entire journey. I thought I'd lost you when you hopped on the plane but, fortunately, you stopped in a hideaway lodge for a couple of days. So here I am.'

As he stood up and looked at Carson, Stanley realised he was still wearing the motorcycle helmet. Poppi edged over, resting a reassuring hand on his shoulder. Aside from the shock of Stanley's baldness, Carson was calm. His explanation rang true: he had plenty of time to access his Heartbeat, he knew exactly where it was. His next question was obvious.

'OK, fair enough, I suppose. But why did you shoot John Lennon?'

'What?' gasped Carson. 'Are you serious? It wasn't me who killed him. It was John.'

'John? John? Why would *he* kill Lennon?' Stanley retorted. 'That's the answer of a desperate man. Everybody knows how much you hated him. He stole your idea for Leaf 4 and you've spent the last twenty years telling anybody who would listen. You're lying, Carson. John had no reason to kill him. Put the gun down and turn yourself in to the Council. I'll put in a good word for you.'

'Don't be stupid, Flash,' cried Carson. 'Don't let him fool you. Most of what comes out of his mouth is lies. I've never told you a lie in all the years I've known you. I'm the one you can trust. I'm not putting this gun down until we have him locked down or dead and, to be honest, I'm not bothered which it is.'

'Poppi, what do you think?' Stanley asked.

'I'm not sure,' she replied. 'I believe Carson, I think. I invented that machine, so I know there's no way it could be manipulated. The programming required just to make it work is immense. To add sequences within it – and in real time – is just not possible.'

'But what about the guy in the helicopter?' Stanley responded. 'He told us the full story about how Carson killed John Lennon. He must have done it!'

'Maybe John paid him to say that. I've never seen him before - he may not have been who he said he was. Have you ever seen him before, Flash?'

'How could I see him? I had a bag over my head, if you remember. I did recognise his voice, but I couldn't place it.'

'What shall I do?' Poppi asked, her voice trembling.

'Tick-tock, tick-tock,' John mocked. 'It looks like it's up to you, Flash; the decision is yours. If you tell Poppi to point the gun at him, then I will pick up mine. Hell, I might even shoot him for having the audacity to point that thing at me. If she keeps aiming at me, then how do you rate your chances of becoming an Agent again after letting our top target escape from our very own headquarters?'

Stanley was in a tight spot. But what should he do? The facts were confusing and contradictory; everybody appeared to be telling the truth and lying at the same time. Of course, they were. They were highly trained Agents – what did he expect?

'Tick-tock, tick-tock,' John baited. 'We can't stay here forever. Eventually somebody will come down.'

Stanley couldn't understand why John was being so provocative. Why direct such belligerence towards someone pointing a gun at him? Shouldn't he be on a charm offensive? He must be confident to adopt such a risky strategy, but then he had always been arrogant. Carson, on the other hand, was a straight shooter, but Stanley couldn't get past the John Lennon shooting. It was too much of a coincidence. He had an idea.

Stanley said calmly, 'Carson, I'm going to ask you three questions. OK?'

'OK.'

'One: Why did you kill John Lennon? Was it because he stole your idea?'

'I didn't kill him.'

'Two: If you didn't kill Lennon, then why are you on the run?'

'I'm not on the run.'

'Yes, you are. The entire Council are after you. You are public enemy number one.'

'No, I'm not. I've walked straight in here today. Logged in at reception. I'm not on the run as I haven't killed anyone.'

'Three: How many steps are there from reception to here?'

'What?'

'You heard me, Carson. How many steps? You said earlier that you had never lied to me in all the years you've known me. When I thought about it, I couldn't recall any lies until I remembered the time in the park, nears Sal's Place, when you told me about your step counting. I never did figure out whether you were telling the truth or trying to ingratiate yourself to get information. So, I'll ask you again. How many steps?'

'But ... but,' Carson spluttered.

'But, but', Stanley teased, 'but I don't know because I thought I could pull a fast one on my stupid friend.'

John roared joyously with laughter.

'No,' Carson replied. 'But how would YOU know the answer to such a question?'

'Because ever since you told me about it, I've been doing it myself. It drives me up the wall. That one little lie has stuck with me all these years.'

'Sixty-nine.'

'Sixty-nine? Is that your final answer?'

'Yes,' confirmed Carson. 'Including the step down into this room. There are always steps down into these rooms to stop things from trickling under the door. They do some crazy stuff down here. Could be water, petrol, chemicals or blood, even. Gruesome really but the step is needed. There are seventeen steps between each floor for the maximum riser height on a stair to meet building code - it may be a top-secret building, but they still need to meet code. Anyway, listen to me, I'm starting to bore myself. Sixty-nine. The answer is sixty-nine. I have been here so many times I could have told you from the outside.'

A wave of ecstasy washed over Stanley. His guile had found the truth and defused an impossible scenario in a matter of seconds. To have done it whilst pitted against two of the best Agents in the world made it even more extraordinary. Maybe he was still the Lion of Uruguay, after all? But he was ecstatic for a different reason: at least one of his friendships was real. Looking back, Carson had never done anything to make him doubt their friendship. He had never been as close to John, but his straightforward, targeted approach to life gave him the attributes of a trustworthy leader. He never faltered and when others did, he was there to pick up the pieces. He had played his part well, but now the cracks were beginning to show.

'Well done!' exclaimed John, sarcastically clapping. 'Well played, Flash... I have to say, I didn't see that coming as your performance since we picked you up in New York did nothing to suggest you were going to spring into action and become an Agent again.'

'Maybe I was playing along with you, acting dumb,' Stanley quipped.

'No, you weren't,' John laughed 'Dumb, yes. Acting, no.'

'Can I shoot him now?' pleaded Carson.

'I suppose you think you're clever, Flash, after your pyric victory? John continued: 'But you're too late. I'm still on my first Leaf; I will come back stronger and finish my work.'

'Which is the reason I'm not going to allow Carson to shoot you - although it's tempting. We need to keep you alive and pass you on to the Council. The Senate will know what to do with you. I'm sure Poppi can extract a few secrets, with one of her fancy machines.'

'The Senate. Those stupid old buffoons! What are they going to do? Yes, that's right, Flash, I hate the Council - and the Senate. You weren't expecting that were you?'

'I had my suspicions,' he lied, trying not to appear surprised as, for once, he was in control.

'Of course, you did,' John replied theatrically.

'No, really I did!' Stanley snapped with embarrassing desperation.

'Can I shoot him yet?' Carson repeated.

Again, John laughed. 'The Council are a joke. Even Carson knows that – he's said it enough times. We need to return to the days of the Gammadions – and we will. It's closer than you think.'

'We? Who's we?' scoffed Carson. 'Have we met any of these people? Do they even exist?'

'Flash has,' John responded. 'Twice.'

'What? When?' Stanley quizzed.

'You met one of them in the helicopter. He's the one who told you the story about Carson killing John Lennon. Of course, you know it's made up now but at the time he had you fooled.'

'I didn't see him, but I recognised the voice. I recognised the voice …' Stanley repeated, trailing off as he attempted to put a face to the voice.

'Maybe this will help you?' John said in a deliberately contrived high-pitched voice: 'Do you want shelter from the storm, sir?'

'The guy at the motel. Seriously? He's who you're working for? But he's an idiot.'

'He's no idiot, he just wanted to meet you face to face, so we concocted the whole motel scenario,' explained John. 'But now you know who he is, you must die.'

It was Stanley's turn to laugh. 'But aren't you forgetting a couple of things? Firstly, it's us with all the guns – and, secondly, you've also revealed his identity to Poppi.'

'Then she too must die. After you, before you – makes no difference in the end,' John claimed.

'Not if I kill you first,' growled Poppi.

'You haven't got the minerals to do it!' John taunted.

'I know you like a bet,' Poppi replied. 'But this is one wager too many - even for you!'

As the ensuing silence shattered, Stanley fell to his knees. The proximity of Poppi's gun ensured his ears would be ringing for a while, his heart pulsating as he gasped for breath. Even though he knew John's luck would run out sooner or later, he was still surprised. Maybe he wanted to be shot so he could get a head start in the next life - why else would he repeatedly incite anger into two people holding a gun directly at him? Two people he had betrayed and must surely hate him. The boom echoed and hung in the air, suspended in time before disappearing.

    He was on his hands and knees. He could smell smoke, not the strangely pleasant chemical nitro-glycerine from the gunshot, but cigar smoke. It smelled like one of John's cigars. Perhaps he was mortally wounded, savouring his last smoke in this life. But why would Poppi not have shot him in the head? She couldn't have missed from where she was. Shakily, he stood up. Directly in front of him was John, smoking his trademark cigar. To his right was Poppi, still holding the smoking gun. To his left was Carson, slumped on the floor, with a clean gunshot wound to the centre of his forehead.

CHAPTER 29

'You shot Carson, 'he gasped. 'Poppi, why have you shot Carson?'

'Because he was pointing a gun at John – that's why?' she replied. 'From the moment he came barging through the door I've been itching to shoot him. Everything I said was to get him on side so he would lower his weapon. I thought it was never going to happen, so I made him think I was going to shoot John myself. When I said I would shoot him, I glanced at Carson for approval. He nodded, smiled and lowered his gun, so I spun around and shot him in the forehead.'

'But I thought you said the images were true - John shot me.'

'Yes of course. But I knew they were. The purpose of today was to extract the information and dispose of it.'

'But if you dispose of it, I will expose your lies,' Stanley threatened.

'Really?' asked Poppi, pointing at Carson on the floor. 'You think you are in a position to make such a threat?'

'You are on John's team?'

'2-4-6-8 who do I appreciate? J-O-H-N - John – WOOOOO!' she screamed, dancing around the room like a cheerleader, waving mock pom poms in the air. 'Yeah, that's right, Flash. Team John all the way'

'So, everything you said to Carson was rubbish?'

'Everything I have said since we picked you up in New York has been rubbish aimed at gaining your trust just long enough for you to let us do the dream sequence. Well, lies and a little female persuasion.' she taunted.

'You made everything up?' Stanley muttered, 'Even the story about John calling himself Christian Surname? I liked that story.'

'Yes,' she laughed. 'I was proud of that one - although John went mad at me after. He said nobody would believe that he was so stupid, but I said it showed a vulnerable side. And we all know that you're a sucker for a sob story, Flash.'

'So, it was you two who killed John Lennon after all?' Stanley snapped, changing the subject to banish the hurt building up inside.

'No, we didn't kill him.'

'But why would Carson kill him after all these years?'

'He didn't,' she replied.

'What? Then, who killed him?'

'It was the guy in the news, the fan. I can't remember his name. Mark something, I think. Just a Normal who was obsessed. You know how the Normals can get?'

'But I thought he was just a distraction. There are already conspiracy theories out there saying he was just a patsy.'

'Yes, we know. We started them,' she continued: 'We figured it would muddy the waters a little. Within Clover circles it would appear more of an execution than a simple murder. This way, we were able convince you that Carson had done it, thus gaining your trust.'

'You expect me to believe it was just a coincidence? After all the things Carson had said over the years, he just happened to get shot when you were trying to win me over?'

'Well it was - we couldn't believe our luck. Although, had it happened a few months later I would have had the machine fully finished. But it worked out in the end, I knew it would. But yes, a pure coincidence.'

'So', Stanley continued, in a state of astonishment, 'you're telling me that John Lennon, a final Leafer, was shot in the back by a Normal. You expect me to believe he just went wandering around New York without his Skin? And what about his protection? High-profile Clover like him would be surrounded by bodyguards; the thought that a Normal could just walk up and shoot him in the back several times just doesn't add up.'

'That's true. But John Lennon was a Normal.'

'What? But Carson said … everyone knew he was …'

'No, Flash. It was an assumption made by Carson. And a bad one. You know what happens when you assume: it makes an ass out of you and me. But mainly you,' John chortled. 'In fact, just you, really.'

Observing Stanley's hangdog expression, he maintained the lecture: 'All of the Beatles were Normals, you know? All of them. I heard there was originally a Clover in there, but he got thrown out. Lack of creativity, apparently. Sounds unlikely until you take a step back and think about it: the Beatles songs were about love, life and vulnerability. But what do we Clover know about any of this? Our multiple lives make us less vulnerable and life less precious. And as for love, well it's not as important as self-actualisation, is it? We kid ourselves we will love in the last life; we will fall in love, have children and live happily ever after. In reality, we spend three lifetimes striving so hard to achieve a successful final Leaf that we forget what love is. The obtainment of material possessions and status become more ingrained into our soul with each transition until, by the end, we can't differentiate between the journey and the destination.'

'Sounds cynical, if you ask me.' Stanley mumbled.

'That's because you're different, Flash. Your soul is not as easily corrupted. You empathise with the Normals like no Clover I've ever seen. Carson understood and tolerated them but that's as far as it went. You actually like them - sometimes it appears that you even envy them. It's no coincidence that the most creative people on the planet are Normals. It's a resource we tap into, particularly here at Headrock. There's a direct correlation between depths of poverty and levels of creativity: they need to be creative more than the rich and privileged do. I don't know anything about the Beatles, but you can bet they are from poor backgrounds. I know it sounds odd, but am I making any sense?'

'For the first time in your life,' scowled Stanley.

'This creativity is born from a desperation to escape their plight. But, of course, it's a poisoned chalice.'

'Why?'

'When success elevates them from their surroundings, they no longer have an appetite for creativity. They don't need it. Some of them even manage to achieve their version of self-actualisation. It's not dissimilar to ours but they don't have as long to enjoy it and are often too old to be able to appreciate it.'

'So why did you kill us both - in Uruguay, I mean?'

'For the money and the power. What better reason to betray your friends?' John sneered.

'But why kill me at the end? I don't understand - the mission was over so killing me changed nothing: you dragged me into the refuge pod, and we were picked up shortly afterwards. The mission was over! There was no point in killing me.' Stanley repeated.

'Your mission was over, pal, not mine. I had to kill you before the rescue squad picked us up.'

'But why?'

'So, I could switch the DNA samples, of course. The guy you killed wasn't our mark. Didn't you think he was remarkably easy to kill?'

'But I thought Mouse had incapacitated him.'

'Didn't you think it odd he had an English accent? Everybody knew he was German.'

'So, who did I kill then?'

John shrugged his shoulders. 'Dunno. Just some Normal lookalike from England. We left him there for you to discover and warned him of what might happen to his family if he didn't play ball. I can't tell you how much it wound me up seeing you being lauded as the "Lion of Uruguay" when all you did was strangle the wrong person. Still, I had the last laugh - you fell right into our trap. Didn't you think it odd that the buildings were empty? They knew we were coming; I didn't scan the fish that night. I sent a GPS of our location warning them to evacuate.'

'So, it was a set-up, I get it now. I thought it was odd that the guy had an English accent and that the whole place was empty. I thought he was pretending to be English so I wouldn't kill him. But what could I do? I was in the middle of a mission, so I had to finish it and hope for the best. I was right about scanning the fish, though. I knew something wasn't right.' Stanley explained.' What I never got my head around was all the bodies sucked of their blood. What was all that about and who were they? Were they construction workers?'

'Yes, well done,' John patronised. 'Although you were bound to get something right sooner or later. They were the people used to build the compound; obviously, we couldn't let them back into their villages afterwards. You know what the Normals are like – a few glasses of wine and they'd be blabbing away all our secrets. Besides, we needed a few bodies for our experiments, so it was a case of killing two birds with one stone. In this way, the Normals came in useful not once but twice.'

'Experiments? What experiments?' Stanley asked.

'Ha, ha, ha,' John chuckled. 'Before I explain the experiment, you have to see the big picture. You need to understand the big picture.'

'What big picture? What are you talking about?'

'You need to know who I have been protecting.'

'Well who is he then?'

John raised his arms into the air and screamed 'HE IS THE DEMIURGE!!'

CHAPTER 30

John was a man of big gestures, but Stanley had never seen him so manic. He was boiling to the point of derangement as he prepared to explain "the big picture"; but Stanley had a big picture of his own. Once John had finished his self-indulgent rant, he would inflict the same fate upon him as he had Carson. The odds of his escape looked slim, but there was always hope. Feeding John's ego would give him thinking time – or at least delay the inevitable. Plus, it was always handy to gather information for the next life. There was no reason for John to explain himself, but he would; he just couldn't help himself – he was like a James Bond villain. John's biggest problem would be getting his big head back out the door after explaining his masterplan. Poppi was a different problem altogether – quiet and indifferent, *and* she still had the gun pointing at him. John's gun remained on the floor - it's difficult to pick up a gun when you are patting yourself on the back. Stanley certainly wasn't patting himself on the back – could he pick it up? But John's patience was wearing thin as his revelation seemed to have fallen on deaf ears.

'You do know what the demiurge is, don't you?' he enquired.

'No, John, of course I don't. If you dragged a hundred people off the streets and asked them what a demiurge is, I would be surprised if three of them knew,' Stanley responded. 'Not everyone has your level of education,' he continued, deciding it wouldn't hurt to throw in a little flattery for good measure.

'True, true. The demiurge is the soul of all creation. He is the coupling between our earth body and astral spirit.'

'What are you talking about, John? This time you've really lost it. You've finally stepped off the reality pavement,' Stanley ridiculed.

'I understand your reluctance to accept the concept of an astral plane running in parallel with the earthly existence you recognise. I was like that too until I opened my mind. You see, the soul exists on two levels, the astral and etheric.'

'Are you for real? You shot Carson and betrayed the Council on the back of this nonsense?'

'It's not nonsense, Flash,' Poppi added. 'Just give him a chance to explain. Go on, John. Open his mind.'

Stanley couldn't believe his ears. Even Poppi had fallen for his mumbo jumbo.

John continued, unperturbed, 'You see, Flash, the human body is just a vessel made primarily from oxygen, carbon and hydrogen. That's all it is, a shell, a house for our soul and spirit. Wrapped around the earthy vessel is the soul but in two skins. The first skin is the astral soul, which gives you a personality, opinions and passion. Without this layer, you would be no more interesting than a cauliflower.'

'A bit like Erik, up at the space station, then?' Stanley joked.

'Exactly,' John laughed. 'The second skin is the etheric soul, which gives you unique physical characteristics. Not DNA characteristics, you understand, but the body's energy and life force. I like to think of the astral skin as red and the etheric skin blue so I can separate the two - as it can get confusing. Wrapped over these is the earthly skin we all recognise.'

'And you seriously believe all of this?'

'It's true, Flash, believe me,' John beseeched. 'A lot of research has been done on the subject. Did you know that our red skin is only a quarter the thickness of that of the Normals', per life? It's only in the final life that our red skin is the same thickness.'

'Red skin?'

'The astral skin, the one which gives us our personality traits and all the other strengths and foibles. During our first life, it's seventy-five per cent thinner than that of the Normals, the second life fifty per cent and so on. This is why the Normals have such complex personalities. I'd always thought it was desperation and lack of planning because they only have the one life. But it's not. It's because they have more heart and soul than us. We only catch up with them in our final life. But you've already spotted that, haven't you, Stanley?'

Stanley's sensibilities were knocked off balance; he wasn't expecting a forthright and plausible explanation to a concept he himself had no belief in whatsoever. Nevertheless, it made sense, kind of. He had attributed the lack of personality and soul within the Caste as an over-reliance on technology. This was a new concept to Stanley, an entirely different train of thought. Could he ride the train or was it a journey too far-fetched? Either way, it presented him with an unexpected opportunity. John had revealed this fact to entice him into his world. He knew of the affection he had for the Normals and was using it as a method of indoctrination. He had even gone to the trouble of calling him Stanley. John hated that he had chosen to call himself Stanley when he left the Council because it was out of chronological order: he was using his Leaf 1 name in Leaf 2. Even when he was called Jack, John had still referred to him as Flash. Yet on this occasion he had strategically dropped the name Stanley into the mix.

'So, what does the blue skin do, again?' Stanley found himself asking.

'It gives us our unique physical traits,' John enthused. 'But this time we have an advantage over the Normals because this is what creates our muscle memory. As the etheric, or blue skin, is interconnected throughout our four lives, so is our physical appearance, which is why we are physically stronger and have greater stamina than the Normals. This isn't there from birth but manifests itself in late childhood or early adulthood. You wouldn't have beaten Carson on Mount Sentinel that day because your memory map had yet to activate the muscle memory. Carson's had triggered, so he had far greater stamina than you – not to mention the Skin and Heartbeat.'

Stanley was intrigued and under different circumstance would ask more questions, but there was no time for a long theological dissection within his mind on the possibilities of split-level souls - but he could play along for a while to get closer to John's gun. John liked to gesticulate wildly when explaining himself, strolling randomly around the room whilst doing so. Although Poppi still had her gun, she was distracted and sickeningly awestruck with John's antics. Seemingly unnoticed, he had been edging towards the gun for some time. If he could get it while she was distracted, he had a chance.

'Of course, I don't believe it for one second, but it does make sense in a kind of weird way. You've got me thinking because if that was the case, the Normals would be of great use to us. They're a wasted resource - we could learn a great deal from them,' Stanley concocted.

'You're right. That's what the base in Uruguay is all about. We're trying to find a way to use them to help us achieve additional lives. And not just that, if we can capture their red skin, we can benefit from their complexities. Like you say, we're learning from them.'

'That's not what I meant. I was talking about learning what makes them tick and how we can benefit from their experiences – not sucking the lifeblood out of them and experimenting with what's left. I still don't understand why you've done this? Why suck the blood out of them?' Stanley queried.

'Because we're trying to use their bodies as vessels for soul attachment during metempsychosis. The process of parthenogenesis, or cuckoo conception, is the trigger for the beginning of the next life. Each time the cuckoo conception is activated we move on to the next Leaf and one of our lives is gone! If we can bypass this process by taking control of a living body, then we will have infinite lives,' explained John.

'Oh. I see,' Stanley mused. 'That makes sense - I suppose. But they aren't live bodies; they've been sucked of their blood. They're dead.'

'True. We haven't got to the bottom of it yet. You see, we thought we would bring a Normal to the point of death, all the way down to unbearable despair and desperation, where all hope is gone and holding onto life is too difficult. Too painful. At that point the soul of a Clover can transmigrate into the body and overcome the spirit of the dying body, casting it out into the ether. Unfortunately, we seem to have underestimated the strength of resolve within the Normals and the tight grip they have on their lives. You should see them, Flash. We put them in ice cold water and drag them to the depths of hyperthermia. It's an awful death, but they never give in. They fight it to their dying breath. Maybe it's because they only get one life, but they are crazy awkward in letting go. There's no way a Clover would hang on like that but, then again, we usually have another life following on.'

'This is sick,' gasped Stanley. 'How can you treat them like lab rats?'

'It's not just the Normals that are dying, Flash. We kill Clover too. We specifically train Leaf 1 or 2 Clover – not Lions, obviously – to take over the body and dispel the soul of the Normal. It's not that easy to get volunteers, as you can imagine, but the rewards for sacrifice are high, instant Lion status, for example. But still many don't have the insight, or intelligence, to appreciate what we are doing. We are developed in the womb via cuckoo conception, so why not push a soul out of a body the way a cuckoo pushes the other eggs from a nest? Unfortunately, it's not that simple and we've been having a few teething problems, but we'll get there in the end, though - of this, I'm sure.'

'But, again', Stanley pleaded, 'if you're trying to take over their mortal bodies, then why have they been sucked dry of their blood?'

'We only do this afterwards, when the experiment has been a failure. We suck the bodies dry and replace the blood with a cryopreserving fluid, so the body is preserved. We are also looking at ways of transmigrating our souls into dead bodies and bringing them back to life. This is proving even more difficult, but it doesn't hurt to have a few bodies lying around. Just in case we need them.'

'Do you have any idea how ungodly this whole thing is? Taking over souls and storing dead bodies – it's sick beyond belief. You can't bring dead bodies back to life; they aren't Frankenstein's monster!' Stanley screamed, pointing his finger at them both in outrage.

'Ungodly?' laughed John, 'Since when have you been religious?'

He was right to question Stanley's faith. He had never been religious, but he *had* been edging towards the gun, which was now clasped between his feet. Poppi had lowered hers and he saw that his chance was now. While they were waiting for him to explain his faith, he had a piece of divine inspiration of his own, and sliding the gun over his right foot, he flicked it into the air and caught it.

With the gun aimed between John's eyes, he yelled, 'Don't even think about it, Poppi!'

CHAPTER 31

Stanley couldn't believe he had pulled it off. He'd only ever done it once before – and that was with a soccer ball. With hindsight, he should have pointed the gun at Poppi, who was still armed - but he wasn't going to beat himself up about that. He could see from the corner of his eye her weapon was still lowered. He fancied his chances in a shootout, if she did.

'Wow! I'm impressed,' John gasped. 'Who taught you that little trick?'

'Fred Spikesley,' Stanley countered.

'Who's he? Is he Leaf 4?'

'No. He's a soccer player, from my first Leaf, back in England.'

'Oh yes, I remember you saying. Did he play for your favourite team? Who was it now? Sheffield Thursday, who really played on a Sunday?'

'Yes, he did. And it's Sheffield Wednesday, who played on a Saturday.'

'Well, I was close,' John sighed. 'It's OK, Poppi, drop the gun.'

'What?' she exclaimed. 'I can take him. Just give me the word.'

'A couple of hours ago I would have agreed. But now I'm not so sure. He seems to be regaining his mojo, and after that piece of fancy footwork, I wouldn't bet against him. And you know how much I like a bet.'

'But I can do it,' she pleaded.

'No, drop the gun,' he affirmed. 'And that's an order. Besides, I think I can talk him round now he's beginning to see things our way.'

'Well, that's where you're wrong,' Stanley countered as Poppi dropped the gun. 'The tables have turned. I don't need to pretend this thing is anything other than abhorrent to me.'

'Are you sure?' John quizzed. 'I gauged your reaction when I explained about the astral skin and how the Normals have a greater depth of personality. This is where you could come in, Flash. You understand the spirit of the Normals better than any Clover I know, and I've no doubt your involvement would speed up the process. This thing is going to happen with or without you. The quicker we find the solution the fewer Normals and Clover will be sacrificed. You could make sure the Normals and their families are looked after with dignity. Who knows, maybe one day we will be able to give them infinite lives, too? How would you like that? You know I'm right, Flash. Trust me – the demiurge is the future of the Clover Caste *and* the Normals.'

'You're not the only one capable of holding back information when it suits. You see, I lied when I said I didn't know what a demiurge is. As it happens, I do know a little about the subject.'

'Oh, I see,' John responded, clearly taken aback. 'So, what exactly do you know, then?'

'I know that the demiurge is the soul of creation; but a soul that lacks a universal mind and spirit,' Stanley replied.

'You don't know anything. The demiurge is the Creator of the new breed of Clover Caste. He will lead us forward,' John growled, maintaining his ground.

'That's so typical of you, Carter,' Stanley scoffed. 'You know a little about something but a lot about nothing. The demiurge has no true core spirit and is centred around passion, urges and impulse, which it cannot resist due to an inherent lack of spirit - the demiurge lacks spirit; you lack spirit. It's a mythical being which does *not* exist. Whoever you are working for is taking you for a ride; you're being tricked, John. You're a fool. You've been hooked in with the positives without even considering the negatives. '

As John fell silent, Stanley was in ascendancy, with no sign of yielding. This guy had killed him once and his best mate twice. He deserved everything he got – he must pay for his sins. One of the things he was going to get was a bullet in his forehead. But first he wanted to make him suffer - he hadn't felt this urge since he strangled whoever he strangled in Uruguay.

Stanley prolonged the insults. 'Remember the time you read that book by Albert Camus on existentialism and suddenly you were an expert? You kept coming out with what you thought were profound philosophical statements, but they made no sense. We used to laugh at you behind your back. Especially Poppi. She used to say, 'he's off again – pretending he's clever.' To me, that sums you up. I'll make sure it's written in your epitaph after I've shot you: Here lies John Carter – he wasn't as clever as he thought he was.'

The noise created as he pulled the trigger was much louder than before despite the gun being further away from his ears. John stood in front of him with a knowing smile on his face. Stanley, realising the bullets were blanks, dived across the floor and grabbed Poppi's gun. It was no surprise to discover it was also carrying blanks.

Looking down at Stanley, sprawled on the floor, John derided: 'Here lies Stanley Webster - he's not as clever as he thinks he is!'

'Do, all the guns have blanks in them?' Stanley questioned.

'Well, yes – apart from this one,' John answered as he revealed a gun hidden behind his back. 'Oh, and I imagine Carson's gun is real as he came here with the intention of popping a cap in my ass. If I was you, I would have gone for that one.'

Stanley groaned in defeat. 'So, what now?'

'Mmm', John pondered, 'I think I am going to have to shoot you. It's not like I didn't give you enough chances to join us. The guns, you see, well, they were the final test which, obviously, you failed. It's a big shame as you would have been perfect for us - we could have done with someone with a degree of virtue. But before I kill you, I want to introduce you to the demiurge.'

CHAPTER 32

He was pushed to his knees, arms behind him, and a gun to the back of his head. Even without the round rimmed glasses, the giant head on the screen was familiar, the brown hair, now cropped around the ears, was covered by a green army style baseball cap.

'I take it from your positions that he's decided not to join us?' the giant head questioned, with the squint in his piercing blue eyes suggesting the picture on his screen was not as clear. Perhaps it was a reflection from the glaring sunlight behind him in the familiar backdrop - he was standing outside the cadaver building in Uruguay. 'That's a shame – I had high hopes for him but it's hardly the end of the world. Still, it won't hurt for him to see what's about to happen. He'll have something to think about during purgatory. Maybe he'll see sense.'

The picture became blurred, bouncing around as he relocated inside the building. When the image became still and clear, he was inside the "Perfusion room", with a body on a trolley pointing feet first at the camera. Stanley remembered the room well: it was cold and had a trap door in the floor, with a hoist above to carry the grisly cargo.

'On the table is Vessel VF822. This specimen has been submerged in water no more than two degrees in temperature to lower the body temperature to the point of hypothermia. We believe these are the ideal conditions for a soul takeover. Our lack of success is due to the fight put up by the Host's spirit, which we had underestimated. To counter this, a synthetic substance called UPX5 has been developed, a form of tetrodotoxin administered prior to the Clover agent being sent on their mission. The UPX5 will further slowdown the heart rate to the point of death and will remain in equilibrium for fifteen minutes. This fifteen-minute period is the window of opportunity for our agent to take over the astral part of the soul and subsequently the body. Of course, the astral soul in a Normal is much thicker and stronger than that of a Clover. Around four times as thick.'

'Have you considered sending a Leaf 3, or even Leaf 4, on this mission? Their astral soul will be closer to that of a Normal?' John enquired.

'Yes, I have,' replied the demiurge. 'But nobody is willing to volunteer at such a late stage in their lives because the risks are too high. Would you? So, we must use Leaf 1 personnel for this - who are tempted by the carrots we dangle - but weaken the resolve of the Host to even up the chances. Are you ready Doctor Johnson?'

Appearing on the screen was a slimly built man dressed in hospital whites, making it impossible to identify him as the campus doctor.

'Yes, sir, I am ready to administer the UPX5,' the doctor answered. His voice was unmistakable: it was Bones.

'John are you ready to send the agent on their mission?' asked the demiurge.

'Yes, I am.'

'You must be kidding me,' Stanley screamed as he watched Doctor Johnson inject the body. 'You think I'm going to help you with this nonsense? I'm not going to try to take over the soul of a Normal. Even if it was possible –and you seem already to have proved that it's not – it's highly unethical. I won't do it. And you certainly won't be able to talk me into it in fifteen minutes.'

'Shut up, you fool,' laughed the demiurge. 'You think everything is about you. Well this is bigger than you. Much bigger. And now you've made your choice, you are no use to me anymore.'

Poppi approached the screen and looked up at the demiurge. It was only then that Stanley noticed that the body on the trolley was female.

'I'm ready to serve you,' Poppi announced.

'No, Poppi, no!' Stanley wailed. 'Don't be stupid!'

'I can be a Lion. You know what that means to me,' she revealed, turning around to face him.

Her body slumped to the floor, a couple of feet from Carson. John's aim was true, with the barrel of the gun being returned to Stanley's head so quickly he had no time to react. With his best friend, and the only woman he had ever loved, lying motionless, he was still in shock when a loud scream resonated from the screen. Doc Johnson and the demiurge were bent over the woman who, despite being strapped down, was jolting violently.

'Get out, get out!' she shouted.' 'I repent thee. Jesus, I come to you as my deliverer. You died for me and rose again. I confess you as Lord and renounce all influences of Satan in my life. Lord, you know the demons that oppress me, that harass me, that entice me, that enslave me. Help me, Jesus. HELP ME!'

And with those words, she fell silent.

'Doc, doc, what's happened?' The demiurge shouted.

'She's gone. She's dead.'

'But how? That was never fifteen minutes. Why didn't we get fifteen minutes? You promised me fifteen minutes! You must have got the dosage of UPX5 wrong.'

'No, I didn't - it was the right amount. You picked the wrong subject. She was religious. Her faith carried her through Poppi's attempt to take over her soul. You need to pick subjects with less faith and who are not strong minded. You need weaker souls. Anyway, don't you think you ought to turn that thing off?' he snapped, nodding towards the screen which, moments later was dead.

'Aside from the mental scars, which I will carry with me for the next couple of lives, I was really impressed with your demonstration,' Stanley mocked sarcastically. 'I can see you're making great progress in a non-weird and non-barbaric way. You must be proud of yourself, getting involved with this lot. It's not too late. Drop the gun and we can go to the Council to stop this.'

'Shut it,' John growled, pushing the gun harder against his head. The barrel felt cool against Stanley's shaven scalp. 'You still don't understand. That's just a little setback. Success and failure are the same thing. The way you react to either shows what kind of man you are. You heard them; it was the wrong kind of subject. They'll find another, more suitable vessel and I will have infinite lives. I'm Leaf 1, so I have plenty of time left for these little problems to be ironed out, unlike you; you are on your way to Leaf 3. Half of your lives are gone!'

'You're right. There is something I don't understand. Why have you told me all about what you're doing? There was no need for you to show me what just happened. If you'd shot me ten minutes ago, I wouldn't have known what you are up to, what the demiurge looks like, the fact that Bones is involved or even that it was you who shot Poppi. Is it pure arrogance? If you think you are some ultra-criminal genius revealing his masterplan, then you're delusional!'

'Why, what are you gonna do about it with a gun to your head?'

'Like you just said yourself, John, I still have two lives left. I will return and inform the Council.'

'It'll be too late by then. We'll have achieved infinite lives and the leverage needed to persuade the Caste to go back to the ways of the Gammadions. Some of the Council are already on board, and we will hunt you down in childhood and kill you,' John warned.

'Kill me? How? You won't have the first clue where I am. When I get to purgatory, I'm going to pick a Host for cuckoo conception you won't be able to find. Somewhere remote. And don't forget, this is my second transition, so I won't be disorientated. I'll know who and what I am from an early age. There'll be no easy giveaway signs for you to pick up if I'm somewhere without the facilities for early medical detection – and there's plenty of those in the underdeveloped world. I can be a shadow. I could disappear – like Fergus Leahy did!'

'Well if you're going to tell the Council and try to avenge your death – well, deaths – you'll have to have a quick trip to purgatory. The longer you stay up there, on the horizon, the less you will remember. It's 1980 now – nearly '81. You'll start to show signs that you are Clover in your early teens, so we'll be looking for you then.'

'You won't be able to find me; it's a big wide world out there,' Stanley rationalised. 'Good luck finding me - before I find you!'

'You see', John retorted, 'you will start to display some secondary signs of being a Clover before you realise what you are. These signs will be picked up by people around you - maybe your parents, who want to send you to a good school, or maybe your teacher, who wants you to aim for the next level of education. Perhaps it's a particular sporting prowess that gets you noticed. Who knows? But there will be something.'

'Maybe. But, if I pick somewhere remote, who will notice some minor achievement reported in a local rag at the back of beyond? You're clutching at straws, John.'

'But what if I were to tell you this?' John hissed. 'We are going to release the Circle of Lives to the Normals.'

'What?! But why would you do that? It's the most advanced area of technology the Clover have. Why give it to the Normals? There's far less advanced technology we don't deem them worthy of, so why the Circle? '

'Because with the Circle we'll be able to keep track of what they're up to - a form of self-surveillance – you've said this much yourself. Genius, really. We're going to explain to the Council progressives that we want to release it to give them access to information to augment their lives but really, we'll be spying on them. Of course, it won't be called the Circle or be as good as our version, but it will be similar.'

'But if you give them access to the Circle, they will be able to communicate with each other much easier. That's why it was invented. If they can communicate quicker, they will spread the word about the Caste if they find any information about us.'

'In theory you're spot on Flash, but we'll also be able to monitor them easier and pinpoint who and where they are. We can weed out any troublemakers or anybody who has accidentally found out about us. Plus, it will be easier for us to deal with.'

'How?'

'Any dangerous information we can flood with false information to throw people off the scent. Turn it into a conspiracy theory and discredit it. It worked with JFK,' John gloated.

'But there will be more people with access to this information. What if a large chunk of people believes it? What if your plan fails? It's a big gamble.'

'If we feel the number of Normals onto us is dangerously high, we will use Operation Purge,' John announced, casting the bait in Flash's direction.

'Operation Purge?' bit Stanley.

'It's a virus.'

'A computer virus?'

'No, a real virus. We have lots of them ready to be used. They are all basically a strain of the 'flu but, unlike the 'flu people in the Caste will not be affected – only Normals.'

'I don't understand.'

'OK Flash, if we know there are a large collection of people in one area - say Florida – who concern us we will introduce the virus into the area. When people begin to pour into the hospitals, we call a national emergency and lock down that area. No one can enter or leave, so the targets are sitting ducks. We just mosey on in and deal with them. If we inject them with a deadly strain, their murders can be explained legally. I've used Florida as an example, but this could be any state, country or even the entire world.'

'You're happy killing God knows how many Normals with a deadly virus?'

'I wouldn't say happy and it's a worst-case scenario, but we will do what's necessary – we always do. You used to understand that. We need to give the Normals access to the Circle. This is a game changer for us.'

'But how will they gain access? Their computers are nowhere near advanced enough.'

'Good point, Flash. It's a shame I'm going to have to kill you. We'll gradually ramp up the Normals' technology over the next few years to be able to cope with the Circle of Friends. Obviously, we'll have to drip feed it so it doesn't look too suspicious, but by the mid-1990s - when you're in your teens in the next life – they will have computers powerful enough to cope. We can kill two birds with one stone, as well.'

'What do you mean?'

'Such advancements in computer technology will make a lot of people wealthy, which will be attributed to final Leafers for their actualisation,' John explained.

'Isn't it all a bit drastic, just to find me?'

'Not just you, Flash, there are a few out there - like you and Mouse – who we've killed over the last few months. We'll be hunting them down, too. Plus, as I've already said, we can keep an eye on the Normals. We're even going to give them a Heartbeat. Obviously, it won't be as good as ours. We'll give it poor battery life – maybe just a day – which will limit the number of things it can do, but we'll be able to track them wherever they are. We'll even put a camera on it, so they can take pictures of each other. We will know where they are, what they look like, who they are with – even where they holiday.'

'You see, John, that's where your plan falls down. You assume the Normals are like us, but they aren't. The thought that they will put such personal information on a network for all to see is ridiculous. Do you remember when I told you about my first Leaf, when I lived in England?'

'Is that when you used to watch Sheffield Saturday, who really played on a Wednesday?' John interrupted.

'Near enough,' Stanley sighed. 'Every year we went on holiday to the seaside. My parents would warn me not to tell anybody we were going in case a thief found out and broke into the house. Do you honestly think people like that are going to announce their personal business all over the Circle for anybody to see? And as for having to charge the Heartbeat every day, what kind of idiot would use a device they need to charge every day? They won't allow their privacy to be abused like us; they aren't as vain as we are. You've underestimated them, John. Trust me, I know them better than you do.'

'No, Flash, you've overestimated them. They will do what we tell them to do. By the end of the century we will know everything about the Normals. You'll see I'm right.'

'Well I wouldn't bet my life on it,' Stanley scoffed.

'But that's the thing,' John pointed out. 'You just have!'

PHASE 4 – HORIZON

CHAPTER 33

What happens when you die? Is it the end, or the beginning of something new? If you're a Normal, who knows? How could any Normal know? If you only get one life, how can you tell others what happened to you after your death? But for Clover Caste things are different.

"Borrowed diction" is a term used to describe words or phrases from Clover Caste culture seconded into Normals' culture. Despite a significant effort to remain clandestine, some aspects are discovered by the Normals and spread by word of mouth before the Caste can intervene. In the curious case of Fergus Leahy, the eponymous anti-hero was intercepted by an agent before he could "spread the word." But what would have happened without this intervention? What if Fergus had addressed the drinkers in the tavern, but without being drugged by Thomas Evans?

There is a department specifically commissioned to address such eventualities known as the Cloaking Department – with operatives referred to as the "Cloak and Daggers". Had Fergus articulated himself in the tavern, the outcome would have been the same, but more work would have been required. Even without Fergus passing on information, the Cloak and Daggers still went to significant lengths to discredit him, including giving his hare traps the appearance of leprechaun traps. Instead of the tavern-based humiliation, he would have been carted away to the "loony bin" to confess to seeing the little red and green men. Instead he was allowed to roam free as a cautionary tale - a warning to the Clover Caste.

Similar manipulation is applied to Clover words overheard to have a different meaning within Normals culture. An example of borrowed diction is the word *purgatory*. At some point, a Normal will have discovered the Clover word purgatory and its meaning to the Caste. This Normal will have come to a sticky end but not before having shared information with others. This is where the Cloak and Daggers intervene to manipulate a word's usage within Normals' culture so the literal meaning is different to that ascribed to it in Clover culture, thus protecting the shroud of secrecy. Normals believe purgatory to be a physical state after death where those destined for heaven must cleanse themselves before entering. They may be required to carry out a task of virtue to prove their worthiness before walking through the pearly gates. This is the definition added to their dictionary to disguise its true meaning.

Borrowed diction often associates words with holy and spiritual issues making them deliberately vague, less accessible and nonsensical to the masses. In the case of purgatory, some Normals believe and some do not, which is the perfect scenario for the Cloak and Daggers. But in the world of the Clover Caste purgatory is very real.

For a Clover Caste Host, purgatory is where the soul remains in a state of flux after death until transmigration into a suitable vessel. It's a waiting room for the soul. Much is known and taught during elucidation about purgatory, but there are still unknowns making each individual transition unpredictable. Recollection of purgatory is sketchy and often described as akin to a recurring dream. If a Host consciously attempts to recollect their previous experience of purgatory, they will be met with blank minds, but during the Host's life, snippets subconsciously appear at random intervals, and it is through these snippets that the teachings of purgatory have been formulated. During purgatory no physical being is present, within the earthly realm, but the Host is still connected to the Host's memory map.

The selection of the surrogate is a vital aspect of purgatory; usually, this will be of a linear nature, with Hosts choosing surrogates residing close to where they lived in their previous life. A proximity to large cities is encouraged, by the Council, as it enables early detection in an area where mentors and greeters are commonplace. The sooner elucidation takes place after the awakening (the first of the three transition stages), the smoother the transition and the more information can be retained from the previous life memory map. However, sometimes the Host chooses a surrogate in an underdeveloped and sparsely populated area of the world to avoid detection. This is highly frowned upon by the Council.

But what does purgatory look like? Because of its appearance, it is known as the *horizon*. The horizon is a body of light linking the soul to the physical body, with a curvature so shallow it resembles the horizon, with the curves forming four concentric circles – one for each life cycle. When a Clover dies, the soul leaves the physical body and divides into the astral and etheric souls, each returning to their own plane. To understand the horizon, one must understand the astral and etheric planes. In Normals' culture there are many different interpretations of astral and etheric which, due to the work of the Cloak and Daggers, are complicated and contradictory; within the Clover Caste they are simple and universally understood.

An etheric projection takes place within the physical (earthly) plane on Earth and is separate from the physical bodies around it. As it is on a higher frequency within the earthly plane, it can pass through physical objects such as walls and doors. The etheric plane sits between, and overlaps, the physical (earthly) plane and the astral plane. Etheric projections can pass through all three planes. The etheric soul contains the unique physical characteristics, life force and the muscle memory of the physical body.

An astral projection takes place on the astral plane, which overlaps the etheric plane whilst having no direct contact with the earthly plane. Astral projections pass through the etheric plane and manifest themselves on the earthly plane as etheric projections. The astral soul contains all the unique emotional and personality characteristics and the full life memory map.

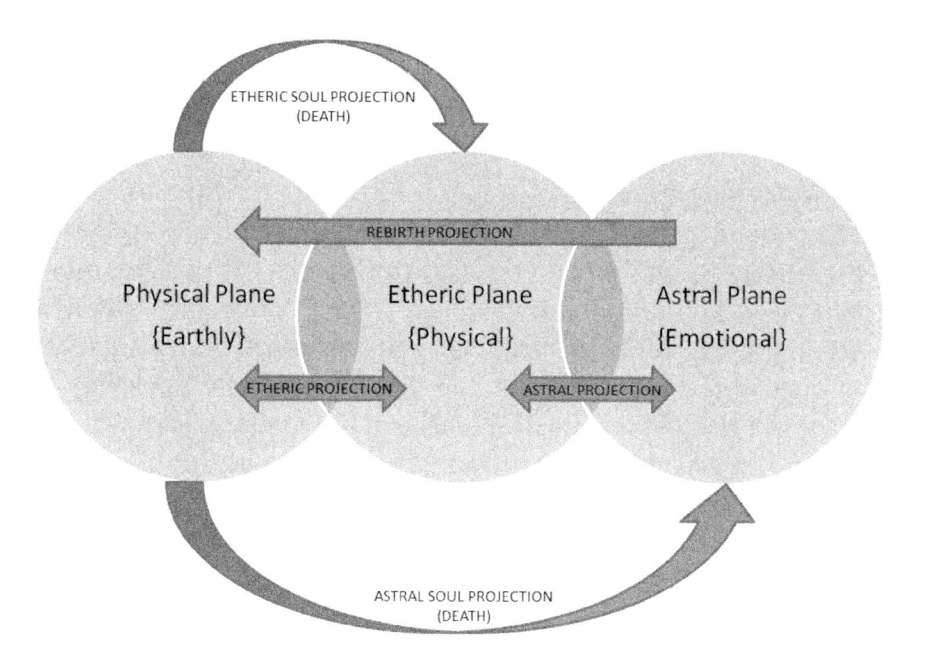

```
                    ETHERIC SOUL PROJECTION
                           (DEATH)


              ←─────── REBIRTH PROJECTION ───────

   Physical Plane      Etheric Plane       Astral Plane
      {Earthly}          {Physical}         {Emotional}

              ←─ ETHERIC PROJECTION ─  ←─ ASTRAL PROJECTION ─


                     ASTRAL SOUL PROJECTION
                           (DEATH)
```

The four horizons occur on the astral plane, with the Host's emotional characteristics (cast off after death) orbiting the astral body as it awaits rebirth. Only three of the rays of light forming the horizons link to the physical body in the astral plane. As the fourth horizon is detached from the astral body, when the fourth transition begins the astral body descends into a decaying orbit. At this point, no more rebirths occur.

The Host maintains all the attributes present during their previous lives, other than the mortal body, with many describing the transition within the Horizon as a gentle floating sensation.

Despite claims that the horizon is spiritually enlightening and emotionally cleansing, the selection of the surrogate is its only tangible purpose; the longer the Host stays within the horizon, the more the memory map becomes depleted. Aside from vital aspects of personality, the memory map contains the embodied knowledge accrued throughout the various lifetimes; without a healthy memory map, the advantage over the Normals, upon each rebirth, is decreased. Also, as the horizon is not connected to Earth from a time perspective, there are no benefits of staying within the horizon; it is not possible to return to earth years after death, the return is instantaneous regardless of how long the Host is away. Consequently, it is beneficial for Hosts to return to an earthly body as soon as possible.

When the Host is ready to seek a surrogate, the astral body, travels as an etheric projection through the etheric plane and is connected to the earthly realm. The etheric characteristics of the Host are projected into the earthly realm, manifesting as an aura of swirling light. Most often, the light forms a small "orb", varying in size from a grain of sand through to the size of a tennis ball. On rare occasions the light manifests itself as an identical replica of the previous earthly body. It is not known why there are such variations in the size and shapes of the projected manifestations or why the projections can be seen on Earth by some Normals but not others.

Originally, this phenomenon proved to be a headache for the Cloak and Daggers, but eventually, orbs were explained away as light reflecting upon dust particles; thus, dismissing the Normals' theory of the spiritual presence of a soul departing the earth after death. Ironically, this theory was spectacularly wrong as although they *are* the spiritual presence of a soul, they represent a soul about to be reborn, one which is re-entering the earthly realm not one which is leaving.

Explanations for the auras of light manifesting themselves in the form of an earthly body proved a bigger challenge. This was exacerbated because the spirit is difficult to control during the etheric projection and often, by default, returns to a familiar place on Earth – usually the place of death or a childhood home. The return of a familiar looking projection has "freaked out" many Normals over the years. However, the Cloak and Daggers task is made easier as only a small percentage of Normals can see the projections. Therefore, with far more non-believers than believers, it is now policy to ignore ghostly sightings, leaving the Normals to argue amongst themselves for an explanation of the phenomenon.

Once projected into the earthly realm, the etheric manifestations seek out the most suitable surrogate donor for their next life cycle. Although this may appear to absorb a portion of time, as there is no connection to earthly time this disappears upon return to the horizon, with the process being timeless. Due to the nature of cuckoo conception, the process must be instantaneous as the window of opportunity to fertilise an egg by parthenogenesis is limited.

But where does all this leave Jack, Stanley or Flash? (Whichever you choose to call him.) It is traditional for Clover Caste to carry the same nickname through all four lives, so we will call him Flash. Well, not many people have been killed on two separate occasions by a gunshot to the back of the head, fired by the same person. Even for a Clover Caste agent this is unusual. To make matters worse, the same gun killed his best friend and the only girl he ever loved. He concluded Poppi must been indoctrinated by her eventual murderer – that was the only explanation for her behaviour. He was equally convinced he could talk sense into her during the next life, knowing that having been killed together they would both be the same age in the next life. Sometimes, friendships within Clover Hosts are broken by staggered life spans, with the age gap too large to bridge.

As he floated around within the horizon, his earthly memories and emotions remained. So how was he feeling? He wanted revenge – well, wouldn't you? He also wanted to warn the Council. But most of all he wanted revenge. It wouldn't be easy; he was a target, particularly vulnerable as a baby and a small child. But enlightenment would arrive sooner in Leaf 3 and be less disorientating; if he could survive into his early teens, his chances would greatly increase. Mouse would be taking similar precautions – and if they could connect with each other before John did, they might have a chance.

It was vital he selected a prime surrogate in the prime location; the more isolated the better. He knew John would be looking for him. He knew the odds were stacked against him. But it wasn't over yet; he still had skills. This was his second visit to the horizon, and he knew what he must do. He must select his surrogate and get out quickly to maintain his memory map, to maintain his anger. He made his choice. He was ready.

Game on.

Printed in Great Britain
by Amazon